PRAISE

"With kink, sensu... ...ion that flies off the page, Eden Bradley has a winner in *Dangerously Broken*. Loved it!"   —J. Kenner, *New York Times* bestselling author

"*Dangerously Broken* is dark and sexy, romantic and edgy—this book will keep you up all night."

—Lexi Blake, *New York Times* bestselling author

PRAISE FOR THE NOVELS OF EDEN BRADLEY

"Intelligent, haunting and sexy as hell . . . For you people who like story and heart with your erotica, I'd definitely recommend any of Eden's books."

—Maya Banks, *New York Times* bestselling author

"Honest, tender and totally sexy—a feast for the senses and the heart."   —Shayla Black, *New York Times* bestselling author

"Brilliant, seductive and dangerous. All of my favorite things."

—R. G. Alexander, author of *Possess Me*

"A hot and steamy ride to the climactic end . . . This story will steam up your glasses."   —*Library Journal*

"An exciting, erotic page-turner that does not disappoint . . . Ms. Bradley's wonderful storytelling ability [and] knack for description . . . transports you right into the story and holds you there until the very last page."   —Night Owl Reviews

continued . . .

Titles by Eden Bradley

DANGEROUSLY BOUND
DANGEROUSLY BROKEN

Writing as Eve Berlin

PLEASURE'S EDGE
DESIRE'S EDGE
TEMPTATION'S EDGE

Anthologies

EXCLUSIVE
(with Jaci Burton and Lisa Renee Jones)

DANGEROUSLY
Broken

EDEN BRADLEY

BERKLEY BOOKS, NEW YORK

BERKLEY

An imprint of Penguin Random House LLC
375 Hudson Street, New York, New York 10014

This book is an original publication of Penguin Random House LLC.

Library of Congress Cataloging-in-Publication Data

Bradley, Eden.
Dangerously broken / Eden Bradley. — Berkley Trade paperback edition.
p. cm.
ISBN 978-0-425-26999-2
I. Title.
PS3602.R34266D35 2015
813'.6—dc23
2015018450

PUBLISHING HISTORY
Berkley trade paperback edition / October 2015

PRINTED IN THE UNITED STATES OF AMERICA

10 9 8 7 6 5 4 3 2 1

Cover photograph: "lock and chain" © PIER / Getty Images;
"wrought iron" © Purestock / Getty Images.
Cover design by Judith Lagerman.
Text design by Tiffany Estreicher.

Penguin
Random
House

To the beautifully haunting city of New Orleans—
you are always pure magic to me.

ACKNOWLEDGMENTS

I want to thank my dear friend author Erin Simone for exploring New Orleans at midnight with me. Our quiet walks through the dark French Quarter, breathing the city in, glorying in the architecture, sharing my longing for the place, inspired me in ways I will never quite be able to put into words. Someday we will go there with our little dogs and hole up in an apartment for a month, writing all day, walking the city after dark, creating new stories together. Promise.

I must also thank the real Dennie, beta reader and one of the sweetest people I know, for letting me use her sassy personality and the strength of the friendship she offers as a model for Summer Grace's best friend. Thank you, doll!

THE SOUND OF leather hitting naked flesh reverberated like a low hum in his veins as Jamie entered the main play space of The Bastille. Bodies writhed beneath the dim red and pale gold lights, seemingly in time with the trancelike ambient music. Everywhere were the scents familiar at any BDSM club. Leather. Desire. And very faintly, a little perfume. But the leather—floggers, cuffs, whips—was only one element of kink to whet his appetite. It was always the primeval glint and clank of chains that really did it for him.

A small frisson of heat shivered over his skin, creeping up the back of his neck as he paused to admire a giant web of chain attached to the sleek, black-lacquered wall. It was one of his favorite play stations at the club. The Bastille was his home club, infamous among the kink folk in New Orleans and all over the country. The club was as decadent as the city itself, as sensual as

New Orleans's sultry air. With its dramatic black and red décor, the spectacular equipment, the subs and slaves blindfolded and bound into the wall nooks where one would normally set a tall vase of flowers or a statue, it was the kind of place one only ever read about. But these beautifully still people were as decorative as a vase of flowers, in his mind. And this place was far from "normal." Tonight The Bastille, this wicked den of far-from-normal appetites, would serve him well—as soon as he chose a play partner from among the many gorgeous submissive women available.

They were scattered throughout the club, seated on the plush red velvet settees and chairs in the front lounge area, or watching the activity on the main floor. They were easy enough to spot whether or not they wore the club's white collar of protection and availability. It was in the furtive glances they cast at him, lashes down, hands clasped in front of them, posture perfect in their rigid corsets. And then there were those who dared to stare boldly at him, lashes batting, a smile on their pretty lips. These were the ones who interested him most, although they always proved to be the most trouble in the end. But he liked a feisty submissive. He liked the challenge.

He liked having a reason to punish them.

Ah, and there she was—the tall brunette who'd made a point of introducing herself the last time or two he'd visited the club. What was her name? She was smiling at him, and there was little coyness in her glance. He smiled back, started to move across the room toward her when his attention was caught by a scene to his left. Maîtresse Renee, an attractive Domme. Like him, she was a regular at The Bastille. She was paddling a petite woman bent over a spanking bench. The girl had a truly spectacular ass that was pinking nicely. It was perfect, really—a perfect heart shape.

And she had long, silky blonde hair that hung down almost to the floor, obscuring her face. But there was something familiar about her small frame . . .

Maîtresse Renee grabbed the girl's hair and pulled her upright and his groin tightened as her flawless, small breasts came into view, tipped with pale pink nipples. He'd love to get his hands on her, loved a woman with that build—slight and athletic, yet still utterly feminine. And she had a gorgeous tattoo of a phoenix on her side in brilliant color. He loved tattoos on a woman, especially one of this size and exquisite detail. Beautiful. Who was she? Someone new, that was for sure. He stepped closer, something about the tiny blonde drawing him.

The Domme pulled her head farther back, elongating her throat, and he caught sight of the girl's profile.

Jesus. Fucking. Christ.

Summer Grace Rae.

His hands fisted at his sides, all thought of the brunette gone in the wake of discovering his best friend's little sister in the club. The girl he'd sworn to protect as her brother Brandon lay on his deathbed twelve years ago. The same little sister he'd lusted after since she was fourteen years old, although he'd never admit that to anyone. The same girl he was lusting after now, even as anger suffused him.

He took a few hard strides toward them before managing to stop himself just short of invading their scene space—stopping so fast it rocked him back on his heavy, booted heels. His head felt like it was about to explode.

What the hell was Summer Grace doing at the club? *His* club! The fucking *kink* club! And even worse, under someone else's hands, Goddamn it.

He couldn't stand to watch, yet he couldn't look away as

Maîtresse Renee pulled her hair harder, Summer Grace's back arching. When her entire slender frame was elongated, the Domme started to use a small leather paddle on the front of her delicate body.

He shook his head, his blood boiling. He had two choices. He could barge in on their scene and risk getting himself banned from the club in the process and ruining his reputation as a Dominant, or he could get the fuck out of there and deal with this later, after he'd had some time to get his head back on straight.

As if.

He knew damn well he should leave, but he couldn't resist circling the scene until he stood in front of Summer Grace—and knew how utterly stupid he'd been when she glanced up and caught his gaze.

Jesus fuck!

It was like a punch in the gut, even from a good eight or ten feet away: those sky-blue eyes, the shock there, and on her lips as they made a small O. The raw *zing* of desire and the knot of emotion. And he was damn irresponsible. He stepped back, his own sense of shock threatening to paralyze him. Blowing out a breath, he took another step back, then forced himself to turn away and head for the front door. He'd almost made it when a hand on his arm stopped his momentum.

"Jamie? You okay?"

It was another beautiful brunette—Allie, Mick's girlfriend. They were two of his closest friends, and they'd all known each other since they were kids—Allie and Mick. Brandon and Summer Grace.

So damn hot, naked on that spanking bench, the tattoo down her ribs, just beneath those perfect breasts . . .

Jesus, he did not want to talk to Allie right now. He was too fucked up. Over seeing Summer Grace. Over his behavior—looking right at her during a scene when he should have walked the hell away.

"Fine. I'm just . . . I'm taking off."

"Like a cat with its tail on fire. What's going on?"

He didn't want to talk about this. "Where's Mick?"

"He's out of town, working, which I'm pretty sure you already know. And you're deflecting why?" Allie smiled, undaunted by his gruff demeanor.

He ran a hand over his buzz cut as if that would clear his brain. "Allie, look . . . I just saw someone in there and . . . Wait. Did you know she was here? You and Summer Grace have been hanging out since you got back to town. Shit, Allie, did you know about this?"

"Don't be so accusatory, Jamie. Yes, I know she's here. I'm the one who brought her. I was just getting something out of my locker—"

"You fucking *brought her* here?" he exploded, then sucked in a breath and tried to calm himself. He'd gotten too close, and she'd *seen* him. And God knew what it had done to her head space. Unforgivable. He knew better. "Hell. Fuck. I'm sorry. But you should have told me. Warned me. Jesus, who thought this was a good idea?"

He needed to calm the hell down. Allie wasn't looking too pleased with him right now. But damn it, this was Brandon's little sister. In his club. Fuck.

"Actually, she asked me not to discuss it with you, Jamie. She wanted to do this on her own."

Of course Summer Grace had asked Allie not to tell him. He would never have allowed it.

"And you let her? She sure as hell hasn't been in here before or I would have known about it. Do you know if she's been to other clubs? Played with someone else before tonight? Before showing up here and bending over a spanking bench, for fuck's sake. How new to the kink life is she? Jesus, Allie, is anyone watching out for her?"

Allie drew herself up, fire sparking in her brown eyes. "Jamie Stewart-Greer, you need to change your tone right now. What do you take me for? *I'm* watching out for her. So is Rosie. I wouldn't let *anyone* come into this without guidance, especially someone I've known most of my life. As for the rest, that's her business to tell you, not mine. You should know that." She reached for him again, her tone softening as she rubbed a soothing hand over his arm. "Come on, Jamie. Take a breath and think for a minute. You know I'd never be irresponsible with Summer."

He blew out a breath. "Yeah. Okay. I know that. I'm just . . . I'm gonna go. I'm sorry I blew up at you. I wasn't expecting to see her."

Naked. Being spanked by someone else. Getting her hair pulled by someone else. Commanded . . .

Allie shrugged. "I can understand it. She's always been everyone's baby sister. But, Jamie? Baby sisters grow up."

He nodded, not wanting to tell her that he'd never thought of Summer Grace as *his* baby sister. He didn't want to tell her he'd spent years fantasizing about her—about doing those things to her himself. And just as many years knowing he never could because of the promise he'd made to her brother.

To see her with another Dominant, even a woman . . . It was more than he could stand.

He pulled Allie in and brushed a kiss across her forehead. "You're right, as usual. I'm just gonna do everyone a favor and go."

"That might be the best idea. Are we good, Jamie?" she asked, looking up at him.

"What? Yes. We're good. Of course we are. This is all me."

He tried to get himself to move but he had to get one last look. It was too crowded and he was too far away, but he thought he heard her crying out in pleasure or pain.

Summer Grace.

Fuck.

She'd done this just to drive him crazy. She was good at that. Three years his junior, Summer Grace had been coming on to him all through her teen years and into her twenties. But in the last year it had stopped, and she seemed to be avoiding him. Not that he could blame her—he'd always rejected her blatant advances. Although seeing her now made him wonder how the hell he'd managed it. Summer Grace had been one hell of a sex kitten since she hit puberty.

Jesus. He was getting hard remembering her crawling into his sleeping bag on more than one of the camping trips he'd taken with the Rae family. Remembering what it felt like to wake up with her straddling him . . .

Allie squeezed his arm. "Jamie? You said you were going?"

"What? Yeah, I'm out of here. I'll talk to you later."

Allie raised one dark brow. "Drive carefully. You seem a little shaken up."

You have no idea.

"I will."

He got out of the club and to the parking lot on the side of the big converted warehouse that housed The Bastille. His auto shop's white tow truck was parked there—he didn't like to leave his vintage Corvette Stingray in the warehouse district. He swung open the door with the "SGR" insignia on the side a little too hard—"SGR" for Stewart-Greer and Rae. He and Brandon had planned to go into business together as soon as they got through the automotive technology program over in Lafayette. The least he could do was add Brandon's name to the business. If only Brandon were there to run the shop with him . . .

If only Brandon were here, this night would never have happened. Summer Grace would never have been naked and submitting in one of the most notorious kink clubs in the country. And Jamie would never have been forced to resist the temptation she offered—not on this scale. Not on his home turf. Temptation he could never give in to. Not only because of the promise he'd made, but because he refused to bring her any closer. He was dangerous to people he cared about, whose lives intertwined with his.

Don't think about that part.

But now he'd seen her naked, and temptation was brought to a whole new level. Temptation and ideas about the possibility of them being together that made his chest ache.

"Jesus fucking Christ," he muttered, scrubbing a hand over his head again.

He pressed his fingers against his temples and then his eyes, where a steady pressure was building.

That wasn't the only place pressure was building.

How the hell could he be so damn mad and so turned on at the same time? He should be used to this by now—that was how things had always been with Summer Grace. He'd chased her out of his bed—his sleeping bag, his tent, off the Rae's family room couch—at least a dozen times over the years. Every time he'd gotten angry. Every time he'd had to deal with the raging hard-on of his life. But he wouldn't—couldn't—do that with her. Not *her*.

But now he knew she was exploring kink at *his* club. If this turned out to be more than a one-time thing he would see her there again and again. They'd run into each other and he'd be forced to watch other people have what he'd denied himself. Watch Summer Grace submit to someone else. See her naked body—her beautiful naked body and that perfect heart-shaped ass growing gorgeously pink as she was spanked, paddled.

He groaned, pressed his hand against the hard bulge in his jeans. "Down boy," he murmured, his throat raw with need.

He started the truck and pulled onto Magazine Street, gunning the engine, then braking for the summertime tourist traffic. "Fuck."

He needed to get the hell home. Needed to either get into his 'Vette and drive off this tension, or get into his bed or the shower or just inside the damn door of his flat so he could work it off properly—with a good, hard orgasm and then some good, hard drinking and swearing until he inevitably got hard again and the cycle repeated.

He came to a red light and waited impatiently, then switched on the radio.

All along it was a fever, a cold sweat hot-headed believer, Rihanna sang.

He sure as hell had a fever. For *her.* If he'd ever tried to deny it before, it was impossible after tonight, when she'd stepped into his world and given herself over to it. Without him. He might have been strong enough to shrug off her youthful attempts at seduction, but whether she knew it or not, she'd just starred in his own personal forbidden fantasy.

He was so screwed.

The lyrics took a heavy emotional turn and he impatiently switched off the radio. It only made him think of that moment when their eyes had met in the dim light of the club. The electricity that went way beyond mere recognition. That forced him to face head-on the fact that he'd always wanted her, wanted her to *belong* to him.

The light changed and he moved through the sluggish traffic, finally hanging a left on Canal Street and driving through the French Quarter proper, drumming his fingertips on the steering wheel.

"Take care of her. Take care of Summer Grace if I'm not here to do it, Jamie. You have to promise me."

He'd never forget Brandon's words. Never forget the oath he'd sworn to his best friend that day as the stark white walls of the hospital room seemed to close in on him. He wasn't forgetting it now. Desire was not the same as taking action. But who the hell was going to protect her from everything and everyone else at The Bastille if he didn't do it himself? It was the same damn situation Allie had wrangled Mick into. With his help, he had to admit. But this was different. Wasn't it? He had a feeling Summer Grace hadn't done this because of him.

He'd seen the languorous lines of her body under that Domme's hands. Had seen the way she responded to being hit with the leather paddle. She was *right there*, her body, her mind, committed to the moment. Oh yeah, she was all in. That wasn't something anyone could fake. Even if she knew he was into kink—and if Allie had brought her to the club, he was pretty sure she'd known before they'd seen each other tonight—she was obviously there because it was what she wanted.

Summer Grace. With the same dark desires he had himself.

Which could lead her into some dangerous territory.

He tried to shake off the thoughts about her in some other man's hands. Being spanked. Flogged. Taken into subspace, where she would be vulnerable. The glossy blue of her eyes.

"Damn it! You're not thinking about her safety—you're just hot for her!"

His stiffening cock confirmed it. So did his hands, gripping the steering wheel so hard his knuckles hurt as he silently berated himself. He sighed in relief when he finally found a parking spot right in front of the three-story building he'd bought last year. Painted in muted tones of sage green, brick red and ivory, the building was one of the newly remodeled Victorians in this neighborhood that was still recovering from Katrina. He was always glad to get home—the first home he'd ever owned, which was a point of pride—and now maybe more than ever, with need still pumping through his system like rocket fuel.

He adjusted the tight bulge under his jeans and took a moment to be sure there was no one else around before jumping out of the truck and striding toward the front door. He fumbled with his keys for a moment, swearing under his breath. Then he was up the stairs to the third floor and in his living room. He tore his shirt over his head as he moved down the narrow hall to the bathroom, kicked his boots off as he hit the light switch. His jeans were next, the zipper catching for a moment on the hard ridge of his erection.

"Fucking Goddamn it," he muttered, not really caring except that it meant another second of delay before he could get his cock in his hand.

He twisted the handles in the shower and stepped in while the water was still cold. Not that it helped. Not that he cared. He leaned back into the cool, green slate tiles and closed his eyes as he fisted his cock with a sigh.

"Oh, yeah, that's better." Only it wasn't. It wasn't her. But it would have to fucking do tonight.

The water warmed against his skin, and his mind swirled

with pictures and memories of the girl whose image he'd come to maybe hundreds of times.

Summer Grace in those too-short shorts and tiny halter tops she wore all summer long, her bare feet and pink-painted toes making her seem even more naked somehow. Her pink mouth that was always a little soft and pouty, even when she laughed—and never more than when she'd kissed him out of a deep sleep that night in his tent on one of the Rae family camping trips in Colorado.

Jamie groaned at the memory of those plush lips pressed against his, sliding and seeking. Soft and warm and knowing. Jesus, the girl could kiss like crazy, even when she was barely fifteen, hardly more than a kid. And if he was perfectly honest with himself, he'd let it go on a few moments even after he realized he wasn't dreaming.

"Summer Grace, stop it."

"Why? I can feel it, you know, Jamie," she whispered in the dark. "I can feel it against me. You want me."

"I was . . . I was sleeping and . . ."

"And you got hard as soon as I climbed on top of you," she finished smugly.

It was then he realized he had his hands on her waist. So slender. Without meaning to, he gave her a squeeze before yanking his hands away. "That doesn't mean anything. Come on, now. Get off me."

The little minx leaned in then and brushed her lips over his again and his cock nearly burst.

"You don't really want me to. Tell me the truth, Jamie. You want to kiss me. I know you do."

"No."

Yes.

He *had* wanted to kiss her. He wanted to kiss her now. *Now.* He wanted to feel those lips under his as he pressed her back against the shower wall. As he stripped her naked, pulled her legs up around his waist and plowed into her, his fingers digging into the flesh of her fine, tight ass, bringing a little pain along with the pleasure. He wanted to fuck her right through the wall, to make her scream his name, to make her beg for more.

"Ah!"

He pumped his hips into his tightly fisted hand, sensation coursing through him, a hard pulse-beat of endless need. He pulled in a breath, thought he caught her familiar scent, like violets and rain.

"God. Fucking. Damn it," he ground out as he started to come.

Pleasure tore through him—into his gut, his balls, his mind, leaving him breathless. And still aching for her.

He pushed off the tiles and into the stream of water, letting it pound against his head.

"Fuck it."

Summer Grace may be the one woman he was not supposed to have, but enough was enough. Because no matter how many others he'd been with—and he'd had more than his share, even if he kept it a bit more under the radar than Mick had before he got back together with Allie—it had always been Summer Grace. It always would be. Even as he'd stood in front of a judge and married Traci, it was Summer Grace who'd been on his mind, and not only because he'd felt bad about not telling her he was getting hitched. No. There was always more to it with Brandon's little sister. He'd denied himself for twelve long years. How much was one man supposed to take? He'd been Saint Jamie for long enough. And maybe he was going to hell for it—for breaking his promise— but he had to have her. He couldn't go on like this. She'd sealed that bit of fate when she'd shown up at The Bastille tonight. And in the end, there was no other way he could protect her.

The whole thing was making him feel a little crazy, and a lot more out of control than he cared for. The battle between doing what was best for her and the driving urge he felt to have her in his arms was pure torture. But he knew now what he needed to do. He had to find a way to keep her safe. From the world. From the inevitable predators she would come upon at the BDSM clubs. And from himself. But he had to try.

He shut off the water and stepped onto the bath mat, looked at himself in the mirror as he grabbed a towel from the rack and roughly dried himself.

"That's right," he told his reflection. "We are gonna do something about this insane situation. It's past time. I'll face the music on the other side when the time comes. But the time to be with her is *now*."

He'd give her a day or two to come down off the post-play high, give her time to recover in case she had any subdrop, the sometimes negative side effect of kink play that happened when all the lovely chemicals released in the brain suddenly went away. Oh yes, he'd respect that. Of course he would, as would any Dom worth their salt.

He reached out and slowly but purposefully traced her initials in the steam that fogged the edges of the mirror.

"But then . . . watch out, Summer Grace. Because this time *I'm* coming after *you*. And there's no one left to say no."

SUMMER STRETCHED AND inhaled the rich scent of coffee brewing in her kitchen. Her small blue and white cottage in New Orleans's Gentilly district was a little on the funky side and in need of repair—the old floors creaked, the white tile on the counters was cracked in places—but she loved it. It was July and one of the warmest months of the year in the sub-tropical city, but since it was not quite nine o'clock yet, she had the windows open to catch the cool morning air. The cat that had come with the house—an enormous female with short white fur and blue eyes—was sitting on the counter, washing her paw in a pale ray of sunshine.

"Good morning, Madame. Catch any mice last night? No? Still too slow? Good thing I decided to adopt you and keep that big belly full." She stroked Madame's fur and the cat narrowed one eye at her. She sighed. "Ungrateful wretch, as ever."

She was trying to pretend this was just another day. Not that it really was. She'd been processing her first real play at the club the other night. It had been amazing. But she'd been up half that night getting herself off over and over—with her hands, the showerhead, her toys—with Jamie's face in her mind's eye, making her come so damn hard she had to stifle her screams. She didn't know how many times she'd come since. She swore she'd nearly come when she looked up to see him watching her at The Bastille. She'd dreamed of him as she slept a fitful four or five hours the last two nights, bringing herself to orgasm in the middle of the night and again each morning. Everything had been a sensual blur since her night at the club. Sensual. Sexual. When she squeezed her thighs she could still feel that jagged stab of desire along with the soreness from using herself again and again.

The coffeepot beeped at her, and Summer poured the dark liquid into a large ceramic mug, adding a few drops of cream. Not that she needed the caffeine today, with her heart a small hammer in her chest. Desire. Confusion. Anxiety. What she needed was to calm the hell down. Moving to the window next to the kitchen table, she looked out at the small garden that was all hers. Well, almost. She was leasing with an option to buy, and she was hopeful things would work out. Her salary managing Luxe, one of the most expensive lingerie shops downtown, helped, but it was a struggle. Still, she'd spent a small portion of her "play money" on plants for her garden. Nothing made her feel as peaceful as working her hands into the earth, seeing her little garden flourish—and God knew she needed some peace this morning.

She swung open the screen door and took her mug outside, Madame following her. The backyard had come with the two tall magnolia trees whose creamy white blossoms gave off a gorgeous perfume, but she'd added the small fig tree, the different varieties of lilies, the pink and red Rangoon Creeper—her favorite variety of honeysuckle—the rosemary that smelled almost as good to her. The scents of her garden were always present, like a subtle perfume, the humidity of New Orleans releasing the fragrance. She moved down the narrow brick path, reaching out to stroke her fingers over the leaves of a large fern that grew in the shade of one of the magnolias, and remembered the sensual touch of Maîtresse Renee from the other night.

It had been a wonderful night—her first real foray into the BDSM scene, other than what she now knew was called "bedroom play." She'd let a few guys tie her to their beds, had let one guy spank her. She'd asked a lot of them to pinch her, to bite her. But being with someone who actually *knew* what they were doing—and in that amazing environment—had been incredible. Like every dark fantasy she'd ever had come true. Well, almost. Because Jamie Stewart-Greer, who'd starred in nearly every fantasy that had ever tumbled through her head, hadn't been a part of the real-life scenario. Other than that wide-eyed look he'd given her. Had he really been that surprised to see her there?

"Good thing I've sworn off him," she murmured to Madame, or maybe to herself. "He's always underestimated me."

She'd chased Jamie most of her life, but finally about a year ago she'd come to her senses after yet another breakup with a guy who was nice and smart and seemed to really care about her, but . . . he wasn't Jamie. She'd decided right then that she had to find a way to let go of her juvenile obsession with him or she'd spend the rest of her life alone. And the fact was, she'd had to start figuring out who she was besides Brandon's little sister, the girl whose brother had died. The one who wanted what she couldn't have.

"Enough is enough," she told the cat, who looked surprised at the emphasis in her tone. "I mean, if he doesn't want me it's stupid to keep chasing after him. I've never had to chase any other man. *Ever.*" Madame turned and sauntered into the garden. "I'm not chasing you, either," Summer muttered.

She blew on her coffee to cool it down. So what if she'd practically had to re-create the way she thought about men and sex and *herself* to get Jamie out of her head? She'd done it. And life was good. She had a great job, great friends. There was her darling Dennie, who she'd known since kindergarten—a girl couldn't ask for a better best friend. Allie was back in town and they were closer than ever. And since Allie had taken her to get her tattoo a few months ago, she'd become friends with Rosie, the artist at Midnight Ink who'd done the beautiful phoenix in red and orange and gold—the color of flames—that now covered the left side of her ribs. An appropriate symbol for the changes she'd gone through.

That had been the beginning of the discussion about getting into the kink scene. Rosie had revealed her involvement easily enough, and it hadn't taken Summer long to put two and two together. When she'd asked Allie if she was involved in kink her friend had admitted it to her and agreed to help her learn what real BDSM was about. Allie and Rosie had both helped her, giving her reading to do, answering questions, taking her to BDSM 101 classes, and eventually taking her to a munch—an event where kinky folk met and talked. And now, finally, her first play party.

Her body was still a little sore, and her bottom carried bruises from her play. She'd experienced what might have been a little subdrop on Saturday morning, but a workout at the gym followed by a hot shower and lunch with Rosie had cured that. Now she simply felt good. Amazing, really. Except for her agonizing obsession with the ridiculously sexy Jamie, brought back to life when their eyes met. While she'd been getting her first real kink play ever. She'd been enjoying herself, loving it. But then she saw Jamie watching her and every sensation she felt the rest of the night had been magnified times ten. Times a hundred. She'd been electrified by nothing more than knowing he'd *seen* her.

Calm. The fuck. Down.

She sipped her coffee carefully, testing the temperature, enjoying the acrid flavor on her tongue. She felt more alive since the other night. More acutely aware of the world around her, every sight and flavor, every texture and scent. More aware even of her own body.

She'd watched herself getting off in the mirror over her dresser the other night, imagining it was Jamie who saw her. And it wasn't only Jamie. She imagined Renee watching her, too—Renee watching Jamie watching *her.* It wasn't that she wanted to sleep with the beautiful Domme who Allie and Rosie had referred her to for her first play. She felt some stirrings of attraction to Maîtresse

Renee, but she wasn't as sexually attracted to women as she was to men. It was more the kink play itself. Giving in to the taboo, giving in to the fantasies she'd had in her head for years. The whole new fetish she may have discovered knowing Jamie had been watching.

She let out a small sigh, suppressed it with a sip of her coffee. Jamie was nothing more than fantasy, one she'd come to realize was best left where it had always been, where *he* had always been—in her imagination. Him being at the club didn't change that.

Liar.

She closed her eyes, letting her head fall back until she felt the morning sun on her face, on the rise of her breasts that curved against the pale pink silk of her short nightie.

God, if only it could be him, just once.

Her body heated all over from more than the gentle sun—it was imagining Jamie spanking her, pulling her hair, as Maîtresse Renee had the other night. His arm coming around her throat and tightening . . .

A soft moan escaped her.

"Hey, Summer Grace."

"Jesus!"

She jumped, her coffee splashing onto the brick walkway as she whirled, her face going hot when she found Jamie in all his six-foot-something glory behind her. Damn, but he looked good in his low-slung jeans and the white wifebeater that showed off the leanly cut muscles in his arms, the breadth of his shoulders. The small, curved bar piercing his eyebrow caught the sunlight, giving his beautiful face, which had always looked a little sweet to her, a hint of the bad boy beneath. The piercing and the scruff on his chin, his jaw. No man should look this good at nine o'clock on a Sunday morning.

"Sorry to startle you," he said, his tone low, the lopsided grin on his generous mouth letting her know he wasn't sorry in the least.

"You don't just sneak up on a person like that, Jamie," she fumed, not sure whether she was more pissed off at being taken by surprise or that her nipples were going hard at the sight of him. She tried to cross her arms over her chest, but couldn't figure it out with the mug still in her hand and had to give up. What she wanted to do was flail. Jamie at the club. Jamie *here*.

Keep your cool.

"Really? he asked. "Like you did to me, oh, a few dozen times?"

She sighed and shoved her hair from her face. "Yeah, okay. But at least I had being young and stupid as an excuse. What's yours?"

He paused, searching her face, his brows drawing together over green eyes that looked as if they were sprinkled with gold in the sunlight. Still the most beautiful eyes she'd ever seen. Still the hardest-cut jawline and most perfectly molded chin. Still the most adorable dimples when he smiled—if "adorable" was a word one could use for the hottest man on the planet. The hottest *Dominant* man. A fact that was making her crazy even though she should know better.

He stuck his hands in his pockets and shrugged, but his gaze on hers went dark and stormy, letting her know the casual attitude was a sham.

"I just wanted to see you."

She studied his face, and his green gaze settled on hers. And she was consumed for several long moments, just like at the club. Desire. Confusion. Anxiety.

Desire.

No.

"You 'just wanted to see me.' Out of the blue? After seeing me at The Bastille, it's out of the blue?"

"No, not out of the blue. I'd like to say so, but the truth is I've wanted to come talk to you since I saw you Friday night."

She waved a dismissive hand, pretending to be unaffected by the idea of him watching her even as everything in her contracted with razor-sharp arousal. "If you came here to give me one of your lectures, you can save it. I'm a consenting adult and I know exactly what I'm doing."

He took a step closer and she hated that her pulse went thready.

"I didn't come here to lecture you. How could I? I was there, too, and I may be a lot of things, but I'm no hypocrite." He paused, and she saw his throat working as he swallowed hard. "I also saw Allie and we talked, so I know how you came to be there, and I understand she'd have warned you I'd probably show up at some point."

She nodded warily. Jamie wasn't going to lecture her? That was a first. "She did. She informed me of *all* the risks I'd be taking. Nice place, The Bastille. Nice and roomy. Surely there's enough space for both of us there. If it makes you too uncomfortable, I'll schedule around you and go when you don't plan to be there."

He took another step toward her and her hand tightened around the ceramic mug, her pulse sputtering.

"Why would you want to go and do that, Summer Grace? It may seem like I don't appreciate how much you've grown—that you've grown up. It may seem—and granted, you'd probably be right—that I've mostly treated you like a child. But—"

"You think?"

He cracked a grin then, his dimples flashing again. "I know. And I'm sorry. It's time I stopped. Hell, it's time I stopped denying what you seem to have known about us since you were just a kid."

She blinked hard. "About *us*?"

"I think you know what I mean."

She thought she did, too—she simply couldn't believe it. "And this realization about *us* hit you on Friday night?" Her stomach knotted and a small rage burned through her. "Friday night, when I was naked at The Bastille and getting spanked? That's when the stars aligned and you had this epiphany about wanting to play with me, or wanting to have sex with me? Seriously, Jamie?"

He had the grace to look surprised. "What? No, it's not like that. Is that what you think of me?"

His tone was laced with that trace of Scottish accent that only came out when he was worked up about something, or sometimes when he'd had a few beers. He'd been in the U.S. since he was seven years old, and the accent was mostly long-buried. Something deeper was going on with him.

"No. No. I just . . . What is it then, Jamie? What are you trying to say?"

There was a long pause while his features relaxed. "Maybe it's that I've woken up, and about time, too. All these years I've turned away from you, from what I've wanted, and now I'm not sure I even know why."

"Because you're so damn noble?" she teased, still half mad but unable to restrain her desire to make him smile. "The White Knight of New Orleans, saving fair maidens from having to make their own decisions."

The dimples were back. "Yeah. I deserved that." His tone softened. "I don't want to turn away anymore. I want you, Summer Grace."

"Jamie . . ."

She turned her back to him and took a few steps down the

brick path, emotion roiling inside her. She'd been mad when she spit out the words, but he *had* just seen her naked. He *had* just found out about her desire for kink. And now he'd shown up in her garden on a Sunday morning telling her, after all these years, that he wanted her.

He wanted her.

How long had she been waiting to hear those words? How many times had he laughed her off or turned her down when she came on to him, denying the chemistry she *knew* was between them? Too damn many.

She whirled around, ready to give him a good scolding for being a superficial prick and send him on *his* way for a change, but as her body turned she collided with him. His arms went around her, yanking her in tight.

"Jamie? What the—"

He cut her off by crushing her mouth to his and she melted into him, her head bent back as he leaned over her, his hot, wet tongue parting her lips with a silent demand. And oh God, he tasted good. Like coffee and warm flesh and sex. His arms tightened until she could barely breathe, but it only made her go wet, her legs shaking. It was *Jamie* kissing her like this, with a hunger and a heat that went through her like a shot of pure desire.

When he paused they were both breathing hard. He hadn't let her go. She couldn't make herself open her eyes, afraid it would stop. Afraid he'd kiss her again. Afraid he wouldn't.

No. Oh God, yes . . .

"Jamie," she whispered, not sure if she was going to argue or ask for more.

He didn't give her a chance to make up her mind. He buried his fingers in her hair until they were close to her scalp and *pulled*, exactly the right way. His mouth came down on hers once more, bruising her lips. She loved it. She loved . . .

No!

She dropped the mug on the brick path with a crash and pushed hard on his shoulders, pulling her mouth from his.

"Damn it, Jamie! Don't do this to me. You've never wanted me before and now . . . Goddamn it, I liked that mug," she sputtered.

"Shh. Come here, Summer Grace," he said softly, his grip on her waist like iron as he moved her away from the shards but didn't let her go. His hold on her was so hard. So commanding. "I've wanted you for years. You know how much. You always have." He leaned in and pressed a kiss to her neck, paused to bite just hard enough to pinch the skin between his teeth, then kissed the tender spot again.

Her head was spinning, her body melting. But she was furious, too.

"I'm not that kid anymore."

He laughed softly. "Oh, I can see that. I can feel it."

She tried to struggle in his grasp, but he took both her hands in one of his and held on tight, pressing their hands to his chest, the other arm still like a vise around her waist.

"Damn it, Jamie. You can't do this—just march into my quiet Sunday morning like you think you have the right. Like you can simply take what you want after telling me to run along."

He pulled back to look into her eyes. "Tell me you don't want this, Summer Grace," he demanded, his tone a low growl. "Tell me you don't feel the same and I'll go."

"No."

"No, what? No, you don't want me here, kissing you, touching you?" He lowered his voice until it was a purr filled with heat and gravel. "Or no, don't stop?"

She shook her head, her mind and body at war. "I don't fucking know!"

He was quiet a moment, his gaze hard on hers. "Then answer this question: Are you all right? Are you still in subspace from Friday night? Subdrop? Did seeing me there fuck with your head space?"

"What? No, I'm fine," she lied.

"Swear it to me."

"I am fucking fine, Jamie. I was perfect until you arrived." She tried to pull her hands away but he only tightened his grip.

"Do you want me to stop? Because you've been at the club and apparently mentored by Allie and Rosie, so you understand how this works. You know damn well I need consent, even with you. Hell, maybe even more because it's you. I should have fucking had it before I kissed you."

"Still the white knight?" she asked.

"Yeah. Still am. To a point." He lowered his head until his lush lips were inches from hers. Until she could feel his warm breath on her skin. "But I need to touch you so badly that if you don't tell me to go right now, the white knight act is gonna disappear in a hurry, and I will be all over you like an animal, Summer Grace. So what's it gonna be? Yes? Or no?"

Her sex was wet with wanting—a wanting she couldn't remember ever being without, but multiplied by a hundred with him so near. His lean, muscular body was pressed tight against hers, and she could feel the length of his hard-on against her thigh. She needed to feel it inside her so badly she was shaking. It pissed her off to know he could feel her trembling in his hands. That he could still do this to her after everything she'd done to get over him. But how could she say no to the man who had been her fantasy forever?

She was mad.
She was more turned on than she'd ever been in her life.
"No," she said through clenched teeth.
His frown was fierce. "No?"
"No. Don't you dare leave now, Jamie."

CHAPTER

Two

S UMMER WENT HOT and loose all over as she watched the change come over his face, his eyes glinting a hard, glassy green, almost as if they were lit from within. There was fire there. And stark command. And Jesus, it was *Jamie* looking at her like he was going to eat her alive.

He kissed her again, and it was all hunger and need and hurting, he kissed her so damn hard. It was everything she'd ever needed. Her body surged against his, everything just out of control. She couldn't think. It was as if he'd shocked her senseless, and all she knew was his hot tongue in her mouth, the flavor of him, the scents of something dark—sandalwood or patchouli mixed with a little motor oil—and all of it so deliciously male she never wanted to stop breathing him in. She was soaking wet simply from kissing him, from feeling the authority in the way he held her.

You are in big trouble.

She didn't care.

"Your bedroom," he muttered from between clenched teeth.

Somehow she stumbled into the house. He was right behind her, holding her wrist hard at the small of her back, his body tight against hers, kissing and biting her shoulder as they moved into the bedroom. He whirled her body in his arms, everything happening so fast she had no time to think. He stripped her nightie off and it fell around her feet, leaving her naked. Then he took a step back and tore his shirt over his head.

"Oh . . ." It came out on a sigh of pure, burning desire.

His body was amazing. Broad shoulders, muscular chest. The washboard abs, the narrow waist. Even his tattoo was sexy—she'd always found tattoos sexy—the words *memento mortalitatem tuam*, Latin for "remember your mortality," she knew, tattooed in a line down his ribs on his right side in bold calligraphic script. And oh, God, when had he gotten his nipples pierced? The two small, steel rings made her want to curl her tongue around them.

Her gaze flicked up to his, then down again as she heard him unbutton his jeans, the quiet *snick* of the zipper coming down. The fact that he wore nothing underneath made her sex clench. But he kept the damn jeans on, the solid ridge of his hard cock hidden beneath the worn denim, tempting her. She could hardly stand it.

She licked her lips. "Jamie—"

"Shh, Summer Grace. I need you to be quiet now, sugar. No discussion. Because now isn't the time to negotiate and I am going to have to rein myself in to keep things under control."

"Don't, Jamie. We don't need control."

He stepped forward and slid his hand around her neck. She gasped in pleasure, felt his fingers flex in response.

"Yes, we damn well do, sweetheart. No arguments. Just fucking kiss me, girl."

She sighed through the slight constriction of her throat, loving the way he held her at that edge as she tilted her chin and his mouth closed over hers. She opened to his searching tongue, losing herself in the sweetness of his mouth. In his utter command.

When he pulled away, she was panting.

"Right now you are mine," he whispered against her cheek, his hand still on her throat, his breath warm on her skin.

"Yes," she murmured.

Her body already belonged to him. She couldn't think of anything else at that moment but the desire—the *need*—coursing through her flesh, taking her over. *He* was taking her over. If he didn't really touch her she was going to explode.

With his hand wrapped around her neck, using only the slightest pressure, he backed her up step by step until she felt the mattress behind her legs.

"Down you go, now," he said, his tone quiet. He was so damn commanding he didn't need to use a harsh tone, a raised voice. She'd imagined a thousand times what being with him would be like—and, as she'd gotten older and discovered her desire for kink, what being dominated by him would be like. But never had she imagined it being this good. This natural.

He exerted the tiniest bit of pressure, guiding her to sit on the bed, her damp thighs hitting the cool sheets.

He leaned over her, clamping his hand a bit tighter. "This time, Summer Grace," he told her, "it's just gonna be you and me and the tiniest edge of kink. Because I fucking need you right now. Do you understand? Later, if you want to, we can do full negotiations. But I have to admit I am in no shape to do that. And judging by your eyes, your breath, your silence, by how beautifully hard your nipples are, neither are you, sweetheart. So tell me again. Is this still a 'yes'?"

"Oh yes," she breathed, the words whispering on a long sigh. There was no other possible answer.

He smiled, his dimples making small, charming divots in his cheeks, and she had a flash of Jamie at sixteen. That was when she'd first fallen for him. It had only taken fourteen years to get to this point. Fourteen years and her decision to finally end her pursuit of him. But he was right in front of her and she was naked and he was touching her—had kissed her! The kissing was a revelation in itself, the flavor of him still warm on her tongue. The answer had to be yes.

He kept his gaze on hers as he slid his hand down and his fingers bore down on the tender pressure points just below her collarbone, hurting her the tiniest bit. Letting her know his power, that he understood very thoroughly how to cause pain with the simplest touch. Then he moved a bit lower, between her breasts, pressed down, making a small hurting spot deep in her flesh. She sighed into the pain, needing to be touched. Needing to feel that little bit of pain. Needing *Jamie*. As if he heard her need, he gathered both breasts in his hands, kneading gently, his thumbs teasing her nipples, and pleasure arced into her like an electric current. He pinched one nipple and she gasped.

"Oh!"

"You like that, do you, sugar? Oh yeah, I can tell you do. No, no. Hold still for me."

He pinched again and she had to bite her lip not to move. It felt so good.

"I can see how hard you're trying. Good girl. Now try harder."

He pinched her again, both nipples this time, and she cried out.

"Ah, God!"

"Still," he ordered.

To her surprise he leaned down and pressed his lips in that space between her breasts where he'd dug into the pressure point there. She let her head fall back with a sigh of pure pleasure. The contrast of sensations was making her head spin. He was making her head spin. That little bit of mind-fuck and the fact that it was *Jamie*. That fact was mind-fuck in itself.

"Oh yes . . ."

She arched into him, and he pulled away. He stood there simply staring at her, watching her, exploring her body with his eyes—eyes heated with lust, glittering in the soft morning light. And all the while her body heated even more, her system going into overdrive, flooding with desire, a hard-edged need unlike anything she'd ever felt before.

He placed one knee next to her bare thigh on the bed and even the touch of denim on her skin was enough to send a new surge of lust through her.

"Jamie, please . . ."

"Please what, sugar?"

"Do . . . something . . ."

He grinned, the dimples flashing again. "Oh, I plan to. I'm just taking my time to soak you in, girl. And to calm the hell down so I do right by you." He reached out and traced his fingertip slowly over her throat, then down her side, over her ribs. "I love the ink on you, by the way. Beautiful. And so damn hot." His finger feathered over her skin, leaving tiny firelights of pleasure in its wake, a small trail of sensation.

Between her thighs was an insistent pulse-beat of *wanting*. She waited, doing everything she could to hold still and take it, knowing that was what he wanted. Fucking torture for a control freak like her, but especially because it was him touching her. She couldn't find it within herself to speak.

He used two fingers on her breastbone to push her back onto the bed. With the other hand, he spread her legs wide, so wide she knew she was completely open to him. But she wanted him to see—wanted him to see her, to see what he'd missed out on all these years. To see how wet he'd made her.

He bent over her, one palm flattening between her breasts, the other pressing hard—deliciously—on her thigh.

"I'm going to taste you, Summer Grace. I am going to bury my face between your lovely thighs and lick you and suck you and fuck you with my tongue until you come. And then I'm going to really fuck you. But that'll have to wait."

With his hands on her waist, he scooted her up on the bed, then he slid his hands down to her knees and roughly forced her thighs farther apart. She loved it—the manhandling. Loved his soft voice and his rough touch. So much it was making her dizzy.

In moments he was kneeling over her on the bed, his mouth between her thighs. And oh God, she thought she might actually die.

Soft lips and wet, seeking tongue—it was everything at once as he used one hand to hold her hip down, hard enough to hurt, while with the other he spread her open until her clit peeked out from under its hood. He began to flick his tongue at the delicate nub of sensitive flesh. Pleasure was like heat lightning, striking over and over, deep into her body. He moved down, lapping at her swollen lips, her clitoris, her waiting hole with his soft tongue.

She grasped his head, his buzz cut like velvet under her hands, and hung on, moaning. Panting. When he took her clit into his mouth and sucked hard, scraping the tip with his teeth as he thrust two fingers inside her, she came up off the bed, the first edge of climax shivering through her. He must have felt it—he added a third finger, and maybe a fourth—she wasn't sure. All she knew was the sensation of being filled up. And at the same time he sucked so hard that the line between pain and pleasure was a blur. But she loved it. She screamed as she came, her body convulsing, drowning in sensation.

Before the last shivers of her climax had subsided, he began again, this time pinching the lips of her sex between his fingers and licking her clit, then pushing his tongue inside her. It was so soft and wet, the sensation nearly indescribable—that and the contrast of the pain from his pinching fingers. And his scent all around her, seeming to surround her, envelop her, as the heat of their bodies grew together. Soon she was coming again, shaking with it, crying his name.

"Jamie! Ah, God, Jamie . . . Yes!"

He lifted his face and wiped his mouth with the back of his hand, grinning, all dimples again, and even that was hot to her—the pleased look on his face. The damn dimples that had always made her swoon.

"You want to come for me again, sugar girl?"

"Yeah . . . I do. I need to."

"Mmm, those might be the sexiest damn words I've ever heard."

He stood, stroked the solid ridge of his erection through his jeans and she held her breath, waiting for him to reveal the flesh she'd dreamed of for years.

"I need to see you," she told him. "To touch you. Come on, Jamie."

"You want to touch me?" he asked, his voice a low rumble. "Come on then. You take it out. Take my cock out and suck me."

She shivered at the way he was talking to her. Oh, she had

never in a million years imagined what a filthy mouth he had. Somehow she'd always thought of him as more straight-laced than she was. But he had a hell of an edge in the bedroom. She hadn't thought anything could make her more irresistibly drawn to Jamie Stewart-Greer, but oh my . . . that beautiful, masculine face and that dirty, dirty mouth. The man made her shaky, she needed him so badly.

She sat up on the edge of the bed and placed her hands on his hips. Looking up at him, catching his gaze with hers, she smoothed her palms over the front of his jeans until she felt that hard shaft. She drew her fingertips over it, drawing a groan from him. The desire blazing in his green eyes went through her like a surge of heat up her spine, and she suddenly—blindingly—became aware of her own power. The power of being utterly female. Of having this incredible man at her mercy. At the mercy of his desire for her. And the mercy of her sexual confidence, which was blossoming with every moment.

She ran her fingernails up the thick shaft, swallowing hard at the size of him, then back down, tearing her gaze from his face long enough to see his abs clench with need.

She brought her gaze back to his. "I can't wait to have your cock in my hands," she murmured. "To stroke you. To take you in my mouth. To suck you."

"Fuck, Summer Grace."

"No, don't call me that now, Jamie. Call me anything else."

He grabbed the back of her head and yanked her in until her face was an inch from his open fly.

"I will call you anything I want, sugar girl. We may not have negotiated full-on play yet, but never forget that when you're with me, *I* am in charge. Completely." The command in his voice scared her a little. She loved it. "And"—his tone and the grip on her hair softened—"you are always Summer Grace to me, even though you hate it when I call you that. You are always that sweet and sexy girl I've known forever. Wanted forever."

"Oh . . ."

Had he? All those years that he'd turned her away? But she couldn't think about it now. She could barely think of anything but doing exactly what she'd said. She licked her lips.

"You call me anything then, Jamie. As long as I can touch you."

"Yeah, touch me, sweetheart. Do it."

He WATCHED HER as she pulled on his jeans, one small hand snaking in and wrapping around his cock.

He groaned. And thought he'd explode when she freed it from his jeans. The look on her face was pure sex: her blue, feline eyes narrowing, a sultry smile on her lips. Lush pink lips that opened to take the head of his cock into her mouth.

"Ah, yes, sugar."

Pleasure was some strange combination—the liquid heat of her mouth and something that sliced into him like a knife. That sharp. That keenly edged. Because it was *her.*

Control.

He pulled in a gasping breath, then another, deeper this time.

He exhaled as she slid her tongue over the tip, into the hole for a moment, and some vague part of his lust-addled mind wondered where she'd learned that trick. Then his brain went empty as she swallowed him whole.

"Jesus!"

But she didn't stop, didn't even pause. With her hand still wrapped firmly around the base of his erection, she slid her mouth up and down the shaft, pausing to lick at the head, to nibble, to scrape her teeth lightly over the swollen flesh before sliding her lovely pink lips down again. He'd never in his life seen anything so damn hot as Summer Grace's mouth on him, her lips wrapped around his hard cock—harder than he'd ever been in his life. He had to close his eyes or he was going to come in her mouth like some sixteen-year-old. Like he had into his fisted hand thinking about her as a teenager, over and over.

"Oh yeah."

"What are you doing here, Summer Grace?"

There was just enough light coming in through the window of the Rae's family room for him to see she was wearing that skimpy outfit she called pajamas, but was really nothing more than a midriff-baring tank top and tiny cotton knit shorts. He could see her nipples under the thin fabric of the top. The sweet floral print did nothing to make it any more innocent-looking. His dick jumped.

She crawled onto the couch, straddling his body. He was too stunned to do anything but lie perfectly still. Could she feel his erection through the cotton sheet covering him?

"I came to see you," she whispered. "I came to see all of you."

She slowly pulled the sheet down, already the temptress at fourteen years old.

Fuck. Fourteen years old!

He grabbed at her hand as the sheet came down and revealed his tented boxers.

"Goddamn it, Summer Grace."

He yanked the sheet back up.

She leaned down until her mouth was mere inches from the rise under the sheet.

"Come on, Jamie. Let me see it. Let me kiss it." She batted her baby blues at him. "I know how."

Fourteen. Fuck.

"*Go away. You have to go. Go!*"

She wasn't going now. He wasn't about to tell her to. And he wasn't going to jerk himself off tonight to the image of her hard nipples under that floral top the way he had for too many years. No, now he was going to come with her. Inside her.

Yes.

"Enough, sugar. And tell me you have a condom in here somewhere."

She licked her lips. Sexy as hell. Why had he waited so many years? "Of course I do."

She turned and rolled over onto her stomach, and he watched the curve of her perfect little heart-shaped ass as she reached into the nightstand drawer, pulling out a small foil packet. Instead of handing it to him she tore at it with her teeth, making him smile. Oh, he liked this girl. Every bit the sex kitten he'd always known she was, and yet more, somehow.

She took the condom out as he kicked his way out of his black boots, then his jeans, climbing onto the bed, one knee on either side of her hips.

"Put it on me," he instructed her.

She slipped the latex down over his hard shaft, and he had to bite back a groan at her touch. He warned himself one more time before he was inside her.

Control.

But as soon as she lay back and opened her sweet thighs for him, her naked little pussy glistening with need and come, as wanton as any woman he'd ever seen and twice as beautiful, he almost lost it. He had to bite the inside of his lip, to take a breath to center himself. And he pressed one hand down hard on her shoulder, exerting his command over her so that *he* would know it as much as she did. He touched the tip of his cock to her opening, and she smiled, her eyes gleaming. One small tilt of his hips and he was in.

She gasped, but she never took her gaze from his. And even in that moment when he thought all he'd be considering was finally being inside her body, the ecstasy burning like a fuse up his spine, something in him broke open. Let go. She felt it, too—he saw it in the way her pupils went wide, in the parting of her lips, the look of awe on her lovely face. And in that moment something shifted. A small voice in the back of his mind told him he'd lied to himself about why he'd come here. It wasn't about settling some kind of old debt of mutual lust. It was *her*.

Summer Grace.

He was fucked.

But there she was beneath him, all big blue eyes and plush pink lips. He laid a hand between her breasts, felt her erratic heartbeat. Her small fingers wrapped around his wrist, holding him there.

"Jamie . . ."

"What is it, sugar?"

"I need you," she whispered.

He shook his head. He couldn't figure it all out now. Not with her naked body twined around his. He'd think later. He couldn't do anything, couldn't feel anything but *this*. *Her*.

"I'm here, sugar girl," he murmured, capturing her hand in his and raising it over her head as he slid deeper into her.

Then it was all sighs and moans, desire met by the rapture of touch and response. Building, coiling. Inside she was like satin, tight and smooth, surrounding his flesh. He pushed into her, slid out easy as silk, she was so damn wet. Her other hand came up, grasping his wrist, and he'd never seen anything more beautiful than her pleasure-torn face, her arms over her head, entrapped by sensation, as lost in it as he was.

With his other hand he brought both her knees up and together until they were pinned between his chest and hers, and he pressed her down with his body. He needed to command her completely, to make her entirely his. Surging in and out of her, slow and rhythmically, then hard and fast, then slow and steady again, desire spiraled impossibly. She was panting, moaning, whispering his name. He swore he could feel every detail of her body: the velvet texture inside her dragging at his rigid cock, her baby-smooth skin all over. He'd never seen anything as exquisite as Summer Grace's face, those feline blue eyes as he thrust, pleasure shimmering into his body until he was gasping, biting back his climax.

"Come for me, sugar," he muttered through gritted teeth. "Come on, now."

"Ah, God, Jamie. You feel so damn good," she panted. "I can't . . . I can't believe how good you feel. How you fill me up."

"Then come again, sweetheart. I want to feel you like a fist around me. I want to feel your need, your clenching. Come, my girl."

"Oh." Her voice trembled. Her body trembled. And then her sweet pussy clenched, over and over. Tightening around him like a glove. Like the purest pleasure he'd ever known.

"Ah, yes, sugar girl. Yes, yes, yes . . ."

He shivered as the first wave of orgasm slammed into him and shook him to the core. The last thing he saw before sensation blinded him was her face. The flush of her climax on her cheeks. Pleasure like a thousand glittering stars in her eyes. Beauty like he'd never seen before in his life. Then the world went black as he shuddered and groaned.

"Ah, Christ, my baby girl. Yes!" He could barely breathe, sensation making his gut clench, his balls, his brain. He pulled in a gasping breath, muttered, "Oh yeah. Yes, sweetheart. So good. You feel like fucking heaven, I swear it. So good."

He let her legs go and gathered her in his arms, holding her tight, crushing her small body to his. She was squirming a little, just flexing her hands on his back, her nails digging in. Didn't matter. All that mattered was whatever was buzzing though his system. Inside his chest. He didn't know what it was. Didn't understand. Didn't matter. She was there with him. His Summer Grace.

Finally he realized she really was squirming, and her gasping had switched from panting breath to what he thought were small sobs.

He pulled back to look at her. Sure enough there were tears pooling in her eyes.

"Fuck. Did I hurt you, sweetheart? Injure you? I was holding you so tight."

She sniffed, pushed at his chest. "It's not that, Goddamn it, Jamie."

"What, then?"

"It's this. *Us.* I don't know why I thought I could do this. All these years of wanting you and you rejecting me. And now you come to my house and take me to bed and it was fucking amazing!"

"I . . . may still be mostly brainless from the best orgasm of my life, sugar girl, but I'm not understanding what the problem is."

Yet some part of him did. This was fucking dangerous, if she was feeling anything like he was. Things he wasn't ready to look at too closely. He wasn't ready to let her go. *Fucking amazing* was right.

"God, men are so dense." She pushed at his chest again, trying to get out from under him, but he wasn't having it.

"Let's just calm down here. Because this was good, and we barely even took the time to make it everything it could be. Everything it should be, Summer Grace. I'll admit I've been dense. I've been a damn idiot. But I'm here now."

"Yes, *now*. And you think we can do this—be together in my bed—as if we'd just met? Had no history? We have a damn complicated history, Jamie."

His chest was going tight. "You wanted this as much as I did," he said, his tone low.

"Yes. I did. More, maybe. But now . . ."

"Now what?"

"Yes, exactly. Now what? Where do we go from here?" She sounded so vulnerable it made him ache.

Focus on this—on the reason you came here.

He drew in a long breath. "Okay. This is what I know. I want to see you again. I want us to have those negotiations. I want to play you. Here, at the club, however you want it to be. Can you tell me you don't want those things?"

Her tight shoulders slumped. She sniffed again. "No. I'd be lying if I did. But Jamie, I feel like this whole situation is too . . . loaded. Do you know what I mean?"

Her eyes were so big. He saw fear there and it made his chest go tight. He stroked a few strands of her silky blonde hair away from her flushed cheek. "I do know. I don't think anyone but you and I could possibly have any idea how deep this goes, how complicated it is, not even the people who know us best. There's always been a connection that belongs to just the two of us. It's taken me a long time to realize it, and feeling that punch to the gut seeing you at the club—I'll admit that. But I know it's there."

She bit her lip and blinked a few times, her features softening. "Jamie? Will you kiss me? Because when you're kissing me I sort of stop thinking and I'm pretty sure that's what I need to do right now."

He smiled. "Anytime, sweetheart."

He bent and pressed his lips to hers, and she opened up to him, her tongue warm and seeking. And together they lost themselves in each other, letting the worries of their strange and unique situation fall away.

SUMMER DRIFTED, HALF asleep, half dreaming. Brandon. Why was she thinking of her brother now, with his best friend lying next to her, his breathing shallow with sleep? Sleep that invaded her body, her mind, forcing her into its depths.

Brandon came into the kitchen, slamming the back door behind him like he always did. Mom hated that, but he did it anyway. It was a guy thing, she knew.

He ruffled her hair as she sat at the table with her history book opened in front of her. "Hey, little sis. I brought you some of that saltwater taffy you like." He tossed a white bag down on the table. "Strawberry, right?"

"Thanks, Bran." She reached eagerly for the bag as he sat down across from her.

"What are you doing, Summer Grace?"

"Studying. World War One. Ugh!" She bit into the taffy and it melted on her tongue.

"No, I mean what are you doing with Jamie? Seriously, what the hell?"

Her heart sank, the taffy suddenly like chalk in her mouth.

"Brandon," she tried to say, but the taffy seemed to expand, and she couldn't swallow enough to talk.

His blond brows drew together. "Tell me, sis. Tell me why you're doing this to me," he demanded, his features full of pain. "Tell me why you're doing this to Mom and Dad."

Shaking her head, her chest flooded with panic. She had to explain. She tried to spit the candy out into her hand, then tried to pull it out, but it was stuck. She was stuck. With her mouth full of candy. With what she'd done.

Her big brother shook his head. "I can't believe you, Summer Grace. I can't believe you'd do this to us—I can't believe you'd do this to your family. It's all your fault. Everything *is."*

No!

If only she could tell him . . . Tell him something. Explain herself. But all she could do was choke on the sugar hardening in her mouth—choke on her own actions while her brother stormed out the back door. She knew he'd never come back.

Summer woke in a cold sweat, clutching the sheets to her chest.

Just a dream.

Brandon would never talk to her like that. He would never judge her so harshly. Would he? He used to tease her about her crush on Jamie, but he was her brother, and he'd never thought in a million years that Jamie would feel the same. Maybe. Why had he said that about their parents? They wouldn't even care that she was with Jamie. That was crazy. Wasn't it?

Fuck.

She threw the covers back and threw on a tank top and a pair of shorts and quietly crept from the room, leaving Jamie asleep in her bed.

She went outside and sat in one of the white wicker chairs on her small brick patio, her arms wrapped around herself, trying to shake off the nightmare. The sun was high in the brilliant blue sky and it was far too hot to be outside in New Orleans in July, but she felt like she had to *breathe*.

It was just a bad dream. It wasn't real.

No, only her time with Jamie was real—that and the apparent emotional repercussions.

They'd stayed in bed for hours, exploring each other's bodies in a way she'd never done with any other man—and she'd had her share. But this was different. Maybe too different. Especially when it came to her dreams turning into some kind of crazy reality she still couldn't quite believe. And because she'd realized when she came out of her pleasure-soaked stupor that he was only there because he'd seen her at The Bastille and felt jealous when he'd seen her playing with someone else. She'd laid there for a good half hour but the knot in her stomach hadn't gone away. It had been a relief to finally drift into sleep.

She was sure the possibility that maybe next time she'd be bottoming for one of the male Doms at the club had crossed his mind. And she was equally certain he hadn't liked it. He'd let her know he felt possessive when it came to her. She'd reveled in the idea when they were naked together, but after the second time they'd had sex—mind-blowing sex, damn it!—he'd dozed off, leaving her to stare at the ceiling and come back down to earth. And the truth.

Jamie felt some ownership over her. Always had. She understood it, to some extent anyway—to the small extent she could accept anyone feeling that way toward her. Her big brother had asked Jamie to take care of her when he lay dying in the hospital, and Jamie took the promise he'd made seriously. She knew that. She also knew he desired her, but that didn't necessarily equal anything *more*. She'd been a fool to simply fall into his arms without really fully considering their history. All she knew about him. All she knew about herself.

Madame came strolling out from behind a bush and rubbed against her bare legs, her white fur soft on her skin. She leaned down and petted the cat, who put up with it for several moments before sinuously slipping away and settling on the bricks a foot or two from Summer, blinking in the sunlight.

"There was good reason why I gave up on him last year," she told the cat. "I'd finally come to my senses. And now where has all my sense gone? Blown to pieces beneath the force of the irresistible Jamie Stewart-Greer. It's those damn dimples." She sighed, blew out a breath, coiling her long hair into a knot on top of her head and holding it there, baring her neck to the tiny breeze blowing through her garden. "I bet you never had to deal with dimples, Madame. Being a cat must be so much easier than being . . . me."

"Hey, sugar."

She turned to find Jamie standing in the doorway, wearing nothing but his jeans. They weren't zipped up all the way. She did her best to ignore it as she got to her feet, wondering how long he'd been there.

"Hey."

"Want to go grab some lunch? I'm starving. Worked up an appetite."

"Oh, um . . . I actually need to . . . get in a workout today. I always hit the gym on my days off. I work long hours sometimes so it's the only time I have all week."

He arched one dark brow. "Don't you want to eat something first?"

"I'll grab a protein bar."

Stepping out onto the bricks, he took her hand and pulled her to her feet. "What's up, baby? Everything okay?"

"Yeah, sure. Great. I just really need to be sure I stay in shape." She forced a laugh. "I have to now, to keep up with you, don't I?"

One corner of his mouth quirked. "I'm pretty sure that won't ever be a problem. But you go have your workout. I'll probably do the same. But come here and kiss me first, sugar girl."

Oh, don't think, don't think!

She steeled herself as he leaned in to kiss her, but her body betrayed her, melting into a hot pool of need and desire and jumbled thoughts.

Take a breath. Take some distance.

She laid a hand on his chest, gave him a small push. "Okay, okay." She laughed. "I should get going."

"I'll call you later," he said, all sunny, dimpled smiles as he bent and kissed her forehead.

"Sure. You go on and get dressed. I need to water the garden before I go."

She turned and walked over to turn on the hose, taking her time, pretending the nozzle needed adjusting. When she glanced up he was standing in the doorway, looking at her over his shoulder. She flashed him a smile, willing him to just *go*. He must have believed it because he smiled back and disappeared into the house. She kept her teeth clenched until she heard her front door shut, then she breathed a long sigh—partly relief, partly a strange sort of grief.

Sex never used to be complicated for her. It was fun, often thrilling. But mostly she'd been able to leave afterward, her body sated, without needing anything else from a guy. She hated that she needed so much from him.

"Fuck," she muttered, turning off the hose and stalking back into the house. But when she reached her bedroom it smelled of sex. It smelled of Jamie. She had to get out of there.

She found her car keys in the living room, grabbed them and her small leather purse and headed out to see her best friend. Dennie would help her get her head on straight. If that were even possible under the circumstances.

Goddamn Jamie. Goddamn her stupid, girlish fantasies and her out-of-control sex drive. It was time she grew up. And there was nothing to make a girl grow up like a broken heart.

CHAPTER

Three

SUMMER PULLED HER Jeep to the curb in front of Dennie's grandmother's place in the pretty Lakeview area, close to Lake Pontchartrain. It was a neat, gray clapboard house with brick steps leading to a wide front porch. Dennie and Annalee were forced to evacuate during Hurricane Katrina, and the house had sustained some damage, but they'd managed the restorations in less than a year. They'd been luckier than some in the area and certainly more than many in New Orleans.

She grabbed her purse and slammed the door of the Jeep a little too hard. She needed to take a breath and calm down before she went in—Dennie's grandma was getting older and she didn't want to worry her. She inhaled, then exhaled slowly before making her way around to the side of the house, where she gave a light rap on the door and let herself into the kitchen, as she'd always done. She was family there—her best friend's house had been a longtime refuge. Dennie looked up from the kitchen table, where she sat with her laptop open.

"Hey, Summer. How are—" Her friend stopped and got to her feet. "Are you okay? You're not, are you?"

She started to shake her head but Dennie was at her side in a moment, taking her into a warm hug.

"I'm okay," Summer said, maybe more to convince herself than Dennie. She pulled back. "I'll be fine. I always am."

"Yes you are," Dennie said. "But that doesn't mean you can't be upset once in a while. Come on and sit down while I get you some sweet tea, then you tell me what's going on."

Summer nodded and sat on one of the old white-painted wood chairs that had been in Annalee's house for as long as she could remember. After Hurricane Katrina they'd simply slapped another coat of paint on them and replaced the flowered seat cushions. How many times over the years since they met in kindergarten had she sat at this table, drinking sweet tea with her best friend, telling her all her secrets? Now if she were going to really be able to talk this out with her she'd have to tell her everything.

She sipped the cold tea, savoring the sweetness on her tongue while she waited for Dennie to sit in a chair across from her. "Thanks, Den."

"It's just tea, honey." She swept her long brown-and-gold-streaked hair over her shoulder. "Now tell me what's got you looking so flushed."

"God, I don't even know where to start." Summer puffed out a breath. "Okay. So this is going to sound weird but do you remember when we went to Europe a few years ago and we went to that club in London?"

"That leather club, or whatever you call it?"

"BDSM club. But yes, that one. You remember how fascinated I was?"

Dennie snorted. "Honeypie, you haven't *stopped* being fascinated. I was wondering when you were going to talk to me about it. And don't look so surprised. I'm your best friend and I've known you forever. Plus you have a tendency to leave the screen up on your computer all the time, and you know how nosey I am."

"Are you mad at me?" Summer asked, a knot forming over the one already pulling her stomach tight.

"For not talking to me about it sooner? Of course not," Dennie reassured her, reaching out to pat her hand. "I don't have to know *every* dirty detail of your sex life. And even if I were mad I certainly wouldn't choose now to lay it on you, when you're so obviously upset. So why don't you tell me the rest of the story?"

She nodded. "Okay. Okay. Well, I've been researching this stuff for a while. A few months ago I found out a friend of mine was into it and she's sort of been mentoring me, taking me to discussion groups and classes. And the other night she took me to the club here in town and . . . I sort of ran into Jamie there. Well, he saw me. And fuck, I'm not supposed to reveal anyone's identity—I really can't tell you who the friend is—but I don't know how else to tell you about *him*. And you have to know it's him so this all makes sense to you."

"Well, well. Jamie, huh? Not that it really surprises me. He's all bad boy under his smooth manners and calling everyone sweetheart—him and his tough cars. We both know that's part of your attraction to him. But don't you worry—I won't tell a soul. It's your business, not mine."

"I know. But I just caught myself and . . . Den, my head is

so fucked up right now. And oh Jesus, shit—am I saying this too loud? Is Annalee here?"

"Nope, she's out at her mah-jongg game, so talk as loud as you want and tell me *everything*." Her eyes sparkled, shifting from blue to green.

"I don't think you want to know everything, Den."

Dennie leaned forward and clasped her hands on the table. "Oh, but I do. Of course, get the hard stuff out first so we can get you feeling better. Just don't leave out the salacious details." She waggled her eyebrows at her.

Summer had to smile. "I sure do love you, Den."

"I love you, too, hon. Now talk to me."

Summer gave her the details of her evening at The Bastille, Jamie showing up at her house and how they'd ended up in bed all day.

"Then you got up, made some excuse and ran over here? Was the sex that bad?" Dennie asked, her brows arching.

"What? God, no. The sex was fantastic, and I mean fantastic with a capital *F*. Everything I ever imagined, but better. God, so much better." She had to bite back a groan.

"So you're here now with me instead of back at your place in bed with him, why?"

Burying her face in her hands she muttered, "Because I'm an idiot?"

"You're no idiot, Summer. You're just confused. Sex can be that way sometimes. Sex you've wanted your whole life? I can only imagine how much weirder that must be."

"Yeah. Weird in a good way. And in a bad way." She lifted her head to look at her friend. "And Den, the kinky stuff—although we didn't do too much of that—just amplifies everything. Makes it so intense. But I just can't get that one thing out of my head—that he saw me naked in his kink world and maybe he thought it was his job to protect me, or he didn't like the idea of some other guy touching me that way. I don't know which, but either way it doesn't necessarily mean he feels anything more for me than he would his own sister."

"Honey, if he spends Sunday afternoons in bed with his sister, then there are bigger problems brewing here."

"That's not what I meant, Den," she growled.

"I know, but look, the fact that he came over and took you to bed is a sign there's more than brotherly interest in you. And frankly, that's not news to either of us, so don't go over-thinking your way out of that. He's wanted you for years, even if he's always fought it. Maybe he's simply done being the good guy—the good guy who does the right thing and ends up empty-handed."

"Because he saw me naked?"

"Because he saw you as the passionate, sensual woman you are—full-blown and unafraid, in a setting he apparently never expected. That might be what it took to shake him loose."

Summer clenched and unclenched her jaw. "I don't want him to want me for the wrong reasons. Just to make sure I'm safe or because he's hot for my body."

"It's not a bad place to start—and don't shoot me that look. You're hot for his body, too, and there is nothing wrong with a man who wants to take care of you. Give the guy a break. Would you rather have had him see you naked and be totally unaffected? Is it really a bad thing that he found you so irresistible he couldn't stop himself from coming over and giving you what you've always wanted? He's finally recognized that you're a *woman* now instead of everyone's little sister, and you're complaining."

"Oh. Oh! Maybe . . . you're right. Damn it. You are."

Dennie nodded and grinned. "I do like to be right."

"So what do I do now?"

"First of all, stop freaking out. Spend some time with him. Everything doesn't need to be dealt with and thought through right this minute. You two need to get to know each other on this new level. Try to just let it happen, Summer. This is what you've always wanted, isn't it? To be with Jamie?"

"Maybe that's what scares me."

"Probably. But this is your chance, honeypie. You know you'll kick yourself until you're ninety if you don't at least give it a shot. And I plan to go at eighty-five, so you'll have to spend those last five years picking up the pieces without me."

"Den!" Summer popped out of her chair and wrapped her arms around her best friend. "Don't say that. You're not allowed to die before me."

"You are so bossy, you know that?"

"But you love me anyway."

"True. Now, what are you going to do?"

"I'm going to go home and get some sleep, and then tomorrow night after work I'm going to find Jamie. But before that I'm going to get some lunch—I'm starving. And oh God, before *that* I think I need to go home to take a shower."

"I *thought* you reeked of sex but I was too polite to say anything."

Summer laughed. "I was in too much of a hurry to get over here and talk to clean up first. Sorry, Den."

"It's okay. One of us should be getting some and it's not me this week. Or this month."

"I don't know why the boys aren't lining up for you."

Dennie sat back in her chair and stretched her long legs. "Oh, I'm pretty sure I've worked my way through this town. Might have to start looking over in Lafayette or up to Baton Rouge."

"Silly girl." Summer grabbed her hand and gave it a squeeze. "Thank you."

"Anytime. I'll send you my bill."

Summer grinned and waved on her way out the door.

WORK SEEMED TO go on forever on Monday, but finally Summer was done and on her way home to get pretty for Jamie. He'd called Sunday evening, but she kept the conversation short, telling him she was tired. She felt bad, but the phone felt too distancing to her somehow. She had to see him in person.

She stopped at the local produce market to buy a basket of blackberries as an offering—they were Jamie's favorite. Once she reached her little house she showered, taking her time, preparing herself for him in a way that felt like a ritual. She'd read about this in one of the books Allie had given her—submissive women paying attention to every detail, focusing on the feel of the soap as they made sure every inch was clean and smooth. Massaging scented lotion into their skin, dabbing perfume behind their ears, between their breasts, transforming themselves into an offering for their Dominant. Was that what she was doing for Jamie?

Tonight they were going to have those negotiations, once she apologized for practically kicking him out of her bed yesterday morning. And after that, maybe they'd have their first real play.

Oh Jesus.

Her heart beat faster and her body heated. Real play with Jamie. Play *and* sex, the air of command in his voice, his hands on her skin. That exquisite contrast of pain and pleasure that somehow blended and became one sensation. She let out a quiet moan. Lord, what that man did to her.

By the time she slipped her sundress on, even the cotton skimming her flesh was like a sensual touch to her.

As she slid her feet into her high denim wedge sandals, Madame came strolling into the bedroom to inspect her. Or to nap in her closet.

"Just in time, Madame. What do you think?" She did a small pirouette. "If this doesn't knock Jamie's socks off, I'll have to go back to charm school. Don't wait up for me."

She got in her Jeep as the sun was setting and drove to his place, but there was no answer at the door. Maybe he was at the gym? If not, she knew where she'd find him. She decided to check his shop first.

Being almost seven-thirty, the place was closed, but sure enough the tow truck was out front and she could see his vintage cherry-red Corvette Stingray parked inside. She found a parking spot and remembered to grab the berries before getting out. As she walked up to the front of SGR Motors she spotted Jamie inside through the big window. He was sitting at the big desk in the office, his head bent. Even the sight of his head made her pulse run hot and thready in her veins. In that insistent, needy place between her thighs. And it suddenly occurred to her that maybe no one had ever had sex on Jamie's desk before. She smiled and stepped inside.

JAMIE LEANED IN over the keyboard, skimming through the coming week's schedule, checking to see that all the parts they'd need had been ordered, saw the note to show one of his customers the special rim catalog tomorrow morning. Since his shop's specialty was restoring vintage muscle cars—like his sweet Corvette—he kept drawers full of stock catalogs, as well as everything available to trick out a hot ride. If a customer wanted anything from custom chrome pipes to fuzzy dice, he knew where to find it. He turned and opened one of the file drawers next to the enormous wood desk, searching for the Wheel Vintiques catalog.

When he came up with the catalog in his hand he almost dropped it. Because there in the doorway stood the luscious Summer Grace Rae, looking like some Southern version of nearly-porn. She was wearing a short—very short—blue and white gingham-checked dress with white lace around the edges that fit her body like a second skin. The halter-style top made for some gorgeous cleavage, and he knew right away there was no bra underneath. The dress was short enough that if she bent over a bit he'd know whether or not there were any panties under there. It also bared a nice, long expanse of tanned legs—or as long as they could be on such a petite girl. She looked cute as a button and sexy as hell simultaneously. But he didn't have time to wonder how she managed to do that before she walked over and sat on his desk, her bottom right on top of the catalog, which made him go instantly hard.

"I brought you some blackberries," she said, all sweetness with that sultry edge she was known for. She held out a small basket of succulent-looking berries, and he took them, barely able to focus.

"Thanks. That was awfully thoughtful."

"I've been thinking about a few other things," she said, her tone lowering.

He set the berries aside and scooted his rolling office chair over to trap her with one arm on either side of her delicate and faintly perfumed body—those violets again. Oh yeah, he was definitely going hard.

"I've been thinking a few things myself, sugar."

She laughed, low in her throat. "I bet you have."

Damn, what this girl—this innocent-faced siren of a woman—did to him.

Get it together.

He cleared his throat. "As much as I'd love to throw you down and fuck you over my desk without even thinking about turning the damn lights off so anyone passing by couldn't see—and I mean that, Summer Grace—you and I have some talking to do first."

"I was hoping you'd say that."

She batted her lashes at him and he nearly lost it, those images he'd just called up threatening to take over his mind. And his hardening cock. He wanted to get her naked and spread her out on his big desk, fuck her right there. Right now.

Damn it. Focus.

"We need to handle negotiations," he said, calling on his years as a Dominant to get his libido under control. "I imagine you've done that at least once with Maîtresse Renee?"

She nodded. "Yes, but Allie was there with me, and I'd had some coaching before."

That sense of hyper-responsibility kicked in hard. "Do you feel you should have a mentor here to help you negotiate with me? It's okay to say you do."

"Not with you, Jamie."

"Is that just need talking? Have you heard of sub frenzy?" He didn't want it to be that, but he *had* to ask.

"Yes, in one of the classes I went to with Allie and Rosie. Do you know Rosie? She did my tattoo."

"Yeah, I know who Rosie is. She's Finn's girl, although I knew her before they met. Real nice woman and talented. Know about her kink, too. Now tell me what you know about sub frenzy, sweetheart."

Summer Grace nodded. "It's that hunger for play that drives a new submissive or bottom to do things that are maybe beyond their limits. But, Jamie, I've wanted you for an awfully long time. I'm not giving away any womanly secret here—I've never hidden that from you, or from anyone. And yes, kink is fairly new to me, at this level, anyway, and I understand my personal desire may intensify the play for me. But I've been very clear on what I want for . . . too long. So yes, I know what it is, and while I *want* . . . it's not a frenzy. It's simply what it's always been when it comes to you, but magnified by the kink factor. Does that make sense?"

Jesus, she was perfect. "It does. Are you ready to begin the negotiations?"

"You're the boss, Jamie."

"Not yet, I'm not. Not until we go through this process and you're still saying yes—if you are. Do you have safewords?"

"I use the most common ones—green if things are good when you check in with me, yellow if I need you to switch toys, to lighten up or if I need a drink of water or something. Red if the scene needs to stop completely. But for the record I am definitely saying yes. It will always be yes with you," she added quietly, something hard and shining behind her pretty blue eyes.

It will always be yes with you.

He forced himself to focus. "Let's start with some of the easy stuff—things we've addressed casually, or that I saw you do at The Bastille. But I'm not going to assume you will do everything with me you've done with someone else. No, don't say anything—that fact is a given until if and when long experience together proves otherwise. I want you to say yes, no or maybe to each of the kinks or toys or activities I throw out there. If there's an explanation or some related detail you think I should know, speak up. Honest communication is the key here. It's the only way we can play and

I can keep you safe—physically, mentally, emotionally. If there's an emotional trigger attached to anything, I need to know about that. Okay? Tell me you understand what I'm asking of you."

"I understand. Allie and Rosie have had a thorough talking-to with me. More than once before they'd let me play."

"Good. Now start by telling me about any health issues or physical limitations."

"I'm healthy top to bottom. And I don't know of any physical limitations. I know I like pain, especially when it's mixed with pleasure. I have no idea how far I can go. It's too new. And I already have a sense that it can be different depending on who I'm playing with—that some of how my body will react is mental connection and chemistry. Is that right?"

"That's exactly right." And Lord, the chemistry they had was off the charts. He had a sadistic side, so he'd have to be careful not to overplay her until they found out what she could really take. God, the things he wanted to do to her. "Tell me how you feel about bondage."

"I'm not into the rope thing in the way Allie is with Mick. I'd rather be cuffed."

"Chains?" He had to ask about one of his favorite fetishes. His hands balled into fists while he waited for her to answer.

"Oh yes," she said with a soft catch in her voice, making him remember how hard he was. "I love how heavy-duty they are. There's something a little dangerous about them, if that makes sense. Exciting. I haven't tried them yet, but I really like the idea. Can a person be bound in chains? I mean wrapped all around your body like you can with rope?"

He stifled a groan. "Oh yeah. And you have no idea how happy you just made me, sugar." She smiled, her face lighting up. Lighting him up. Making him hard again. He shifted in his chair before continuing. "What about spanking? Yes or no? Or maybe?"

"A definite yes."

"How about a paddle? Leather? Wood?"

"Leather, yes. Wood . . . I'm not sure. I'd have to try it."

"Caning?"

He saw a small shiver go through her. "I'd like to try."

"But it scares you?" he asked.

She shrugged. "A little, yes."

He leaned in and said quietly, "You don't have to play the tough girl with me. This isn't the time for that. I already know how tough you are, sweetheart. You have nothing to prove with me."

She looked into his eyes, hers gleaming in the harsh lighting of his office, the pupils enormous. She said in almost a whisper, "Don't I, Jamie?"

He took her hands in his. "Why do you think that?"

"Because of our history—I don't want you to change your mind before we play. And maybe because you haven't even kissed me since I got here."

His hand went into her hair and he drew her face to his. "That was a huge mistake on my part, sugar girl. You had me distracted—you in your tight little dress and your berries. I won't make that mistake again. Come here," he said before pulling her close and pressing his lips to hers.

A small sigh escaped her lips, and he breathed it in as he parted them, exploring, delving with his tongue. And sweet Jesus, her mouth alone, the hunger in her kiss, was enough to nearly bring him to his knees. His cock, his entire body, pulsed with the hard beat of desire. When he pulled back, they were both a little breathless.

"*That*, my sugar girl, is why I didn't kiss you right off. I wasn't sure I could responsibly carry on negotiations after I had your sweet mouth under mine."

"And now?" she asked. Her cheeks were flushed pink. He ran his thumbs over the baby-soft skin there.

"And now it's maybe a good thing we at least got started. That we had a chance to set down the ground rules. But I'm going to sit back and take my hands off your lovely body or things are going to get real dirty real fast and we may never get the negotiating part done. Which means none of the kinky stuff for you, young lady." He grinned, giving her nose a small tap, and was surprised to see her blush.

She was already falling into subspace and he knew it was his own fault. Time to cool down. He pushed his chair back and stood up. "I'm getting a Coke. Want one?"

"Yes, sure."

He went to the mini-fridge on the other side of the room, grabbed two cans of soda and handed her one, careful not to get close enough to breathe in that violet scent that always made his dick hard.

Down, boy.

He sat in his chair once more, careful not to touch her even though his hands itched for the satin of her skin. He flexed his fingers. "Okay. Let's move on. Do you like some rough body play? Really more manhandling in my case, I guess. Do you know what that is?"

"There seems to be different levels of it from what I've learned. But what I think of as manhandling I think I'll like a lot. You sort of did some of that with me already."

"And?"

Her tone lowered. "Come on, Jamie. You saw how I responded."

"Yes, I did, but I need you to tell me."

"Then you saw how much I liked it. The way you used your body to overpower me. Oh yeah, I am definitely into it."

Her eyes were glossy with desire, her voice low and sultry. She meant every damn word she said. She wasn't one of those girls who would say only what they thought he wanted to hear. If Summer Grace said she loved it, then she did. He loved that intensity about her. Her frank sexuality. He'd been an idiot to have held her off all these years—once she was legal, anyway. But what mattered now was that she was sitting there on his desk, all that simmering heat aimed at him. This was one time when he was more than happy to be the target. She'd already hit him dead center.

Do your job.

"Is there anything else you want to try?" he asked, buying himself a moment to get his head back together. "Anything I haven't brought up?"

"I don't know. There's so much variety. It seems endless."

"That's true. I think the best way is to start off fairly simply, look around and see what else piques your interest. If you find anything you think you'd like to try, talk to me about it. Your limits can always be renegotiated later." She nodded. "Okay, hard limits and triggers? Do you understand what that means?"

"Hard limits are things that are just a 'no' for me—that aren't even up for discussion. And triggers are anything that will set off some sort of unpleasant emotional response. Right?"

He nodded.

"Well, my hard limits are the squicky stuff I filled out on my form at The Bastille—the usual stuff, from what I'm told. No scat, animals, blood. No age play. And right now, until I get to know myself better, no electrical play, no whips, no knives, no needles, and I never even thought of this until Allie brought it up, but for God's sake, no damn clowns!"

He laughed. "Don't worry, sugar, no clowns for me, either. But let me ask you this: breath play?"

Her breath caught, as if he already had her in his grip. "That takes a lot of trust. But with you? Yes. And Jamie? You can take it a little further than you did at my house."

He had to suppress a shiver as an image of his hand around her lovely throat crossed his mind. He gave himself an internal shake, cleared his throat. "Anal sex?"

One corner of her mouth lifted in a half-smile. "Yes. Definitely."

"Are you basing that answer purely on theory?"

"No, I am not," she answered, her blue eyes twinkling.

"What about mind-fuck?"

Her lips quirked. "Like you can avoid doing that? But, yes. Please. I think it helps me . . . get out of my head. Which is good because to be honest . . . Well, sometimes I sort of think I'm too smart for everyone else. It's actually comforting to be taken down a few notches. I think too much in general and it's good to be forced out of that pattern. It also means I'm not . . . responsible for everything."

He saw her swallow hard. Scooting the chair closer, he tucked a silvery strand of hair behind her ear. He asked gently, "What do you think you're responsible for, sweetheart?"

She swallowed again, and her glance darted away for a few moments, then back to him before she answered. "For everything. For . . . keeping my family together after Brandon died."

"Aw, sugar, that was never your job."

She shook her head, and he saw how hard she was hanging on to that well of emotion. It didn't matter that the conversation had shifted from kinky sex to something so deep, so profound. No—it did matter, because it was *them*. And maybe no one else in the world could know the inside of this thing—Brandon's death and what it had done to the Rae family. He knew it because he'd become their second son before they lost their own. And because he knew what the loss of his brother Ian had done to his own family. It tore a hole that could never be repaired, only patched in some haphazard fashion.

"Summer Grace, look at me, baby." He took her face between his hands, cradling it in his palms. Her eyes were enormous. "This is *me*. And I've been doing this for a long time. While you're with me, I promise you can let it go. Turn it all over to me. Into my hands. Do you feel how strong they'll hold you?"

She bit her lip, and there was so much emotion in her big blue eyes it made his chest ache with some sensation he couldn't quite get a handle on. Just this raging need to protect her. To make her feel safe. If nothing else, he would do that for her. And suddenly, to his surprise, she flung her arms around his neck and buried her head there. As he wrapped her in his arms, drawing her down into his lap, he heard her soft sigh. Of release. Of surrender. And everything in him—the sex and the emotion, the kink and the chemistry, the heat and the history between them, melded into one thing. Into that moment. There was both beauty and terror there. Old grief and new delight. They would explore it all together, and he would keep her safe. He would not let her down.

There was a small roar inside his head. A fierce need in mind and body—for *her*, to do what he'd just silently vowed. How was it possible that it was all connected? But it was.

"Hey, sugar," he murmured as he lifted her chin. "Do you know how Goddamn beautiful you are? Do you have any idea how much I've needed you all this time? I held back because I thought that was what I had to do. And maybe for a long while it was. But now, well, everything has changed." He swallowed hard at the desire and the trust in her eyes, the swallow expanding until it was an ache in his chest he couldn't think about right then. "I need to hear your consent one last time. It's not like there's no turning back once I have it—you always have that option. But tell me now what you want, Summer Grace."

She shook her head. "It's not what I want, Jamie. It's what I *need*. I need to know what it is to turn myself over to you." She gave one small, slow shake of her head, her silky blonde hair rippling like pale golden silk. "Only you. So yes, you have my consent. You're gonna have me begging in a few minutes if you don't take me out of here and . . . Goddamn it, don't make me beg."

Her words went through him like fire—scorching hot. He got to his feet. "Don't move."

He went to the windows and, one by one, he dropped the blinds.

"Jamie, what—?"

"Shh," he told her as he turned back to her. "I don't want you to say a word now, Summer Grace. Not unless I ask you a question or you need to use your safeword." He crossed the room and came to stand before her. Putting his hands on her waist, he lifted her off the desk. "On your feet now, sugar. I'm going to undress you."

"Yes, undress me," she murmured almost as if to herself while her eyes lost focus.

"Not a word, now."

Her entire posture changed and he recognized the loose set of her shoulders, her mouth, as surrender. He could feel her going deeper by the moment as he reached behind her and unzipped her dress, then untied the halter at the back of her neck. Her breathing slowed, her body stilling. He stepped closer as he slipped the cotton from her shoulders.

"Ah, Christ, if I'd known you were naked underneath this sweet little dress . . ."

His cock pulsed hard. He willed it down. The effort was only partially successful. Taking a step back to look at her as the dress fell to the floor, leaving her in nothing but the pinup girl shoes, he had to draw in a long breath. Her nipples were already hard, pink and succulent. He exhaled as he took her breasts in his palms, and they fit perfectly, the nipples going even harder as she let out a sigh and arched into him.

"Hold still, sweetheart," he told her. It was no less an order for the pet name. It never was, with him. He preferred to seduce a woman into yielding to his command. Most of the time.

She took in a breath, nodded, bit her lip. He leaned in and nipped at her lower lip because it was too luscious for him to resist. When she started to pull away, he bit harder and she groaned into his mouth. He stood back and focused on her breasts once more, not allowing himself to look at the tempting vee between her thighs yet.

Too much.

He could challenge his control, but he knew his limits. And with Summer Grace those limits were shifting and changing by the moment as lust battled fiercely with his sense of responsibility.

Gathering her flawless, firm breasts in his hands, he ran his thumbs over the nipples, then pinched them.

"Oh!"

"Quiet, Summer Grace," he ordered, then did it again, making her gasp.

He pinched the undersides of her breasts, then filled his hands and pressed into the pressure points on the sides, watching her breathe through the pain. She instinctively knew how to take it, how to convert the pain to pleasure. He took in a breath, took in her scent of violets and rain and the scent of her desire, like its own perfume on her skin. Too beautiful. When he pinched her nipples again, much harder this time, she gasped, yelped, sucked air in between her clenched teeth as he held the pinch. He went harder and harder, watching her face. A blush rose on her cheeks, on her breasts, and she squirmed a little.

"Does that feel good, sugar? Answer me."

"Yes. Good and . . . it fucking hurts. But yes, so good."

"Is it making you wet?"

She moaned. "God, yes."

He spun her around in his arms, grabbing her around the waist with one arm and yanking her in tight, using one of his thighs to force hers apart. "Let's find out."

With his free hand he grasped the back of her hair and pulled, bending her over, then he slid his palm down and over the soft flesh of her perfect ass. "Brace yourself on the desk and spread your legs," he ordered before slipping his hand between her thighs—and found as he smoothed his fingers over her pussy lips that she was soaked.

His cock pulsed, lust singing in his veins. Right now he had a handle on his desire. But fuck, he didn't know how long he could hold out.

Give her what she needs.

"Spread wider," he demanded, a bit harsher than he'd meant to.

She did as he asked with only a moment's hesitation, enough for him to know there was still some struggle going on in her. That was all right. He didn't mind if she went down with a little fight. It was Summer Grace, after all. He'd have expected nothing less. He leaned in closer, laid his head on hers, listening to her breathe while he rubbed his face against her soft, soft hair. He stayed there for some time, waiting for her to align her breath with his, and after several moments she did. He cinched his arm tightly around her waist, listened as she had to adjust her breathing to the constriction. Waited a few beats, then flexed his arm, pulling her tighter. She adjusted her breathing once more.

"Very good," he murmured. "Do you know what good girls get, sugar?" he asked. "This."

He thrust two fingers inside her, and her entire body bowed in his tight grip.

"Ah!"

"Shh, stay very quiet, sweetheart. Hold still for me while I fuck you with my hand. I'm going to fuck you hard. It's going to hurt. And it's going to feel so good."

He began a sharp, deep thrust, his fingers plunging in and out of her. She squirmed in his arms, which he knew she would, her body mindlessly grinding onto his hand, then pulling away as he went deeper.

"Come on, baby. You can take it."

"Jamie!"

"Shh."

He shifted his arm and used the heel of his hand to press onto her mound, finding the hard nub of her clit. Her breath hitched, and he felt her insides clench around his probing fingers.

"Ah, ah. Did I say you could come?"

"No," she answered on a small sob.

"Then take your pleasure from me. Take it and hold it until I ask it of you."

"I can't," she panted. "I can't."

"You can. And you will."

Another small sobbing breath, but when he felt her muscles tense all over, then let go the tiniest bit, he knew she was making an effort to control herself.

"Good girl."

He began again, fucking her fast and hard, his fingers piercing her over and over while she grew wetter and wetter. He tried to concentrate on doing this for her, *to* her, ignoring his own body's response. Soon she was gasping, groaning. He paused long enough to pinch the swollen lips of her sex.

"Ah!"

Then he started again, thrusting in deep strokes. When she went up on her toes he knew she couldn't hold out any longer. Hell, neither could he.

"Come for me now. Give it to me like a gift, sugar girl."

Her insides clenched, fluttered, then she bore down hard as she came into his hand.

"Jamie! Oh my God."

She writhed in his arms as he pumped into her, and her orgasm went on and on. His cock was aching, needing her. But the driving desire to do what *she* needed was even stronger. And her body would require pleasure before she would be prepared to take much pain.

She wasn't quite done coming when he slipped his fingers from her and spanked her ass hard, one sharp smack.

"Oh!"

He didn't give her time to figure out what was happening. Instead he began an even pace, his hand coming down on her beautifully pinking flesh. Not too hard at first—he was gauging what she could handle. But she pressed back into his hand with every strike, making him smile. Oh, she was built for this. How had he never guessed?

How had he kept his hands off her for so many years? The idea was mind-boggling, especially now that she was naked and pliant in his arms and more gorgeous than he'd ever imagined in his wildest dreams—and they'd been pretty damn wild. His cock, his entire body, was hot and throbbing with a desire that could be quenched only through sex. And through kink. He had to have her, his fantasy girl. But first he had to hurt her.

CHAPTER

Four

JAMIE TOOK HER hand and began to lead her from the office and through the door that led to the shop. Some small part of Summer's subspaced brain was in awe of the fact that she was naked except for her shoes, her ass warmed by the stunning Jamie's wonderfully cruel hands, her body soft all over after coming at his command. And now he was taking her into an auto shop of all places to do God only knew what to her. She'd never felt more blissful. She refused to acknowledge the small part of her psyche that was screaming at her to run before she got hurt—heart-hurt.

Nope. Not thinking about it.

But what the . . . ?

"What the fuck, Jamie? Really? You keep a play bag at work?" she couldn't help but ask when he grabbed a black duffel bag from a chair by the door and slung it over his shoulder.

"Is 'what the fuck' a safeword, Summer Grace?" he asked with a small chuckle before he must have recognized the look on her face. "Ah. Sweetheart, I have never played anyone else here."

She smiled—she couldn't help it. She couldn't stand to think that he regularly brought women to his shop for play. It was different than The Bastille, in her mind, however unreasonable that might be. But she was unreasonably thrilled that his shop was virgin territory, that he was popping its cherry for *her*.

"But yes," he went on, "I keep a spare play bag in here for those nights I work too late to go home before I head to the club. The equipment is limited, but there's enough in there for me to work with. Don't you worry."

"Lack of toys is not what I'm worried about," she muttered, quietly pleased that he'd let her get away with breaking her silence. She shook her head as he pulled her along behind him. She would never understand how he could be so sweet and still so purely Dom-like at the same damn time. But she had to admit it was working its magic on her. Big-time.

Jamie flipped a switch on the wall and one section of the shop lit up. She'd been there before—she'd dropped by a number of times over the years, hoping to entice him—but never after hours. The place was so clean you could eat off the floor—everything shining chrome and the gorgeous mural on the back wall of vintage muscle cars: a Mustang, a GTO and a Corvette, all done in matte black against a background of gradually deepening shades of blue. The black-and-chrome tool chests were in neat rows against the walls, punctuated by wall-mounted counters. There were work bays with pits, some with different types of lifts—she thought that was what they were called, but her brain was cloudy—in sleek black and red. The place was really some car perv's fantasy. She couldn't help the small giggle that escaped her.

Jamie turned to her. "What are you finding so funny, sugar?" One brow was lifted, and there was both humor and menace in his tone, which she loved.

A shiver went through her. She was naked in Jamie's auto shop and this was crazy! But she liked the crazy. "I just realized that cars are one of your fetishes."

"You just now realized that?" he asked. "And I thought you knew me so well."

"I thought I did, too," she said, only then realizing there was an awful lot about this man she'd missed.

He wrapped an arm around her waist, his biceps flexing deliciously against her bare skin. "Now is when we really get to know each other, Summer Grace."

All she could do was nod. Desire was a simmering fire in her body. Desire and a little titillating fear about what was going to happen. And as if he sensed her fear he bent and brushed his lips across hers, fanning the flames of need, sending a shock of pleasure deep into her system.

Oh yes. This is what I need.

She sank into him as he pulled her in closer, nibbling on her lips, licking them, then kissing her hard and deep, his tongue exploring. *Taking.* If she'd had any doubts about what they were doing he made them all melt away.

"You're going to be just fine, sweetheart. I'll take very good care of you," he whispered against her flushed cheek. "I'm going to do some wonderful and terrible things to you. Is that what you want?"

She closed her eyes, breathed him in, let her tongue dart out to taste him on her lips.

Oh yes.

"Exactly what I want. What I need. I'm just . . ."

"What is it? Tell me."

Her throat went tight, but the words seemed to pour out of their own accord. "Have you ever had your heart's desire right in front of you and suddenly you realize you hadn't ever really imagined it could be more than just a dream? And then it's right there and it *seems* like a dream. I can't seem to get ahold of it. It's like the whole world is wobbling. But yes, I want it, need it. *Please*, Jamie."

He pressed his lips to her cheek, kissing it over and over. Then he said quietly, his voice a low rumble, "Yeah. I know exactly what you mean. We are on the same page, sweetheart, at this very moment. But this is what it means to turn it over. Just give it all up to me. You can do it. This is me, Summer Grace, and I will take care of everything."

"Yes," she agreed, knowing that was utterly true.

He kissed her cheek again. "Come on, sugar girl."

He took her hand once more and led her across the quiet shop, their footsteps echoing on the cement floor. He stopped in front of an odd-looking contraption made of red-painted metal framework set on the floor that had some sort of crane or hoist attached to it. The black vertical arm had "Xtreme" painted down one side in big white letters, a row of large squared teeth like a spine up the back and a rod angled off the top. At the end of the rod hung a length of chain, ending in a large hook.

"Jamie . . . ?"

His grip on her hand tightened as he set the toy bag down on the floor. "I suppose you're wondering what we're doing here? That, I'm not going to tell you, but I will tell you what this little beauty is. It's a portable Spider frame straightener—it's what we use to straighten out the bent frame on a car that's been in an accident. This baby can hold up to ten tons." He dragged Summer close and brushed a kiss over her hair. "Now I need to go get a few things, and I want you to wait for me here. Can you do that?"

He pulled back to look at her, and she swallowed, nodded, her head spinning.

"Good girl," he murmured before kissing her hand, then dropping it and stepping away.

She was afraid to even turn her head to see what he was doing—and her vision was entirely filled up by this torture-chamber device in front of her. She didn't want to imagine what he'd use this thing for. At the same time that fear only fed the lust spiraling inside her naked body, coiling and raging like a storm in her belly, her breasts, her sex, waiting to be released . . . but only within the safety of Jamie's control.

Why did she feel as if she were about to lose control in some way she never had before? As if being with Jamie, facing this fear with him—*for* him—was going to unleash some new element of her sexuality? And being left standing there in nothing but her high shoes seemed utterly perverse.

She waited for him, full of fear and desire and a sort of awe at the force of it all, and she had to keep clenching and unclenching her hands, rocking a bit on her toes in her pretty shoes. When he returned and she heard a hard metallic clink she looked up to see him carrying a long length of heavy chain. Her stomach tightened.

He had an evil grin on his face. She loved it and it pissed her off a little at the same time. But, God, he was gorgeous. Those dimples got her every damn time. And he'd taken his shirt off so she could take in every beautifully muscular line of his tall frame, his pierced nipples immediately drawing her gaze. And that narrow line of dark hair leading its way down into the waistband of the low-slung jeans around his hips was some sort of madly tempting detail of his anatomy. She breathed out on a sigh.

He dropped the chain on the floor with a loud clank that made her jump.

"Need more chain. Don't you go anywhere."

She turned her head and kept her focus on his long strides, the way the muscles rippled across his back when he rolled his shoulders. She couldn't look at the pile of chain on the floor. She couldn't look at the weird device he was apparently going to chain her to—unless this was just some kind of mind-fuck. She wouldn't put it past him.

God, was he really going to chain her to that thing?

By the time he returned with another length of gleaming chain her legs were shaking. He let it fall to the floor, and the sound made her jump again, even though she knew to expect it. Oh yeah, if this was mind-fuck he knew exactly what he was doing.

He came up to her and smoothed her hair with gentle fingers. "You scared, sugar?"

She nodded. "I'd have to be crazy not to be."

"That's my good girl," he said. "Don't think you're not exactly where I want you." He pulled back and winked at her.

"Goddamn it, Jamie," she muttered.

"Yeah, right where I want you." He leaned in closer, brushed a kiss over her cheek, whispered, "I kinda like it when you cuss at me sometimes. Sometimes. Other times it might simply make me do something evil to you. Since you have a little potty mouth, you'll just have to see which way it'll go at any given moment, won't you, sweetheart?"

She wanted to cuss again, but she bit her lip to keep quiet. She wasn't sure she wanted to do anything to make the situation worse. Or better, depending on how one looked at it.

"Fuck," she muttered, turning away from him.

"What's that, baby? I can't hear you."

"Nothing." She ground her teeth.

Suddenly he yanked her in tight—so hard it rocked her off her feet, but his arm was wrapped around her waist, holding her against his solid body. Before she had time to think he thrust his hand between her thighs, his finger pressing into her.

"Oh!"

"You're as wet as I expected you to be. You can cuss all you want, but you *like* this, Summer Grace. You like it a lot. But I want to hear it. Tell me."

"Jamie—"

"Tell me," he ordered.

"I . . . I like it and I hate it at the same time."

"That's exactly what I wanted to hear. That and the breathless tone of your voice, your confusion and your desire. Oh yeah. Makes me fucking hard, sugar. Feel how hard."

He took her hand and pressed her palm to the front of his jeans, and he was solid iron under the denim, his flesh straining at the fabric. At the same time, he stroked at her swollen clitoris, making her groan. As soon as she began to squirm, he pulled his hand away then pulled her hand from his erection.

"Gotta get to work now," he said.

"You torture me, Jamie. And yourself, from what I just felt."

"Mouthy girl. But you're exactly right. Isn't that what this is all about for people like us? Because I've become certain fairly quickly that you *are* like me. I think that, new as you are, you understand the flow of energy within this dynamic, don't you? You get it. So yes, it's torture for us both, but some divine kind of torture. The wanting. The anticipation." He moved back in again, kissed her lips quickly, drawing her lower lip between his teeth and biting down just hard enough to hurt. He whispered against her mouth, "I may create the mind-fuck for you, but it's just as much a mind-fuck for me, having you this close and having to hold back."

He pulled away and caught her gaze, watching her. A slow grin spread over his face, and she couldn't help but smile back at him in silent understanding.

"Okay, then. We begin," he said.

He made sure she was steady on her feet, then turned away and crouched to pull two pairs of leather cuffs—both wrist and ankle—from his toy bag. He straightened, then took one of her wrists, bringing it to his lips and kissing it softly. Then he buckled one of the soft cuffs there, pulling it tight, slipping two fingers under it, testing it to allow for circulation. He loosened it and tested it again before he seemed satisfied. He did the same to her other wrist. And as he buckled her into the cuffs her head began a slow, liquid swarming sensation, and she felt herself slipping into that lovely, cloudy place that was subspace.

He clipped the two cuffs together with a carabiner—a sort of metal clip often used in rock climbing—inserted through the D-rings on each cuff, then laced his fingers around the clip and pulled her toward the big red steel frame. As he moved her into position, straddling the center bar with her back to the tall vertical steel rod, the frame looked like some enormous, intimidating monster. Only the fact that it was Jamie preparing to chain her to the monster gave her any sense of safety. She had to concentrate to prevent her legs from shaking. With nerves. With sharp, jolting shocks of desire.

"Stay still," he told her, and at that moment she couldn't imagine doing anything other than what he asked of her.

He came back with a short length of chain and she heard him attach it to the hook. Then he took her hands and used another carabiner to clip her cuffs to the chain. Moving in close to her left side, he laced an arm around her waist.

"Hydraulic jack," he said, squeezing her waist.

She didn't have time to process what that could possibly mean before she heard a low, groaning hum, and glanced down to see him pressing one booted foot on a pedal on the floor. She heard the hiss of a compressor as the slack in the chain tightened.

"Oh, Jesus," she said.

Jamie grinned, but he kept his gaze on her bound wrists as her body began to elongate, her arms stretching slowly over her head. Adrenaline shot through her system, along with a feeling of being utterly exposed to him. Powerless in the face of this metal machine, the weight of gleaming chains and the sheer force of the calm dominance he exerted over her.

He ran a hand over her ribs, her stomach, the sides of her breasts, his touch reassuring. Sensual, setting her skin on fire. If only he would *really* touch her. Put his hand between her burning thighs.

"Jamie . . ." She bit her lip, wanting to beg, knowing she didn't dare.

"Shh. Be still, sugar girl."

Finally, when she thought she'd be pulled off her feet, the hydraulics stopped. He moved around in front of her, keeping one of his black-booted feet on either side of the center bar, and a hand at her waist.

"You look unbelievably beautiful like this," he murmured.

He ran his hands over her sides, pausing to pinch the skin at her waist a little, then over her breasts, spreading his big hands over them. She tried to arch into his touch, but she was stretched tight, almost having to go up on her toes in her high shoes. He pressed on her nipples with his fingers, then he took them between his fingertips and drew them out, pinching a little, then pressed again. The sensation was one she hadn't experienced before, the pressing, pulling and pinching painful, and all of it pure pleasure. She closed her eyes and tuned in to the sensations. The pressure hurt, more and more as he pressed harder and harder, the pinching and pulling gradually getting harder, too, but the pleasure grew along with the pain. From some distant place she was vaguely aware of her body undulating a little in the chains—as much as it was able to—and of her own panting breath, the small sighs escaping her when something really hurt. When he stopped her eyes fluttered open, and she only had half a moment to focus before he slipped around behind her, with a small kiss brushed across her cheek.

She stood quietly through long moments of silence, but already she was deep enough in that lovely, floaty headspace that she was able to exist in the moment, simply waiting for whatever would come next.

She sensed the cool metal before the chain links ever touched her skin, then he wrapped the heavy chain around her waist. She shivered with the most exquisite desire. With a small chill from the cold chain. And oh God, she was sinking into this—into whatever he was doing to her. Whatever he wanted to do. When he used more of the carabiners to clip another chain onto the one around her waist she stood in patient silence as he crossed them over her stomach, drew them up over her shoulders and crossed them once more over her back, clipping them there. And even though these chains were purely decorative, doing nothing to actually bind her, they made her feel something entirely different.

"Jamie," she gasped.

"Do you need to safeword, Summer Grace?" He laid his hand on her back, the heat reassuring. "Are the chains too heavy for you?"

"What? No. No. I just had to tell you . . ." She had to pause, to draw in a breath. "I just had to tell you what I'm feeling."

"Ah, good girl. And what's that, sugar?"

"It's like . . . being held. Like being in a corset, only so much more so. They don't even have to be tight like a corset. It's the weight of them. It's safety. I don't know if this is making sense."

"Baby, you have no idea how much sense you're making to me. It's my chain fetish come to life. Not everyone gets it. But I can see you do. I can see the goose bumps on your skin." He ran a finger down her spine and she shivered deliciously. "I can see how damn hard your nipples are." He ran his fingertips over the aching tips, making her moan. "And I can see your surrender to the chains."

"Yes, to the chains. But Jamie, it's you I'm surrendering to."

He was in front of her in a flash, tilting her chin in his hand, capturing her gaze with his green, green eyes. Then he grabbed her face with both hands and kissed her. His mouth crushed hers, his hands hard on her cheeks, holding her so she knew she couldn't escape. She didn't want to. Her lips yielded to his, opening to his demanding tongue—demanding yet so sweet, so soft and wet. And between her thighs she was wet, desire like a wave washing over her, heating her body up beneath the cool weight of the chains. At that moment her entire world was contrast: warm and cold, hard and soft. The pungent scent of motor oil in the air and the clean scent of Jamie's skin.

Then he grabbed the chains where they were crossed between her breasts in one fist and yanked her in close, his knuckles digging into her flesh, pressing on the bones. She loved it—his control over her, the way he hit the tender pressure points on her breastbone. The passion with which he kissed her. He kept kissing her as he curved his other hand under the chain at her waist, his knuckles digging in there. Then he released her so suddenly she would have fallen had she not been bound to the frame straightener. He came back moments later with more chain, and her sex squeezed at the sight of the glinting metal links in his strong hands.

Oh, yes, please.

Very quickly he used the clips to attach two more chains to the one at her waist, bringing them under and between her thighs and clipping them to the back of the waist chain, so that it was like a harness. The cool lengths of steel on each side of her damp sex were frightening and intoxicating all at the same time. She wanted the chains to squeeze, to pinch her there. Jamie grabbed the chains around her thighs, sliding them up a bit under her buttocks as he lifted her off her feet.

"Oh!"

"Legs around me, sugar," he told her as he slipped her shoes off.

She wrapped her legs around his waist, her wet, open sex against his taut stomach. She groaned.

"Oh yeah, I love the feel of your sleek little pussy on me." He lifted her up, then let her body slide down an inch or two, just enough to rub her mound and her swollen clit over his muscled abs. "Do you like that, my sugar girl? You're going to like this even better."

He shifted and slipped one of his hands under her, the other still holding her up, and he began to pinch her ass, pausing to slap it, then pinching again before dragging his nails over her skin. She loved it all—the lovely pain, the pace of it. Again he built the intensity until she was panting and squirming and soaking wet, her needy sex sliding against his skin. And all she could think was how badly she needed him inside her, how she never wanted him to stop what he was doing.

Going crazy.

Oh, yes. But a good kind of crazy.

He pinched her harder, going for the same spots over and over again, at that tender juncture where her buttocks joined her thighs, until she started to groan, then to squeal at each hard pinch, her body undulating against him. Pain and pleasure were two sides of the same wicked coin, making her head spin.

"Jamie! Please . . ."

"Please what, sugar?"

"Please . . . God, I don't know!"

"Ah, but I do."

He shifted again, letting her body hang in the chains, her legs still locked around his waist. She heard his zipper come down. She was vaguely aware of the sound of a foil packet ripping, but her body knew it in every cell, every raw, waiting nerve. Then his sheathed cock was at the entrance to her body, poised there while he fisted his hands around her chained hips.

"Summer Grace. Look at me."

She kept her gaze on his, blinking up at him. He was so damn beautiful she could barely stand it as he bit his lip and slammed into her.

"Ah!"

She threw her head back as pleasure drove deep into her body along with his lovely, thick cock. But he let one hip go to grab her hair tight, dragging her head back up.

"I said look at me," he commanded.

She did, and the intensity of sensation she felt multiplied in mere moments. She was on the verge of coming almost instantly.

Jamie tightened his grip on her hair. "Bite it back, baby. Hang on to it. Let's drive it higher. I want you to come with me."

She swallowed her climax down, although it remained a hard buzz in her system, her sex tight with need, tight around his cock. He tilted his hips and thrust deep. She moaned. He did it again. And again and again, one hand gripping the chain at her hip, the other buried in her hair. She was completely taken over as he plunged into her, the plunging turning into a hammering rhythm. He was fucking her so hard only the strength of his hold on her and the heavy chains kept her in place, the metal biting into her skin. Pleasure washed across his face, and his brows drew together in concentration. The green of his eyes began to absolutely glow, the look in them wild in a way she'd never seen before. Primal. Dangerous. Seeing it there made her own pleasure soar, until she was barely hanging on. Her clit was pulsing so hard it hurt.

"Jamie, I can't . . ."

"You can," he insisted.

"When?" she demanded. She couldn't help it.

"Look at me. You'll know."

His eyes were a force of their own, pulling her in. And she saw it all there—his own desire, the exquisite, renting surge of sensation. She felt herself nod as she tuned in to him on some incredibly deep level, as though his sensations were her own. Her body moved in time with his, his hips slamming into her, hard, harder, brutally. Pain and pleasure. Pleasure and pleasure, his features ragged with it. Then they were coming, both of them crying out.

"Jamie! Ah, God! Yes, yes . . ."

"Fuck, sugar . . . Fuck!"

They shivered, hips crashing together, then slowing, undulating as pleasure peaked, peaked again, then eased like the waves on the shore. Still they moved together, both of them milking their orgasms. Trembling. Panting.

His head dropped to her shoulder. "Jesus, Summer Grace," he murmured, his Scottish accent thicker than she'd ever heard it in his low, rumbling tone. "You are unbelievable. Just . . ." He paused to draw in a deep breath. "Truly unbelievable, baby. You're really here with me. Like this. As if we were always going to be here. As if the universe planned this."

She couldn't really think. But she knew he was right. "You know what I've always thought, Jamie?" she asked him quietly, emotions like a hard shift catching in her chest.

"Except for the last year," he said.

"No. The only thing that changed was me deciding to step back."

He caught her face in his hand once more, his hard grip easing bit by bit as he looked into her eyes. Shadows shimmered there, his beautiful eyes going from a dark, mossy green to almost emerald, fevered and brilliant.

"I understand, you know. Looking back, I can't believe you hung in there as long as you did. But now that we're here, I want to keep this going. I want to see what we can be. Do you want that?"

She wanted to swoon, all of her girlish dreams coming true in this moment. But something in her knew to protect herself. *Had* to after all she knew of loss—the kind that happened when someone died. And the kind that happened when the people who were supposed to love you simply stepped out of your life.

Don't be stupid. Be the smart girl you're supposed to be. Except that you never have been when it comes to him.

"Jamie. You're still inside me and I'm still in your chains. Do you think . . . maybe we can talk about this after you take me down and my head is back on straight?"

"What? Of course. Fuck. This isn't the right time. I know that. I'm being irresponsible. It's just that when I hold you in my arms, Summer Grace . . . Well, yeah, let's take you down, baby."

He stepped on the pedal and there was the low groan of metal parts moving, the sensation of her chains loosening. When they'd gone slack, Jamie carefully unwrapped her, handling her body very precisely, and in some way that made her feel . . . precious. As the words he'd spoken a few moments earlier ran through her mind, emotion spiraled, making her chest ache. For what could have been. For what was right now. With fear about the future—or the lack of one.

What if this doesn't work out?

Her pulse fluttered. She'd given him her body, and maybe more important, her submission. The stakes were higher than ever. She wasn't sure she'd land on her feet if he let her fall. Stubbornly, she bit the tears back. She was just subspaced—coming down from the incredible heights of sensation and power dynamic.

Nothing more than that. A simple explanation. It'll be okay. You can do this.

He kissed her skin where the chains had bitten into her shoulders, so softly it made her want to melt inside. But she fought it. There were places she couldn't go, even with him. Or maybe especially with him. Places too deep, too dark. She wasn't sure what was in there herself.

The chains lay in gleaming coils at their feet as he lifted her in his arms, carrying her up the metal stairs that led to a loft area she'd never seen. Her body was soft and pliant against his, seeking the warmth, but inside her a battle was beginning to rage. Her mind was spinning with doubt, possibilities, hope, dread, all at the same time. By the time they reached the top of the stairs and Jamie stepped into a lounge area with a pair of black leather couches, she was biting her lip, biting back the swirling mess of emotion that threatened to come bursting out.

He sat down with her in his lap, pulling a soft, gray blanket from somewhere and wrapping her in it. She was acutely aware of the rough denim of his jeans, the edge of the still-open zipper beneath her thighs. Of his scent—dark, sweet, smoky wood and motor oil and soap, maybe. Familiar. Heady. She could smell his come in the air, and her own. She heard the low whirring of the small refrigerator in one corner, a car going by outside, felt the ever-present humidity of New Orleans. And wondered how she could even notice these things in her present state.

Jamie lifted her chin in his hand, forcing her gaze to his. "Sugar, where are you?"

"I'm here. I'm right here."

He shook his head slowly. "No, you're in some faraway place. Talk to me, Summer Grace. Was the play too much?"

"No, the play was wonderful."

"Then what?"

"It was . . . God, Jamie, it's everything." She knew it was all about to explode, but she couldn't stop it. "It's the play and the sex and the things you said to me down there." She squirmed, her fingers catching the edge of the blanket, her muscles too tense to hold still.

Jamie caught one hand in his, lacing his fingers through hers. He said quietly, "Tell me."

"You don't see it? The promise that kept you away—you held on to it for years. It's hard to believe it's not there anymore, or that your perspective has really shifted. That the shadow of my brother—my wonderful brother—won't get between us again." She stopped, took a breath. "It's us being together exactly as it was meant to be, like you said. But it's also us being together *despite* our history, and my brother, and the years of . . . of yearning and anticipation. I can barely stand it—how *important* it feels. How do we do this? With every other man I've been with, I've always known exactly what to do. And now, with you, I feel like some virgin. *Me*, of all people, wide-eyed and innocent somehow—the girl who spent her adolescence sneaking into your bed. How ridiculous is that? But that's how it feels."

He'd been watching her very carefully as she spoke, his dark brows drawing together as he tried to understand what she was saying. She knew the words had come out in a tumble of confusion.

"Okay. Okay. It *is* everything, Summer Grace. It's intense and a little insane. It's loaded. Brandon's presence will always be in both our lives, and losing him the way we did will always affect us. We have that in common, our losses, our brothers. Ian. Brandon. Even my brother Allister sort of withdrew into himself. And we both lost our parents in a way, when losing a child was too much for them to handle. We had to take care of things, take care of ourselves and grow up fast. Don't think I didn't see that, that I don't get it, because out of anyone else in the world, I recognize it. Yeah, it's all of that. It is important. It will be no matter how this turns out. But how we do this is by existing, being in the moment. That's how I *have* to do this. Because projecting into the future has kept me from being with you long enough. Far too fucking long. And now we have this connection that's powerful and rare, in my experience. Desires we can't express with just anyone. It feels right, doesn't it? It's fucking complicated and insane and beautiful at the same time. It feels so right to me."

The tears pooled, hot behind her eyelids. She did not want to cry. She couldn't stand it if he saw her tears right now.

"Yes, Jamie, but it's still a little Goddamn overwhelming."

He cracked a smile. "You must be coming back to yourself if you're cussing at me."

"I'm always cussing at you."

His face sobered. "Not tonight, you didn't."

"No," she agreed. "Not tonight."

He stroked her hair from her cheek, pushed his fingers into the long strands and held on tight. Her body went loose and she leaned into him. When he released her hair, she looked down into her blanket-covered lap.

"Jamie, I'll be honest with you. This is scary. I don't like that I'm not in control. Of anything. Of myself, most of all."

"What did you think submission meant, sweetheart? You have to give yourself over to it or it doesn't work. And you did. I felt your compliance. Your release."

"So did I. I felt it with Maîtresse Renee, but nothing like this—like it is with you."

He slid an arm around her waist and pulled her in tight, until she could feel the hard planes of his chest against her side. He felt so solid and warm and safe. And yet *nothing* felt safe.

She shook her head, unable to figure it all out. "Jamie, please don't."

"Don't what, sugar? You're safe with me."

God, and now the man was reading her mind. "Am I?"

"Hey," he said, his tone gentle. "You know you are, Summer Grace. I'll take care of you."

"No." She pushed away from him and got to her feet. It didn't matter that she was naked other than the blanket, which she held around her like a shield. Her heart was hammering out of her chest. And all she knew was the need to *run*. She caught Jamie's confused expression as he rose to his feet before she turned and did just that, her bare feet echoing on the metal stairs.

*   *   *

HE HADN'T BEEN expecting her to jump up and run off like some frightened deer. Hell, maybe that's what she was right now. And he'd put her in that vulnerable place.

Fuck.

He got to his feet and went after her. The lithe Summer Grace had reached the far end of the shop by the time he made it to the bottom of the stairs, but as she darted between the pieces of heavy equipment, steel pillars and work bays, he was able to catch up to her in a few strides, his longer legs serving him well. She'd reached the door to the office, her hand on the doorknob when he caught up to her, closing his hand over hers. Christ, he could feel her shaking. He tried to take her in his arms but she pulled away.

"No, Jamie! Let me go."

Yeah—exactly like a frightened deer.

He kept his voice low. "Come on, Summer Grace. Stop a moment. Take a breath. Sit down with me and talk it out. Or we can just sit and be quiet together. It doesn't matter. But I am not letting you leave here like this."

She dashed a tear from her eye with the back of one hand, her full lower lip trembling in a pout he would have found adorable if he didn't know how upset she was.

"I'm not very good at keeping quiet, Jamie," she said sullenly. "Neither are you."

"Good point. So we'll just have to put up with each other yammering on whether we like it or not. Either that or you're going to run out into the street without your clothes—not that I'd imagine you'd much care about that—or, more's the pity, I'll have to turn in my Dom card for being irresponsible about your aftercare."

One corner of her mouth quirked, even though her tone was still moody. "It's not just about aftercare."

"Like hell it's not. What we did was intense. It kicked up a hornet's nest of emotion along with all those lovely endorphins and dopamine. But it *is* part of the equation, and something you can't ask me to ignore. I want to take care of you. And right now you're tempting me to chain you down in order to do my job, which would piss you off even if you liked it—and you would."

"Says you," she muttered.

"Yeah, I do. Now stop being so damn stubborn."

She seemed to be thinking that over for several long moments while his heart raced. He understood what she'd said earlier—this was important, all of what was between them. Which sure as hell didn't always make it comfortable, but he was done denying it. He had to be. There was no place to hide anymore—not after they'd been together. Played together. Slept together.

No turning back.

No. All they could do now was forge ahead.

"Summer Grace." He let a warning tone seep into his voice.

"Okay, okay. You don't have to go all super-Dom on me."

"Apparently I do."

She sighed. "All right. You can cuddle me and we'll talk."

He moved in closer and kissed her cheek. "You make it sound so sweet and romantic-like. Come on. I'm taking you home."

A few minutes later he'd found her clothes, had helped her into the company truck with the blanket still wrapped around her naked body, and they were driving through town toward her little house in the Gentilly district. She was quiet on the drive home—stubbornly so, he thought, which was fine for the moment. He turned on some music and let the rhythm carry them over the streets as a light rain began to fall. There was something almost magical about the two of them in his truck, the inky sky lit here and there by the silvery clouds covering the moon. The mood the night always brought. Or maybe that was just him being poetic again. Occupational hazard for a Scotsman. He glanced over to find her gaze on the wet street. But he saw the lovely curve of her cheekbone, her long, long lashes, the tumble of golden hair over her slim shoulders.

Jesus, but she's lovely.

Damn poetic Scottish blood again, but there was no denying it. If he wasn't careful he'd find himself falling in love with the girl. Or falling for her, at the very least. But hadn't that already happened a long time ago, no matter how hard he'd fought it?

He ran a hand back over his head, scrubbing at the short stubble. He sighed out a long breath—and almost passed her place, too lost in thought.

"Jamie, this is it."

"What? Yeah, of course. Hang on." He pulled to the curb and put the truck into reverse, grinding the gears a bit too hard, then backed up and stopped right in front of her blue cottage. "Hang on and I'll come around. You can use my jacket to keep the rain off you."

"Don't be silly. I'm a New Orleans native. A little rain won't hurt me." She went for the door handle but he reached across and stopped her. "Fine, no jacket. But you *will* wait for me to open your door."

She bit her lip. "Okay."

Glad she knew better than to argue with a Southern gentleman—despite that he'd been born in Edinburgh—he got out and went around to the passenger side. As he helped her from the truck, the sky opened up and the rain fell in a sudden torrential downpour that made them sputter as they ran to her door, her hand held fast in his.

"Keys," he demanded—and was pleased when she shoved her damp hair out of her eyes, dug in her small bag and handed the key chain to him.

By the dim light of the amber streetlamps, he was able to get the key in the door, and they both wiped their feet on the door-mat before she led him into the house. Inside, the air was warm and a bit still. She turned on a light in the entry hall, then went to turn on a lamp in the small living room.

"Leave it," he commanded. She stopped in her tracks, straightening up and turning to him. "Get a towel, sweetheart."

She nodded and left the room, returning with one of her thick bathroom towels in a pale shade of lilac. He took it from her and stepped closer, looking down at her as he gently toweled the rain from her bare shoulders, smoothing the soft terrycloth over her graceful collarbones. Then, when she didn't struggle, he began to dry her hair, taking lengths of it between his fingers and care-fully running the towel over the long strands. While he dried her he watched her. He really couldn't stop looking at her. Observing her stunning beauty. Her submission even now, when there was no play going on, no purposeful roles. Well, perhaps that wasn't entirely true. Now that they'd gone there he imagined there would always be an undercurrent of power exchange between them.

His chest went tight as he turned the idea over in his mind—his chest and his stomach. There was excitement there. Oh yes. It was a definite thrill. But there was powerful emotion, too.

She blinked up at him. "Are you finished, Jamie? I think I'm dry enough."

Hell. "Yeah, all done."

He used the towel to roughly dry his own head, his shoulders and chest. Stepping away, he draped the towel over the back of the ivory-colored chair that matched the sofa, then moved back to her, slipping an arm around her shoulder.

"Sit down, sugar."

She did, surprising him that all the wind seemed to have gone out of her sails. He loved her sassiness, but it seemed they had some important talking to do, so maybe it was good that she was no longer fighting him on everything. Except that she'd sat on the sofa a good two feet from him.

He patted his denim-clad thigh. "Lap. Now."

"I'm fine, Jamie."

He caught her pixie-like chin in his hand, his voice firm. "Summer Grace. Lap."

She rolled her eyes, but she climbed onto his lap and burrowed in, laying her head on his shoulder, leaning into his body with hers. He draped his arms around her, and when he heard her small sigh he held her tighter. It felt good.

She ran a nail over the collar of his shirt. "Is this when we talk?" she asked.

"Yeah. This is when we talk. And I know you're still in subspace, but I don't know that you'd open up the way I think you need to in order for us to really communicate about some things we need to. And I don't know if I can, either, without feeling a little raw, the way I do after play. With you, anyway."

"You're probably right. But I don't know where to start."

He sat quietly for a few long moments, thinking. Finally he said, "I think we start at the point that joins us."

"What point is that? Do you mean when we met?"

"Even before that. We have to go back to the things that connect us, I think. The things we have in common that we don't like to talk to anyone else about."

There was a short pause. "Oh," she said quietly.

"I'll start. Okay?" He didn't want to do this. But it was for her. For them.

"Yes, please."

He took a moment, trying to gather his thoughts. But they were too jumbled, so he decided to simply begin.

Like pulling off a Band-Aid. Just do it.

Only for her. Only for Summer Grace would he be willing to open up the old wounds that never went away.

She wasn't the only one who would feel pain tonight.

CHAPTER

Five

"So," HE STARTED, "you know I came to this country just before my eighth birthday. My family was . . . Well, they were never the same after Ian died. Neither was I. Maybe especially me. Seven is too damn young to experience that kind of loss, and the fact that I . . ." He trailed off, his fingers flexing on her waist as a hard buzzing began inside his head. "Look, I've never told you—fuck, I've never spoken about this to anyone. Not anyone. But I saw him die, you know. And all that shit they say about twins, it's true. I was playing in the yard while Ian was climbing that tree, and I swear to all the gods I *felt* him falling even before I heard him scream. And then he was just limp on the ground and there was . . . Well, it was messy, as you can imagine. And Jesus, I'm an idiot. I shouldn't be saying all of this right after you've been played. What am I thinking? Fuck."

She raised her head and laid a soft hand on his cheek. "You're just telling me the truth. All of it. For the first time, Jamie. It's important. I didn't want to talk, but you were right. We need this. And if we don't do it now, while I'm still open enough, then I don't know when I can. You were right about that, too. Maybe that's part of why I need to submit—because apparently it's the only way I can open myself up to anyone, other than Dennie, and maybe only to a certain extent even with her. And forgive me for saying so, but maybe it's the only way you can, too. Would you be doing this under any other circumstances?"

He looked up to find her blue eyes on him, real concern there. Real understanding. Of course she'd understand. Which made telling this old story—the one he always tried to think of as ancient history—a little easier to tell.

"With anyone else? No. And over a beer or dinner? No."

"Then tell me now."

He nodded and she laid her head back on his shoulder, guessing that maybe it would be easier for him if she wasn't looking at him.

"Well. My parents, they had a hard time after losing Ian. My brother Allister did, too, but he'd always been the toughest one of us, maybe because he was the oldest. But my mum and dad, they couldn't stand to be in the house where Ian had died. Neither could I. I never went out into the garden again after that. It was less than a year later that we came to the U.S. But no matter where you go, your memories follow and none of us was ever able to forget him. To forget that our family was broken. My parents just sort of disappeared. They've never come back. It was almost a relief when they moved to England a few years ago, and I feel like an absolute shit for saying so. But they just keep running. And Allister was a lot older and pretty independent, but that only left me more alone. Not to sound pathetic, but I felt fucking orphaned, if you want to know the truth."

She shifted in his lap and took his face in her small, warm hands. There were tears in her blue eyes. "I'm so sorry, Jamie. So sorry. It was exactly the same with me. It was as if I ceased to exist when Brandon died. Like he was their only child and I didn't count anymore. They just retreated into themselves. And then there was the divorce, and they were both farther away from me than ever. I've only seen my dad maybe four times a year since then. It was like he couldn't stand to look at my mom or me anymore. My family was gone, and I've never quite been able to understand exactly how it happened. How can you ever understand something like that? If it weren't for Dennie and her grandmother I would have been totally alone."

"That's why I spent so much time with your family once Brandon and I met each other. Why I went on every camping trip with you guys, ate dinner at your house every week, spent Christmas Eve over there. I imagine your family got pretty sick of me, but they never turned me away."

But in their grief they'd turned away from Summer Grace. He knew what that felt like. Too well. And damn it, he should have been there for her. His stomach clenched. He'd do better now. It already felt like an oath.

"I was never sick of you, Jamie," she said quietly.

He took one of her hands and kissed her soft palm. "Not until last year, anyway."

One corner of her lush, lovely mouth lifted. "This is the second time you've said that. I thought you understood."

"I did. I do. But I didn't say I liked it. I didn't say there wasn't a bit of stomping and brooding because you'd given up on me. But I deserved it."

She shrugged. "You did—I can't argue with that. But it wasn't an easy decision. I think in a way you were the only thing that

held me together for a long time. You have to have something to
hang on to, you know, Jamie?"

"Fuck, Summer Grace. And I let you down. I was supposed
to look after you—"

"And you *did*. You were so there for me right after he died. It
was you at the hospital letting me cry all over you, letting my
mom do the same. And my father, that first night out in the hall.
I couldn't let either of you know I was there, but I'll never forget
that. I saw his tears. I saw you pat him on the shoulder, which
was the only comfort he ever allowed, I think. From anyone. And
then when I was in high school you chased off all the bad boys I
would have dated—oh yes, don't think I didn't know the whole
time it was you. But that only made you seem more like a hero
to me. And then . . ." She paused, sniffed. "You used the Rae
name when you branded your shop, which has always felt like it
was as much for me as it was to honor Brandon's memory, and I
don't care if I'm wrong about that. It's comforted me. But I've
come to understand things, Jamie. We were both grieving. We
were surviving. If I'd slept with you before now, before you really
wanted to, it wouldn't have been good for me in the end, either."

It broke his heart a little to hear the words come out of her
mouth—the way she'd put him on a pedestal, when he was so
fucking fallible. To hear the pain beneath the words as she remembered those awful days after losing her brother. And to know he'd
let her think he didn't want her. For years. He'd *had* to—or he'd
thought so until recently—but still, it left a dark, burning hole in
his heart. "Ah, sweetheart. If you only knew how badly I wanted
you the entire time."

"You did?"

She gazed at him with wonder and trust in her eyes, in the
softness of her features. So damn pretty, this girl. Prettiest girl

he'd ever seen. It had been true back when she was only fourteen—in his reprehensibly perverted mind—and it was even more true now. But he could let it be. Because Summer Grace was no longer forbidden. How had it taken him so long to come to this place? How had it even happened that they were there together, finally? Talking in a way they should have a long time ago.

He understood how vulnerable she'd allowed herself to be with him just now—maybe even more than when they'd played, when they'd had sex. So had he. It was the connection between them that had allowed him to open up to her. But he didn't want to think of what they'd discussed—not right now. No, now he wanted to touch her. Take care of her. Because something in those beautiful blue eyes told him she was as raw as he was.

He swept her hair back from her cheek, loving the way she blushed when he did it. When had Summer Grace Rae ever blushed? Only once or twice in all the years he'd known her, and both times recently, with him. But it spoke even more deeply about the space she was in at that moment.

"Hey, sugar," he said softly. "You know what I want to do? I want to run a bath for you and let you soak in the hot water. Maybe get in with you. Then I want us to order some food and feed my growling belly. Then I'm taking you to bed."

Her eyes widened. "What happens then?"

He grinned at her. "Baby, if you need to ask then you don't know me nearly as well as you think you do."

Her face sobered. "I think I know you better than anyone."

"Yeah, you do. Come on."

He picked her up and she was like a doll in his arms—that small, that delicate. He carried her to the bathroom, where he set her carefully on her feet. She started to move toward the big, old-fashioned claw-foot tub, but he put a hand on her arm.

"I'm running this bath, sugar."

"Bossy, bossy."

"Damn right." He turned the knobs, adjusting the temperature. "Bath salts?" he asked.

"If you're asking my preference, yes, but unless you want to smell like a girl we'd better skip it."

"I won't mind smelling like you. It'll be like wearing you all over me."

She laughed. "That was a little *Silence of the Lambs*."

He shook his head. "Stop sassing me, girl. Get your bath salts."

She grabbed a jar from a standing shelf next to the tub, opened the top and held the jar out. "Have it your way. Smell like a girl."

He took the jar and whipped her blanket off in one deft move, smacking her bare bottom.

"Hey!"

"Are you complaining, Summer Grace?"

She smiled, batted her lashes, then she turned around and bent over a little, making him laugh. "Only at your insistence on using my middle name."

"You are really asking for it."

"Yes, but you like that about me."

"I do, indeed." Opening the jar, he discovered where that scent of violets came from. He dumped a handful of the salts in the running water, then picked her up. "In you go."

SUMMER HUNG ON to his hand as she lowered herself into the filling tub, the hot water feeling wonderful on her bare skin. "What about you? Aren't you coming in?"

He smiled and began to unbutton his shirt, and she found her entire system aching with need as his beautifully muscled body was revealed inch by inch. He took off the shirt and she nearly sighed over the breadth of his shoulders, the light gold of his skin, the way his pierced nipples hardened as they met the damp evening air. Even the simple line of Latin script tattooed down his right side was like some sort of fetish to her. He kicked off his boots, then unbuttoned his jeans and she sat back to watch her private strip show with the hottest man ever born. The only man she'd ever felt this driving, burning *need* for.

He pulled the worn denim down over his strong thighs, his thick, half-hard cock springing free. She had to swallow another sigh. He really had the most beautiful cock she'd ever seen, so long and thick, the flesh such a lovely pale golden color, the head so perfectly shaped. She squeezed her thighs together beneath the warm water. He moved toward the bathtub, then knelt down on the bath mat beside it.

"Aren't you getting in?" she asked, disappointed.

"In a bit. But I need to take care of my girl first."

Her stomach knotted, partly with barely restrained joy and partly in stark fear. *His* girl? That had come out of his mouth all too easily. Or maybe she was reading too much into it.

Relax. Just enjoy this.

She leaned back in the tub, watching him as he took the giant sea sponge she'd hung over the spout on its attached cord and dunked it in the water. He picked up the bottle of liquid soap and sniffed it.

"Violets, too."

"Is that good?"

"Oh, it's very good."

He squeezed the soap onto the sponge and lifted one of her

feet out of the water. And ever so gently he began to wash her. His face was a study in concentration as he smoothed the sponge over her toes, up her leg, and she couldn't remember any man focusing so purely on her. It made her heart beat faster, the desire simmering with some emotion she couldn't find a name for. It was some exotic blend of comfort and excitement. And some part of her could barely believe this was happening to her—it was like something out of a foreign film, with the bathroom light touching the hair on his forearms, the muscled curve of his shoulder, and all of it softened by the steamy air. She wanted to cry. She wanted to come. She must be losing her mind.

He lowered her foot into the water, lifting the other. His tender ministrations began again, and once more she was in a state of awe at the way he handled her. When he lowered her foot, she couldn't stand it anymore.

"Jamie. Please get in with me?"

He grinned, his dimples flashing, then he stood and climbed in facing her. His legs were so long he barely fit, but the old tub was enormous—she'd always felt a little lost in it by herself—and with his knees bent, he managed. He pulled her to him, turning her body so her back rested against his chest, and she let her head fall back against his strong shoulder. He remained quiet as he washed her, one arm around her waist possessively while with the other he ran the sponge over her arms, then her neck, his touch slow and sensual. When he slipped the sponge over her breasts, she moaned.

"Feel good, sugar?"

"Oh yes."

He moved the sponge down over her ribs, her stomach, then lower.

"Spread for me," he whispered next to her ear, his cock growing hard behind her, pressing into her back.

"Mmm, yes, Jamie."

She did as he asked, and was rewarded by the silky slide of the sponge over her mound. Desire was a sharp ache deep in her body—where she wanted *him* to be—but his slow, lovely assault continued. He moved the sponge down, then up again, over and over her aching clitoris. Sensation was something soft and sultry, undulating like the bathwater through her body. His other hand came up to cup her breast, his wet fingers slipping over her nipple. She arched into his touch, and he palmed her breast, squeezing, releasing, then squeezing harder.

"Ah, yes, Jamie."

"So beautiful, my sugar girl," he murmured.

The sponge kept moving over her needy sex, stroking her pussy lips, pressing against her tight clit. She sighed as pleasure spiraled inside her. When he added his fingers around the edges of the sponge, catching her clit between them, she groaned. He pressed her nipple between his fingertips and she arched into him—her breast, her body—and he rubbed the sponge and his fingers over her clit, harder and harder.

"*Come,*" he whispered.

Just that one word, and her body shattered. She cried out, shaking in his arms, her body convulsing, sensation hot and liquid.

"Good girl," he murmured, making her shiver all over.

Small tremors of pleasure still washed over her body, and she undulated against his hard cock at her back.

"Mmm, you do that for long and I'm gonna have to take you to bed and ravish you, sweetheart."

"Yes, please," she said.

"Oh, yeah—that's it."

He pressed her forward and got to his feet, pulling the plug in the tub as he did so.

"Stay there," he commanded her as he quickly dried himself with a towel.

It was tough holding still, trying to do as he asked—as he demanded—when his beautiful cock was right there in front of her. If she reached out she could touch it. Take it in her hands, in her mouth.

Oh yes. To taste him. To please him.

She shifted and knelt in the tub, needing the porcelain surface hard against her knees to keep her in line—that little bit of punishment. But finally Jamie pulled her to her feet and quickly dried her body before lifting her in his arms.

She looped hers around his neck. "You sure do like to carry me around."

"I like to do everything with you."

She leaned in and breathed in his neck. "And you do smell like my bath salts. Like me."

"I'm about to smell a lot more like you. Your pheromones. Your sweat. Your come, sugar girl."

"Mmm, I like it when you talk sweet to me."

He set her down a bit roughly on her bed. "Sometimes you're the same old Summer Grace. Someone needs another spanking."

"Don't be a tease! And would you still make me come, then carry me naked to bed to do what I have no doubt are unspeakable things to me if I were still the same old Summer Grace?" She leaned back on her hands, arching her back just enough to raise her breasts, blinking up at him.

"The unspeakable things are a given, but I am hardly being mean, my little kitten in heat. I like that you're still who you've always been. That you haven't let life change you to the core. That you don't put it on for me. I just like you. Better gird your loins, sweetheart—I'm about to show you how much."

"Mmm, dirty talk," she murmured as he lowered his body over hers, pressing her down on the bed.

"I thought it was sweet talk?" he said, leaning in to kiss the hardening tip of first one breast, then the other.

"It's all the same for me." She grabbed his head, urging him on. "Anytime, anywhere. Don't you know that by now, Jamie?"

He laid his head on her chest, then dragging it lower he gently bit the tender flesh just below her ribs. "You are a most unusual woman."

She lifted her legs, wrapping him up in her thighs until his solid shaft pressed against her pelvis. She shifted until it hit just the right spot, pleasure surging through her. "We'd both be bored to death if I weren't."

"True. Now I'm going to do all sorts of dirty things to you. And I'm going to do it very, very slowly."

"Mae West said anything worth doing is worth doing slowly."

"She was a wise woman. And it's no surprise you'd quote Mae West."

"No it— Oh!" she cried out as he slid down and put his mouth on her.

Then she couldn't manage more than gasps and moans as he began an assault—it couldn't be called anything else—on her wet, needy pussy. He licked her slowly with the flat of his tongue, long, even strokes that drove her wild with need. He paused to suck just the tip of her clitoris, biting into the tender flesh until she squealed in pain and indescribable pleasure, then licked and kissed his way lower, pushing his whole tongue inside her for a moment before working his way up again.

He must have felt her body tightening as the need to come bore down on her like a heated tide. He pulled back.

"Don't come yet, sweetheart," he told her. His tone was

gentle, but it was a command—there was never any mistaking it with him.

She drew in a deep, gasping breath. "Jamie . . ."

"Shh, my sugar girl. Hang on."

He pushed off her, but she was relieved to find it was only to grab a condom from her bedside table. She watched, her body clenching all over as he slid the latex down over his gorgeous cock. So big, with a pearly drop of pre-come at the swollen tip.

Inside me, yes. Now!

He placed both his big hands at her waist and turned her over onto her hands and knees. She arched her back, waiting for him. It was several moments before he ran a fingertip down her spine, and she waited for him to spank her, to enter her from behind. But he just continued the gentle stroking—with one fingertip, then all his fingers feathering over her skin, down her spine, then up to sweep her hair aside and stroke the back of her neck, making her shiver. When he placed his flat palm on her back, leaving it there for long, breathless moments, need shivered over her skin.

What was he doing? She tuned in to his breathing, which was a bit labored but not entirely with desire. There was more there— she wasn't even sure how she knew it. When she turned her head to look over her shoulder and saw his face, she had to bite her lip not to say something. Not to melt into him. Not to cry. Not to run.

She started to shake her head, and he grabbed her and turned her gently in his arms, one hand behind her head as he slowly lowered her onto her back once more.

"Ah, God, Summer Grace." It was a slow whisper that escaped his lips with words nothing more than a part of his breath. Except that they *were* more.

She blinked at the tears burning her eyes, the beauty of the

moment something so completely unfamiliar it was as if she didn't
know what to do with her hands. So she waited, lying quietly
beneath him. Staring up at him—at his eyes gleaming like dark
emeralds, their expression open to her. And what she saw there
was . . . love?

No. It couldn't be. Jamie cared for her—of course he did.
And she'd always thought he loved her, but she'd never meant
it the way his eyes seemed to at that moment.

You must be mistaken.

Every cell in her being was screaming that she wasn't. Her
heart hammered.

"Jamie?"

With his brows drawn together as if he didn't quite understand
what was happening, either, he stroked her hair from her cheek,
pausing to rub a long strand between his fingertips. "Shh, Summer
Grace," he said very quietly. "Don't talk now. Just be here with me."

She bit her lip. Nodded. And felt something inside her breaking down. No, not down. Breaking open.

He sat back on his heels, pulling her up with him and onto his
body until she straddled his thighs on bent knees. Then he lifted
her, his gaze on hers, still misty with that same confusion as he
settled her slowly onto his cock.

She swore she felt every single inch and ridge and taut vein
as his rigid flesh pushed into her body—every inch exquisite.
She wrapped her arms around his neck, sighing her pleasure,
breathing in his gasping breath as he tilted his hips, his cock
pressing deeper. When he was as deep as he could go she ground
down onto him until it hurt a little. She didn't care.

No. Not true. I want it. Need it. Need him.

He inhaled, leaned in and exhaled against her lips, then into
her mouth as she kissed him. Her body was burning with a wild

need. Her mind was wild with sensation and the sound of his name in her head.

Jamie. Jamie. Jamie. Finally.

He pulled back and locked his gaze on hers once more. Their bodies moved together, one being, flesh on flesh, inside and out. Pleasure was like a ribbon twining between them, graceful and sinuous. His mouth was only inches from hers, but she couldn't tear her gaze from the fire burning in his eyes, more intense with each stroke. The pressure built inside her, and her sex went tight. His erection went rock-hard, and she felt the first pulsing flutters that signaled his orgasm, and hers.

He grabbed her face between his hands. "Summer Grace . . ."

"What, Jamie?" she gasped. "What is it?"

He shook his head, pushing deeper into her and holding himself there. "I don't know. I don't fucking know. But it's . . . *something.* Jesus Christ."

He bucked hard into her, and she felt the heat of his come through the latex of the condom. It was too much for her—that and his words swirling through her head like some crazy aphrodisiac. Her climax rippled over her skin, through her body. Pleasure and pleasure and pleasure until she was panting with him, writhing with him, groaning with him. Then his mouth came down on hers, drinking in her cries as her nails dug into his back, her hands flexing helplessly.

It went on for some endless period of time. Then they were simply rocking together, her head on his strong shoulder, his arms wrapped so tightly around her body she could barely breathe. But she didn't want to. She couldn't get close enough to him.

They were slick with sweat, enveloped in each other and the damp New Orleans air. Finally Jamie sighed and pulled back, lifting her and laying her down on the bed, pausing to squeeze her hand tightly for a moment.

"Be right back," he said before getting up and moving toward the bathroom.

She felt too naked without him beside her. She shook her head at her silliness and waited for him to return, her body sated and limp, a small, happy smile on her lips. Several minutes passed, and she looked at her bedside clock to see if it really had been that long.

Oh, for God's sake—don't be so damn girly.

But more time passed, and soon it had been a full fifteen minutes before he came back and climbed onto the bed next to her.

"Everything all right?" she asked.

"Yeah, fine," was all he said.

She would have been tempted to ask for more but he pulled her into his arms and snuggled his face into her hair.

"Mmm, you feel good, sugar," he murmured.

She closed her eyes and reveled in just being in his arms. Except for the tiny voice in the back of her head that was still asking why he'd disappeared so suddenly after sex—after the intensity that had happened between them—and why he'd been gone so long. But she sure as hell wasn't going to say the words out loud. She wasn't going to ask if what she'd seen in his eyes had thrown him as much as it had her. Made him wonder if they'd made a mistake.

Fuck.

"You okay, baby?"

"What? Yes. I'm great," she lied. To herself as much as to him. Because this was maybe more than she could deal with. Especially right now. But she had to stop. There would be plenty of time to be freaked out tomorrow.

Stop it. Be in the moment.

And the moment was so good, if she only let it be. It was lovely to be taken care of the way Jamie had done tonight. When had any other man done that for her? The bath, his gentle handling of her—when he wasn't being so beautifully rough with her. But what if . . . ? God, she could barely stand to think of it, but what if this was nothing more than an extension of the promise he'd made to take care of her? And after seeing her involved in kink, this was maybe the only way he could do that?

And what if you're borrowing problems where there aren't any and he was just throwing away the condom and taking his time washing up, rather than planning his escape?

She buried her head in his chest and breathed him in, trying to calm herself, and after several long breaths it worked. A little. She had to concentrate very hard on the slowing cadence of his breath to relax. At some point, she slept.

THE SUN WAS just coming up when Jamie stirred, waking her.

"Hey." His voice was rusty, and even in that one word she heard the touch of Scottish accent that usually made her shivery all over, her knees melting. But this morning it only made her shiver, and not in a good way.

Please don't let this fall apart.

But the doubts from the night before came flooding back to her—she couldn't help it. She wanted to run again despite the connection she'd felt with him during sex. During the bath. Hell, during the entire evening until he'd gotten up from the bed. Funny how a mere fifteen minutes could change everything.

Too damn early to go there. She needed coffee. And maybe a lobotomy.

"Want some coffee?" she asked. "I can put a pot on."

"Yeah, I do, but it's almost seven and I need to get to the shop. I'll pick some up on the way."

"Oh. Yeah. I need to get ready for work, too."

He yawned and kissed her forehead. "All right. Time to get up."

That was it? Not even five minutes of morning cuddling? No "sugar"? No "Last night was wonderful"?

Oh, you really do need to cut this girly shit. Just let him go to work, damn it.

"You can shower here, if you want," she offered, but she didn't know how sincere she was. She could use some time to catch her breath, to catch a beat without being distracted by a man who was driving her crazy and turning her into some needy, whiny little girl.

He stretched, sat on the edge of the bed with his back to her for several moments before getting up. She didn't want to look at him, but he was too damn hot to look away. Strong, muscled back, shoulders practically rippling in the misty morning light.

"Nah," he said finally. "Thanks. I'll run by my place. Need a fresh shirt, anyway."

He walked into the bathroom, came back with his clothes on, making her glad she'd gotten up and slipped into a short cotton chemise.

He grinned at her, one cheek dimpling. "I think I left the berries on my desk."

"Well, you'll have something for breakfast, then."

"Yeah. Thanks for that."

She shrugged. "Sure."

He moved toward her then, laid a hand on her shoulder and peered into her face. "Any subdrop?"

"Oh. No. I'm fine."

Doing his duty, anyway. That's something.

No, it's really not.

Maybe you are in subdrop.

He was, of course, oblivious to her silent conversation with herself. "Good. You can call me if you drop, okay? If you can't reach me for any reason, call Allie or Rosie."

If she couldn't reach him?

"Of course. I know what to do. You'd better hurry. You don't want to be late."

"Right. I'd better run."

Still no "sugar" or "sweetheart" or "baby." She hated that her heart sank a little.

"I have to get in the shower in a minute, anyway. I'll just . . ." Her hands fluttered at her sides. "I'm going to put some coffee on and get ready for my day."

"Don't work too hard."

"You, either."

He dragged her in and kissed her, but even the soft press of his lips on hers was missing something.

After he left she stood in the kitchen, mentally shaking her head and her hands literally shaking as she put the coffee on. What the fuck had happened? Were they both so classically screwed up that the intensity they'd felt the night before had shaken them this much?

Yes. That was it exactly. There was no way to deny her emotional crash or his distance. Her instinct might be to run, but Jamie had beaten her to it. Just like she'd been afraid he would.

Madame wandered in and demanded treats. Summer absently opened a drawer and grabbed a few out of the bag she kept there, scattering them on the floor. Madame crunched busily.

"This is exactly why I shouldn't get involved with anyone," she told the cat. "Especially Jamie. This was never going to end well. I knew it. You knew it. What was I thinking? That he was hot? Okay, yes, he *is* hot. Jesus. Like no other man on the planet. You've seen him."

Madame looked unimpressed.

"But I think this proves I was right. The 'taking care of me' stuff—it's what I always knew to expect of him. That doesn't make me special, except that I'm Brandon's little sister so he has to be especially careful with my feelings. He wanted me, but he didn't expect it to come with intimate talks about our childhoods—even if it was his idea—or Holy Grail–level sex. I think we both overdosed on closeness."

Tears pooled in her eyes and she dashed them away with an impatient hand, then grabbed one of her big coffee mugs from the cupboard. "See? This wasn't a good idea, Madame. A few days of mind-blowing kinky sex and a lifetime of regret. This is not good for me." She squatted down and stroked the cat's snowy fur. "Except it sure felt good for a while," she whispered quietly so she wouldn't have to hear the words herself.

She pulled in a deep breath as she got to her feet. "Okay. Enough of that. I have to get ready for work and . . . I think I need to take a step back and reevaluate things. Good idea? Yes?" Madame ignored her. "Yes," she said decisively. She wanted to think she was decisive, anyway.

In the bathroom she turned on her iPod speakers and blasted the most upbeat music she could find to keep her mind busy as she showered, but the act of washing his scent from her skin was almost painful. And Goddamn it, even her favorite violet-scented soap reminded her of him now! She might have to pick up something else at the lingerie shop today. They had rose and lily of the valley and jasmine. She could do jasmine.

"God, what am I thinking? I am not changing myself for him!"

She stepped from the shower and dried herself, then ran the towel over her wet hair. Today she would focus on work. Tonight she would wallow in whatever unbearable muck this was.

But work brought no relief. Luxe was slow, as Tuesdays often were, and the only other task she had was checking in a new shipment, which was mindless work. Too mindless, offering no escape from the endless loop in her head, reviewing her morning with Jamie over and over. She wasn't close enough with any of her salespeople to confide in them—not that she wanted to talk about it, anyway. Which was why she went for drinks with the girls from the shop after work rather than calling Dennie. She limited herself to two margaritas so she wouldn't get too sloppy. That would have been all she needed. By ten she was home again.

She changed into her pajamas and fed Madame, who expressed her displeasure at her late meal by meowing plaintively even after she was done eating. Summer ignored her and Madame started a thorough cleaning of her paws before slipping out the back door into the garden.

Summer found herself at loose ends. She sank down onto the sofa in the living room and flipped the television on, but she rarely watched TV and after trying to get into a movie, then a late-night talk show, then another movie with little success she finally turned it off and went into the bedroom, intending to get a good night's sleep. But the scent of Jamie and sex from the pillowcases hit her too hard. With a curse she stripped off the sheets, stuffing them into her wicker laundry basket and making up the bed with fresh ones. But once undressed and in bed, all she could do was stare through the curtains at the moon rising through a dark, misty sky and think of him.

"Goddamn it, Jamie," she muttered, flipping onto her side. "Why do you have to be so . . . *you!*"

She wished he'd been mean about it. That he'd been lousy in bed. That he couldn't make her laugh the way he did. That he hadn't known exactly how much pain she could take with her pleasure, or what to say to make her feel special.

She rubbed at her forehead, which had started to ache.

She would spend the next few days—or whatever it took—obsessing over it, trying to come to some sort of peace with the situation. But the fact that he hadn't called or texted her all day made it pretty likely he was having exactly the same ideas.

"Damn it, Jamie," she said into the dark for the tenth time that day.

She had a feeling she might be cursing him for some time to come.

CHAPTER

Six

B RANDON WAS SCOWLING *at him and Jamie knew why.*
"Brandon, I'm trying."

Brandon raised an eyebrow at him—honey-gold brows and
hair, just like Summer's. And his eyes that same baby blue.
Summer's eyes. Or maybe hers were Brandon's. Either way, he
couldn't stand that his friend was pissed at him. Even worse,
disappointed in him.

"Okay, okay. I know I fucked up." He paused, searching
his friend's eyes, but he found them empty. Blank. Just like that
day at the hospital. His last day. "Did I fuck this up?"

Suddenly it was that last day and Brandon lay pale against
the white, white sheets of the hospital bed and the smell of
antiseptic was making Jamie feel sick to his stomach, but he
had to hold on for his friend. He'd do anything for him. Except,
apparently . . .

Brandon's voice was a low hiss. "This is *your version of taking care of my sister?"*

"Brandon, no. No. It's not. It's . . . I'll get my shit together. I'll figure it out. I'll take care of her the way I'm supposed to. I will."

"I will!"

Jamie bolted upright in bed, the sheets a damp tangle around his waist. His heart was a hammer in his chest. He pressed the heels of his hands against his eyes.

It was the same dream he'd had the other night. Twice in one week. Twice since he'd left Summer Grace's house the other day and hadn't so much as called her since. Sure, he'd sent a few texts, but she'd answered in the same short, meaningless sentences he'd used with her. "How are you?" "Fine." It was all crap.

Managing to escape the twisted sheets, he got up to stand by the bedroom window that overlooked the empty street below. He folded back the heavy plantation shutter. It was early, the sun barely beginning to rise in a shimmering glow of pink and gold, the streetlamps still lit. He flattened his hand against the glass, absorbing the coolness left from the night air and thinking about the dream.

Today was Saturday. July twenty-fifth. The twelfth anniversary of Brandon's death. Which could be the reason for the dreams, but he knew that wasn't the whole reason. He was being fucking haunted for screwing things up so completely with Summer Grace. Either by starting this with her in the first place or by taking off the other day and hardly giving her the time of day since. He really could be an asshole sometimes.

But maybe the worst thing he'd done had been to encourage her involvement in the kink life. Maybe if he'd left her alone her curiosity would have run its course and eventually she'd have left kink—and his club—behind.

He scrubbed a hand over his buzz cut. No. That wasn't how this shit worked—not for the people who were serious enough to play at the clubs. Or rarely, anyway. And she'd taken to it all too easily. She was made for this life. Or maybe that was simply more of his own selfish desires clouding his judgment.

Selfish because he still wanted her. Wanted to be with her.

He wasn't entirely comfortable with that idea. But when had he done anything in his whole adult life other than make sure things were fucking *comfortable*? It had been years since he'd really been involved with a woman. Certainly not anything long-term. Not since the woman he'd—foolishly—married when he was almost twenty, less than a year after Brandon died. And she'd left him six months later. He'd never told a single soul what the real reason was. They'd both told everyone it was because she wanted to go to grad school in California. And that part had been true, but . . . no, the rest was his secret to carry.

He heard the low rumble of a diesel engine and looked down to see his downstairs neighbor, Astrid, drive off to her Saturday morning nursing shift at the hospital. The same hospital where Brandon had died. Which brought him back to the fact that it was this particular Saturday. Which meant he'd see Summer Grace that evening at the cemetery.

He pulled in a lungful of the damp morning air, blew it out, trying to clear his head. Summer Grace and Brandon and guilt were too heavy on his mind. Guilt around Ian and Traci, too, but that was always hanging over his shoulder, tangled up in everything else. But there was no way around it. Not today.

Today they remembered.

"Miss you, buddy," he said quietly, pulling his palm away from the cool glass, swallowing hard as he went to get a quick shower in before heading to the shop for the day.

* * *

JAMIE LOVED THIS cemetery after dark. Quiet but dangerous, full of memories and mementos, life and death. In New Orleans loved ones weren't buried beneath the dirt and forgotten—they were celebrated and enshrined. It may have originated out of necessity, but now it was a point of pride with the locals as well as being a tourist attraction. Particularly this cemetery.

St. Louis Cemetery No. 1 had always been Brandon's favorite. He and Jamie and their group of friends from high school had gathered here back in the day to drink beer and hang out in the shadows of the ornate marble mausoleums, following tradition by spilling drops of beer on the infamous Voodoo priestess Marie Laveau's tomb as an offering. It was their spot whenever they needed to discuss the really deep issues, like the true definition of getting to third base with a girl and their dreams about the future.

Now the ones left behind met here every year on the anniversary of Brandon's death.

That first year after Brandon died it had simply been where they'd all gathered, showing up one by one, as if they'd ended up there purely by accident. Maybe they had, at first. But Jamie didn't quite believe that. This was New Orleans, and no one could live here for any amount of time without believing at least a little that there was more to life than random chance.

The evening air was moist on his skin, hot even in his cotton wifebeater as he walked down the row past the stone and brick and marble structures with their low, ornate iron fences, past the statues of weeping angels. The scent of old stone and plaster was strong in the air, mixing with the aroma of decaying flowers and the hint of exotic spices that lingered everywhere in the city.

He saw them as he approached their usual meeting place—

at the end of the row that housed Marie Laveau's tomb. Even in the dark he could make out Mick's tall, lanky form, his arm around Allie's shoulders. He could see the long curl of Marie Dawn's hair, her husband Neal—Mick's brother—at her side. Then he saw Summer Grace and every muscle in his body went tight.

He knew it was going to be difficult, but had no idea it would be this gut-wrenchingly hard to see her. No, that was total crap. He'd known it—he'd simply kept himself too busy all day to think about it. But it had always been hard to see her. He should be used to it. Every single time he ran into her over the years his resolve had been challenged. Summer Grace Rae had grown up to become the embodiment of temptation, pure sex in a doll's body. And now he *knew* that body. Maybe even more, he knew *her.* The woman she'd grown up to be. The woman he'd left after having the best sex of his life. The kind most people read about and called bullshit on because nothing in reality could be half that good, that damn life-changing.

He was well and truly fucked.

He watched the silhouette of her delicate figure as she moved in to hug someone. Watched her long, pale hair catching the moonlight as he walked up to the group. So damn pretty, that hair. And everything else. Beautiful.

Don't look at her too closely.

As if she were Medusa, about to turn him into stone.

Oh, she'd make him hard, all right. Always had. Always would, he suspected. Not that he planned to do anything about it tonight. No, they had to talk first. If she even wanted to talk to him. Fuck, if it were any night but this—the anniversary of her brother's death—he'd *make* her talk to him.

But it *was* this night. July twenty-fifth. Damn it.

"Hey, Jamie." Mick greeted him, coming up to slap him on

the back. "I see you made it over the wall. Wish they didn't shut this place down like fucking Fort Knox at three in the afternoon."

Jamie shrugged. "It doesn't keep us out, though, does it?"

"Never." Mick grinned and bent to retrieve a beer from the six-pack on the ground, tossing it at him.

"Thanks. Hey, Allie." Jamie bent to kiss her cheek. He was damn happy to see the two of them back together after all their years apart. And pleased with himself that he'd had something to do with it. It had been a few months and he'd never seen either of them happier.

"Good to see you, Jamie," she said, smiling at him.

"Marie Dawn, Neal. How are you two?"

"We're good," Neal answered. "Just . . . you know . . . we're here."

Marie Dawn grabbed her husband's hand, shooting Jamie a look that told him Summer Grace had confided in her friend about the two of them. Great. Now everyone would know he was an asshole.

"We all still miss him," she said, putting voice to the one thought Jamie knew they all shared. "Especially this year, with Allie home again. It's like we're all back together again except for Brandon." She paused, shaking her head. "It just feels wrong to be here without him."

"Yes." It was Summer Grace, her voice small but with a raspy edge that let him know how upset she was. It would be arrogant of him to assume it was all about what had happened between them. What he'd done to upset her.

God fucking damn it.

He took a breath. "Good to see you, Summer Grace."

"*Summer*," she said stubbornly.

She'd always hated that he called her by her full name. He did it partly to annoy her, he had to admit to himself—never to her, of course. But also partly because he'd known her forever and that was who she was to him. It was what Brandon had called her.

"Jamie," she said more softly, and went into his arms for a hug he hadn't offered.

Well, hell—he *had* to put his arms around her, didn't he? Offer her some comfort on the anniversary of her big brother's death? And pretend in front of their oldest friends that nothing was going on between them, good or bad. But if Marie Dawn knew then Allie knew, which meant Mick knew, and hell . . .

He held on to her as long as he could, trying not to feel every soft curve of her small body, the press of her breasts right up against him, for God's sake. He pulled in a breath and gritted his teeth, waiting for her to pull away. She didn't, which made him feel even more like an ass. Maybe she really did need some comfort from him.

Finally, he pulled back. "You get a beer?"

"I've had two already," she answered. "Could probably use a few more tonight."

"Yeah, we all could," he agreed, thankful she was talking to him at all.

"So," Mick began. "Who wants to start?"

Jamie popped his beer open and took a long swallow. "I will," he said. He was always the first one to talk about Brandon. Mick asking was a formality.

He glanced at Summer Grace but Allie had pulled her aside and looped an arm around her shoulder. He was glad to see someone was caring for her, since he couldn't. Not tonight.

"You have the floor then, buddy," Mick told him as some of the others sat on the ground or on the shallow steps of one of the old mausoleums with their beers.

Jamie took a long swig, swallowed, and did his best to focus on the reason they were all here. "Brandon was my best friend from the time I was eight years old, new to the country and full of fight. Even then, he was the best guy I knew. He never made fun of my accent. Never acted like he cared that I was the new kid. He taught me about New Orleans—taught me to love this place. He was more than a friend to me. He was family." He was quiet a moment, taking another long swallow of his beer while gathering his thoughts. "When someone dies at nineteen, it's just not fucking fair. He deserved more of life. I can't help thinking—all the time—what would he be doing if he were here with us now?"

Mick chuckled, said quietly, "Probably making out with some girl and ignoring us."

Jamie started to grin, the constriction in his chest easing a little. It was true. The girls had loved Brandon—there was always one or two mooning over him—and he'd loved them right back.

"He would have gone into business with you, Jamie," Summer Grace said, the low rasp of her voice soft on the night air, "the way you two were always talking about. He would have rebuilt your muscle cars with you, spent his time covered in grease and happy as could be, doing what he loved. Happy to be working with his best friend. The man who was like a brother to him."

Jamie took another pull from his beer. "Yeah," he said, forcing the lump in his throat down deep, where he kept it, safe and sound, other than this one day each year. Except this year there was another reason for that lump. This year he'd broken his promise—not by being with Summer Grace, but by hurting her.

She looked over at their friends. "We all know it's true, don't we? I mean, everyone here loved him, but Jamie and Brandon were never happier than when they were hanging out together. Unless they were competing over a girl. Or a game of Frisbee.

Or a sandwich. Two peas in a pod, my parents used to say. He was never happier than when he was with you, Jamie." She stepped closer, grabbed his beer bottle from him and took a sip. As she tucked it back into his hand she whispered, "So was I."

Even in the moonlight, he could see the baby blue of her eyes beneath the long lashes. Eyes that seemed to look right through him, to recognize the desire he'd felt for her since the first time she'd crawled into his bed when she was fourteen years old. He'd been seventeen at the time, a walking, out-of-control hormone factory. He'd been staying the night at the Rae house—something he'd done often. She'd woken him with a soft, wet kiss, lying on top of his prone body. No fourteen-year-old should have known how to kiss like that. But this girl . . .

He shook his head. "I'm sorry, Summer Grace," he murmured, letting the others think it was about Brandon, if they wanted to. And it was. But it was also about *them*.

"Come on. Let's walk it out like we always do," Mick suggested.

Allie squeezed Summer Grace's shoulder. "Come on, honey."

Allie had only been back in New Orleans a few months, but Jamie knew she and Summer Grace had kept in touch while she was off doing her pastry chef gigs in Europe, same as she had with him—and now he knew they'd solidified their friendship in a whole new way.

He stayed back and watched the two women walking side by side, their heads close together in the stark moonlight, everything cast in monochromatic shadows. And he knew suddenly that *he* wanted to be the one walking with Summer Grace tonight. Soothing her. Making sure she was okay.

He'd spent too many years underestimating her. She'd been Brandon's little sister for so long—a smart-mouthed temptress who'd tested his patience along with his resolve to keep his hands off her. But lately he'd found out so much more about her. Like how smart she was. How competent. How independent. Maybe a little too much so. He couldn't count the times over the years he was certain her sass would get her in trouble. But she'd come through all right so far, and now that sass only added to the attraction.

But it was more than simple attraction. She made him smile, made him want to ease her fears—and instead he'd only proved them right. He'd told her he wanted to be with her, to see where things led, then he'd left her the next day. "Asshole" didn't even begin to cover it. He was irresponsible, too. He hadn't checked in to make sure she wasn't experiencing subdrop, knowing full well that sometimes people in drop were unable to reach out when they needed to. And maybe most important of all, he hadn't told her that when he'd looked into her eyes that night, he'd felt like he was finally home.

The group had started to move down the path and he hurried to catch up with them, staying quiet as they walked up one row and down another, past the wall crypts and mausoleums. This was part of their yearly ritual, to tread the ground for Brandon. Get drunk together. Celebrate him. Remember him.

It suddenly occurred to him that Brandon might not appreciate their yearly remembrance of him. He'd like that they all found a reason to get together en masse once a year, but he might say "Get over it, already. Move on. Don't mourn for me—live for me. Throw a party, not a wake."

Sometimes Jamie's life felt like one continuous wake. A memorial to Brandon. To Ian. To the other young life he'd lost. Was he so afraid of yet another loss that he was pushing away someone he cared for before they'd even had a chance?

In silent meditation Jamie did his best to shift his thoughts from Summer Grace to her brother, but he was hyperaware of her presence at the edge of his vision, her arm linked through Allie's. He couldn't help but notice the gentle sway of her slender hips in her denim cutoffs, her tiny waist outlined by her tight black tank top.

He was definitely going to hell, because instead of maintaining his focus on the group's silent meditation and their purpose there, all he could think about was tossing Summer Grace over his shoulder, carrying her off to some dark corner of the cemetery and kissing her until he'd gotten his fill of her lips. He remembered how beautiful she'd been in his chains. How much she'd loved it, and how perfectly she'd matched him, need for need.

And Jesus, this was not the time or the place. He subtly adjusted his tightening jeans and kept his pace slow, his friends ahead of him.

When they got back to their starting point, they all sat down on the ground, leaning against the iron gates and stone vases, some empty, some full of wilting lilies, and told their stories while they went through the beer until they were all at least a little buzzed.

Summer Grace was more than a little buzzed, he noticed, and too far away.

"You remember that time Brandon drove his car right across school campus?" Neal asked. "He tore the hell out of the lawn. I thought the dean would have his ass, but he managed to charm his way out of it, like he always did. That was *crazy.*"

"He always did have a wild streak," Allie said. "But that was what the girls all loved about him. I don't think I knew anyone— cheerleaders, stoner girls, theater nerds—who didn't have at least a small crush on him."

"And it wasn't just the students," Marie Dawn said, laughing.

"Remember when he got caught kissing the art teacher's aide in the supply closet at the end of senior year? That French girl, Gabrielle. He almost didn't get to go to graduation. What was that art teacher's name? She almost had a stroke when she caught them."

"Mrs. MacGuire," Neal said. "She was an old crone."

"But the aide was hot," Mick chimed in.

"Hey!" Allie protested.

"Well, she was. Hot enough that he kept seeing her until after graduation. Brandon got all the hot girls. Except you, of course, baby." Mick leaned down and kissed Allie's cheek.

"She was the last girl Brandon kissed," Summer said quietly.

Jamie nodded. "Yeah, she was. Gabrielle . . . She came to the funeral, you know. She stood in the back and left before it was over. But I saw her. I saw her crying."

They all sat silently for a moment, thinking, he knew, of the funeral. Summer Grace got up then and walked off slowly, as if no one would notice her absence. As if he wouldn't immediately feel it.

"Jamie," Allie whispered, reaching out to smack his arm. "Go after her, would you?"

"If I say no, you'll just smack me again," he muttered, already getting to his feet to follow her—as if he wanted to do anything else. The cemetery at night was no safe place for a girl alone, and he knew she was upset, thinking of her brother. Probably upset with him, too, and he couldn't blame her.

But Jesus, the girl moved fast. By the time he peeked down the row she was nowhere in sight.

"Summer Grace?"

He moved quickly, peering down the side aisles through the dark, and was just starting to worry when he finally saw her leaning up against a stone urn in front of a moss-covered vault.

"Hey. You okay?"

She shrugged. "Marie Dawn was right. I love having Allie home again, but it makes it harder, too, you know? Now we're only missing one."

"I know." He stepped closer. "And I know I'm probably the last person you want here, but I need you to know I *am* here. I know you're missing him. Even more than I do."

"Maybe. I'm not sure about that. He was really your brother, too. Neither one of us has much family left. And these anniversaries are so Goddamn hard." She sniffed, wiping her nose with the back of her hand. "As if we don't remember every day. As if we don't remember his smile or him waiting to walk me home from school. As if we haven't heard that story about the last girl he kissed a dozen times."

"Hey." He moved in, steeling himself as he pulled her in close. But he could smell her hair, and her body felt familiar in his arms. So damned good. "It's okay," he told her. "It'll be okay."

"I can't stand to think about that shit sometimes, Jamie. To think about who else he might have kissed after the art teacher's aide. Who he would have ended up with. God, who knows? He could have married Marie Dawn. Or Allie." She paused. "No, Allie was always Mick's, wasn't she?"

"Yeah. Always."

It was true. Allie and Mick—that was pure destiny. It had taken some convincing for Mick to get over himself and see that. And Neal and Marie Dawn were right together, too. Out of the group it was just him and Summer Grace who still ran solo. Or not.

Can't think about that now—not while she's crying over her brother.

"In some ways it doesn't get easier, you know what I mean?" she asked, her voice muffled against his chest. He hoped she couldn't hear the hammering of his heart as he breathed her in. "He's been gone for twelve years and I still sometimes feel like I can just pick up the phone and call him. Like I'll walk around a corner and he'll just . . . be there. Is that ridiculous?"

"No. I feel it, too. About Brandon. Even about Ian."

She turned her face up to his and those big, blue eyes glistened with tears. It made his breath catch to see her hurting. "Really?" she asked.

"Yeah. Really."

"But your brother's been gone since you were seven years old. Do you even remember him that well?"

"Sort of. He was . . . Nah, this is really going to sound crazy."

"Come on. Tell me, Jamie."

When had he been able to deny her anything? Well, almost anything.

"The thing is, Ian was my twin, so my whole life I've had this weird idea that he's grown with me, still looking like me. Like if I look hard enough into the mirror, he'll be there staring back at me."

"Wow."

"See? I told you it was crazy."

"No, I don't think it is. I think it's sort of amazing. And sweet."

"Yeah?"

"Yeah."

"Traci never understood when I talked about Ian like that."

"Yeah, well, you guys weren't married long enough for her to really get you," she said.

It was true. He'd gotten hitched to the first girl he'd hooked up with after they lost Brandon, less than a year later. It had been a stupid move, and she'd left almost as quickly. He couldn't blame her. For a lot of things.

Don't think about her. Not here. Not now.

All he wanted to think of was the beautiful girl in his arms.

Summer Grace snuggled in closer and suddenly he was aware of the soft press of her breasts against his ribs. The fact that they were both a little buzzed on the beer and hurting. And maybe she'd missed him the way he had her this week.

"We should get back to the others," he said, starting to pull away, not wanting to take advantage of the situation.

"Jamie, please. Just . . . hold me a minute."

There was no way he was going to argue with her. He let his arms relax around her, pulling in a few deep breaths of the humid New Orleans air. But it was no good. Despite the ache in his chest, he was hyperaware of every soft plane and lusciously sleek curve of her body against his. He shifted so she wouldn't feel him growing hard.

It wasn't the first time and it wouldn't be the last—he was as certain of that as he was that he should never have touched her. Not Summer Grace. Brandon's little sister . . .

She'd always been the little sister. In theory, anyway. But it was that theory that had allowed him to resist her until so recently. Because when she'd crawled under the blankets with him when she was fourteen hadn't been the only time. No, that was just where it had started.

There was that time he'd gone camping with the Rae's. They'd driven all across the country, and Summer Grace had done it again—slipped into his sleeping bag one morning when Brandon had gotten up early to go fishing with his dad and Jamie was too tired to join them. Her hands had slid all over his body. How she'd known to stroke his hardening nipples like that at barely fifteen . . . and before he'd really woken up and realized what was happening, he'd been lost in a dream where her long, silky hair was falling all over his chest, then dragging lower over his stomach, and his cock had gone so damn hard he could feel the come pulsing in it, ready to explode. When she'd touched him, her fingers tracing his erection through his boxers, his eyes had flown open and she was there—her hands and her hair on him *real*. He'd nearly come right then—he'd had to bite his cheek hard enough to draw blood to keep from grabbing her, tearing off her little shorts and sheer tank top, which had shown clearly in the dawn light that she wasn't wearing a bra. He'd groaned, wanting to take those firm, pink nipples between his teeth and . . .

"Jamie," she whispered.

"What? What is it, Summer Grace?"

She sighed. "When are you ever going to call me Summer, like everyone else?"

He smiled in the dark. "Probably never."

She pulled back enough to tilt her chin, those long lashes coming down like a sooty shadow over her eyes as she blinked up at him. "Jamie," she repeated, the rasp back in her voice.

"Yeah?"

She stared up at him, blinking again. There was so much going on in her eyes—more than he could figure out right then. And too much going on in his own head, too. In his body. Desire and the shared pain of what this night meant to them both. The guilt of having left her on her own all week. The deeper guilt of having violated his vow to her brother, and the really dark shit that ran even deeper. Being the survivor, both of their brothers dead and gone and him still standing there.

With his arms around the one woman he'd ever really wanted.

Too much. It's all too fucking much.

But she was *right there*, in his arms. His hands gripped her tiny waist as he pulled her in and opened her soft lips with his tongue. Jesus, she tasted good. Like the beer, but behind it she tasted the way she smelled—like flowers and heat.

How was that even possible?

But he didn't care. It just *was*. *She* just was. Hot and pliable in his arms, her lips and tongue as hungry as his. So many damn years of wanting. He deepened the kiss and she pressed closer, her breath a soft pant against his lips, into his mouth as he breathed her in.

He was hard as hell, hard enough to ache. He ground up against her. He couldn't help it. She was all heat and need—he could feel it coming off her in waves, echoing his own need—a need he'd kept banked for years. Because she was . . .

Forbidden.

"Christ." He let her go. They were both panting. "Summer Grace, I can't do this."

She shook her head. Her hair was mussed, her lips soft and swollen. "Don't say it. Don't. I've been Brandon's little sister my whole life. But I'm still *me*. And I'm a woman, Jamie. I'm twenty-seven years old, for God's sake! I'm not some kid who can't make her own choices anymore. I haven't been for a long time. How long are you going to run from me?"

He stepped back, braced his hand on the iron fencing behind him. "I'm not running anymore."

"No, you don't. Don't lie to me. God*damn* it, Jamie. You haven't even called me all week." She pounded on his chest with her small fist, and he was shocked at the anger he felt from her— the anger and the power in her. "I was done with you. I was moving on. Why did you have to fuck with my head?"

He heard the tears in her voice, but he let her give him one last shove before she walked away, back toward their friends. He saw her go back to Allie, sink into her embrace, and he felt like absolute shit.

That should be me comforting her. Except she won't let me.
Fuck it. And fuck her not *letting* him.

A small rage was burning in his chest. Rage and certainty and he wasn't quite sure where either had come from. Didn't matter. He knew what he needed to do.

He stalked after her and grabbed her right out of Allie's arms. "We're not done talking. You're coming with me, Summer *Grace.*"

"What the fuck?" Mick demanded.

"Mick, let them go," Allie said, and Jamie would have shot her a look of gratitude if he weren't so completely focused on the woman struggling in his grasp.

"Summer Grace," he said, keeping his tone low. "You can come with me or I'm about to make a hell of a scene right here in front of everyone."

"Like you haven't done that already," she muttered, but she stopped struggling.

"Oh, you haven't seen what I can do if necessary. You coming or do I carry you out of here?"

There was a long pause, but she kept her gaze on his, not even glancing at the others. It was as if nothing existed but the two of them, the tension thick in the air between them. As if nothing mattered but what might happen next.

Nothing does.

Finally she nodded, shook him off, and with her chin held high she headed for the part of the wall they all used to climb into the closed cemetery.

"Sorry, guys," he shot over his shoulder.

"Don't worry about it, buddy," Mick said.

"Go get her," Marie Dawn chimed in. "What? It's exciting."

Jamie caught up with Summer Grace in a few long strides and grabbed her elbow. She kept moving, not looking at him, but she didn't try to shake him off. At the wall he gripped her arm tighter.

"I'm giving you a boost up."

She sighed. "Whatever. I can do it on my own, though."

"You're only five-foot-three."

"I can do it myself, Jamie," she said through gritted teeth. "I always do. I can use a can opener and pay my bills myself, too. I'm a Goddamn superwoman without you around. I can do a lot more than you've ever given me credit for."

"Yeah. I know."

She turned to look at him. "You do?"

"What do you think I'm doing here? Why do you think I'm dragging you out of here with me so we can talk? Did you think it was just to show that I could? Because you know, that move has earned me a lot of points with the crowd."

She surprised him by cracking a half-smile. "Maybe."

"Don't think just because we have some talking to do that you won't be owed a spanking."

She squared her shoulders. "I'm not scared of you. And you might not get to spank me. Your silence was the beginning of renegotiations of our limits."

Fuck.

"I don't think you're scared of anything, Summer Grace. But maybe you should be. And we'll see about your limits."

"Stop with the dire warnings and give me a leg up, will you, Braveheart?"

"Make that two spankings."

"Promises, promises."

He shook his head and clasped his hands for her to put her foot into. "Climb over the damn wall already and you'll see how good I am at keeping my promises."

Except for the one. But he was feeling more and more confused about how to interpret the promise he'd made to Brandon so long ago.

Would his friend have been upset if he and Summer Grace ended up together? He didn't think so. But the kink . . . Would Brandon have known how to react to that at nineteen? How much would the years have changed his perspective?

Brandon would never know, though, would he? Maybe all he could do was his best.

He followed her over the wall and took her hand in his as they crossed Conti Street to where his Corvette was parked. It was a risk parking there at night, but he'd always taken whatever his current hot rod was to Brandon's remembrance night, and nothing had ever happened to one of his cars there. It was as if Brandon were watching over them. He opened the passenger side door and watched with a small smile as Summer Grace's hand stroked the cherry-red paint, lingering there for several moments. She'd always appreciated the muscle cars—maybe almost as much as he and Brandon did.

She slid into the pristine black leather seat and he closed the door behind her, then went around to the driver's side and folded his long legs into the car. He flipped on the headlights before starting the car and the usual small thrill went through him at the purr of the powerful engine. But it was nothing compared to the fact that Summer Grace sat there beside him.

Gotta make it right.

"Your place or mine?" he asked.

"Yours," she said without hesitation.

He raised an eyebrow at her but she looked straight ahead through the windshield.

"Okay. My place it is."

As he pulled onto the street, the rain started, as it so often did in this subtropical city. The only sounds were the quiet thunder of the engine, the windshield wipers going back and forth and the rain splashing on the top of the Corvette as he drove. He didn't let himself look at Summer Grace. He couldn't. He was too damn distracted by her as it was, already formulating what he had in store for her at his place—and by what needed to be said. It was an insane mix of raw emotion and stark desire. But that's just how things were with them. Pure intensity on every level. It wasn't drama, like it was with some women. It was simply true.

When he reached the Pontchartrain Expressway he opened the engine up, the roar of it satisfying, helping him to focus on the drive home. A few minutes later he exited and hung a right onto Kerlerec Street, then pulled into a parking spot just past his house. He finally let himself look at her. She was still staring out the window—he could see the shadowed profile of her long lashes, faintly illuminated by the amber streetlamps as she blinked, the sooty weight of them coming down on her high cheekbones. He couldn't read her from this angle. Was she still mad despite their banter? Hurt? She had a right to both.

"You gonna look at me, sugar?"

She let out a sigh. "Oh, you're calling me 'sugar' again?"

He reached over to take her hand and felt her fingers wrap around his. He gave her hand a squeeze. "I'm sorry, Summer Grace."

"I know you are, Jamie."

"You still mad at me? Upset?"

"A little. If I wasn't I'd be a doormat. No one likes a doormat, Jamie."

"You're not a doormat. You want to talk to me?"

"Not really."

"You just wanna give me a hard time, is that it?"

She chuckled. "Maybe I do."

Ah, there's my tough girl.

"In that case, I have the perfect cure for your mad."

He grabbed her and unbuckled her seat belt, pulling her across the console in one easy move, then into his lap.

"Jamie! What the hell are you doing?"

"I'm spanking you in the front seat of my car."

"You are not!"

"Wanna bet, sweetheart?"

He lifted her until she was straddling him, and with one hand he yanked her shorts down, revealing her nearly bare ass—not that the small scrap of lace she wore would get in his way.

"Aw, you dressed up just for me," he said, stroking his hand over the smooth flesh of her perfect little ass.

"I did not."

"You may as well have. I'm enjoying it either way."

SUMMER WRIGGLED IN Jamie's strong grasp, but he hung on tight. "I bet you are," she sassed, enjoying the banter. Enjoying the way he held on to her. Overpowered her. It made her mind empty out, which was exactly what she needed tonight.

Jamie was what she needed, no matter how hard she tried to deny it. Despite her anger—her justifiable anger—his little cock-fight of a show at the cemetery had told her what she'd needed to know. And his touch was getting to her. It always did.

"Better behave, bad girl," he warned, mock severity in his low tone. Or maybe not so "mock."

"You know me better," she argued, squirming harder. But he

only grabbed a handful of her long hair and wrapped it around his fist.

Oh yes, exactly what I need.

She kept wriggling, and the more she struggled the tighter he held on to her, her body going soft and hot all over in his commanding grip.

"I know you'll love it when I spank you," he said, lowering his tone. So damn sexy she could hardly stand it. "You'll love every single strike on your fine, fine ass. Every smooth stroke of my hand in between smacks as I run my palm over your burning skin. And in minutes you'll be moaning. Wanting more. Oh, I know you, sugar, better than I ever have before. I know what you want. What that hot little body of yours needs. And no one can give it to you like I can."

"Fuck, Jamie," she murmured. Every single thing he'd said was true.

He chuckled quietly. The first smack came and she let out a soft groan. Then another hard smack, and another, and soon she was squirming with pain and the most exquisite pleasure—it flooded her system, making her wet instantly. She laid her cheek against the headrest behind Jamie's head and gave herself over to the spanking. To pleasure. To the heat of his body so close to hers, the burning pain of his hand as he spanked and caressed.

When his hand slipped between her thighs, she gasped.

"Mmm, baby, you are so hot. So wet. Fuck."

"Yes, please," she begged. "Please, Jamie."

Somehow he unbuckled his seat belt—damn, he was good at that!—and slid out of the car with her in his arms. It was still raining, small drops spattering them as she wrapped her legs around his waist and he carried her across the street. In moments he had the front door unlocked, then he carried her up the narrow stairs, through his living room and into the bedroom.

Jamie's bedroom. She had a quick moment to take it in, illuminated by the pale hall light: the sleekly modern four-poster bed in a dark wood, the red blanket folded back to reveal the bed neatly made with sheets in a gray and white geometric pattern. The enormous mirror framed in dark wood leaning against a wall next to the bed—it must have been almost as tall as he was and maybe four feet wide. Which meant that from the bed you could see everything.

Oh, nice.

He set her down on the bed and moved her up toward the pillows, handling her roughly.

"Don't be careful with me, Jamie," she said, even though she knew he wouldn't be. Never any more than he had to be.

"I won't be. I promise." He grinned, those devastating dimples flashing.

She knew he'd keep his word, and at that moment those words were the only thing that mattered.

CHAPTER
Seven

"QUIET NOW," JAMIE said, placing his hand over Summer's mouth and pressing hard enough to let her know he meant business—hard enough that it pressed her head into the downy softness of the mattress a little. And her sex went hot at the utter command in that small action.

He yanked her shorts down over her legs, his other hand still tight over her mouth. He pulled her sandals off and straddled her body, grinning down at her, his face utterly masculine and beautiful in the dim wash of silvery moonlight that shone through one of the open shutters. He looped a finger through the edge of her lace thong. She arched her hips, needing him to touch her, but he let the lace go and laid a heavy hand on her hip.

"Still," he said, his tone full of authority.

She stopped moving, her breath coming out in hot pants against the hand clamped across her mouth. Her sex went tight, making her aware of how wet she was, how swollen.

Need him, need him, need him.

He was making her crazy. But she would do as she was told. He was right—the spanking had taken the fire out of her. Now all she wanted—needed—was to please him. Partly because she knew he wouldn't reward her with the pleasure she craved otherwise, but also purely for the sake of pleasing him.

Jamie.

As she lay there blinking up at him, his grin faded and his expression shifted, his brows drawing together as he slid one hand over her breast.

"No bra. It really does seem like you dressed for me tonight. Good girl."

She wasn't about to argue. Not at this point. And maybe she had, somewhere in the back of her mind.

"But do you remember what happens to good girls, sugar?" he went on. "In case you've forgotten, a lot of things. And I can't ever let you guess which way it'll go, can I? Sometimes it'll be putting my hand between your thighs and pressing my fingers into your hot pussy. And sometimes it might be spanking you until your skin is raw—because good or bad, you *will* get spanked. But you like that, don't you, baby? You'll like this, too."

He drew back and used both hands to pinch her nipples, the fabric of her ribbed tank top grating against her flesh.

She moaned.

"Not enough? You never can get enough, but I love that about you."

He pinched harder, twisting her sensitive flesh between his fingertips.

"Oh, God, Jamie!"

"'Oh God' good or 'Oh God' bad?"

"Both!"

He chuckled. "That's my girl."

His girl. Yes.

Then her entire body tried to arc off the bed as he pinched her so damn hard she nearly screamed, but he was still straddling her, holding her down. And immediately she was soaking, aching.

"Ah, you like that, sugar. Yeah, you do. You're gonna like this, too."

He tore his white tank top over his head. She could never see his body without appreciating the ripple of muscle in his abs, his shoulders, his biceps. Without his ink turning her on. And those luscious pierced nipples.

She groaned.

"Yeah, baby. I like to hear that—to hear your pleasure. I need it like I need my own breath."

He bent over her and pushed her tank top up, baring her naked breasts, and placed a soft, hot kiss between them. She sighed. He turned his head and bit into the soft flesh.

"Ah!"

He shifted and took one stiff nipple into his mouth, stroking it with his tongue, then sucking hard, hurting her. Then he licked at the sore skin before sucking hard again. He was driving her mad, the pleasure and the pain some crazy elixir she couldn't get enough of.

He moved down her body, lower and lower, until he was licking and kissing and nibbling his way around the lace of her thong. He forced her thighs apart with rough hands and moved his face lower. She felt the scruff on his jaw against one thigh, then he yanked the lace aside and plunged his tongue right into her.

"Oh! God . . ."

He began to fuck her with his tongue, hard and fast and relentless. Desire was like a series of electric shocks rumbling through her body. She needed more. Needed to come. But she knew this would be at his pace. Under his control.

Yes.

Suddenly he pressed his fingers into her—she didn't know how many—and spread them inside her so that she was filled up, and he began a hard pumping.

"Jamie . . . I can't take it. I can't . . . can't wait."

"You can do it. Take it for me. Wait to come."

Sensation built, a tight coil in her belly. Liquid heat in her sex. Her hips arched into his thrusting fingers and he pulled them away. She almost sobbed, her hands scrabbling at the cool sheets. But in moments he'd replaced his fingers with his hot, wet tongue and she sighed in relief. Sighed with indescribable pleasure when he began to lick her sensitive clit, his tongue moving fast, pressing hard, until the pleasure itself hurt. But she wouldn't have had it any other way.

Her climax started to shiver through her, and he stopped.

"No . . . please."

He clamped his hand across her mouth once more. "Shh. No pleading. No begging. You'll get what I choose to give you. You'll give me your pleasure, sugar girl. And when I ask for it you'll give me your orgasm, too, won't you? Tell me," he demanded.

He took his hand away and she gasped, "Yes, Jamie."

"Yes what?"

"Yes, I'll come for you. For *you*."

"That's my good girl."

He went back to work with his lovely tongue, torturing her with pleasure while he pinched the inside of her thighs with hard, hurting fingers. The pain made sensation spiral once more, taking her higher and higher, until she couldn't think at all. She was nothing but sensation, riding the rolling waves up and down as Jamie dictated with his touch—or his denial of it. Each time she reached that crest and couldn't hold her climax back any longer, he backed off, forcing her to pace herself. Finally he pulled away completely and sat up. She was too limp with pleasure and pain, her system too suffused by it all, to do anything more than blink up at him.

"Spread wider for me, sweetheart." She did as he asked. "Oh yeah, that's it. Your beautiful pussy, so wet and pink and sweet as a peach in the summertime." He licked his lush mouth and her sex clenched hard. "I love the taste of you, baby. I want to drink you up." He unbuttoned his jeans and she held her breath as his smooth skin was revealed. "But right now I need to fuck you even more."

Then he was naked and sheathing his beautiful cock with a condom he'd taken from the table next to the bed. He dragged her by the ankles to the foot of the mattress and hooked her heels over his shoulders.

"Hands clasped over your head, my good girl."

He held his cock at the entrance to her pussy, brushing it over the swollen lips. Then he plunged.

"Ah! Jamie!"

"Don't you come. You come when I tell you to. Understood?"

"Yes," she panted.

He pulled out of her and she wanted to cry. "Yes, what?"

"Yes, I come when you tell me I can."

"Ah, that's my good sugar girl." He caressed his thick cock, wrapping his fingers around it and beginning to stroke. "I'm gonna fuck you so hard. I'm gonna fuck you until you can barely breathe—until I lose my breath. Until I am so deep inside you will never forget me."

She almost came right then, but his command was even more powerful than the pleasure he brought her. She bit her lip and held it back as he pushed into her once more, his length and girth filling her completely. As he did exactly what he said he would. He fucked her so hard she slid up on the sheets, and she had to force herself to hold her clasped hands over her head, as he'd ordered. But he grabbed her hips and dragged her back to the edge of the bed, then lifted her bottom higher, allowing him to surge deeper inside her in long strokes. And in between she caught small flashes of their reflection in the big mirror—it was one of the hottest things she'd ever seen.

He tilted his hips, his hands digging into her bottom, lifting her. He gave one lovely, savage thrust that really fucking hurt, that made her feel as if she were drowning in pleasure.

"Oh, oh . . . God!"

She was blinded by sensation, her vision swimming. She felt beautifully powerless, giving it all over to Jamie.

The pressure built, but he pinched the top of her thigh hard enough to bring her out of it, away from the ready edge of orgasm.

"Ow!"

"'Ow' is not a safeword, sugar," he panted, his dimples making tiny, irresistible divots in his cheeks.

She started to laugh, tried to swallow it, but she was too high on endorphins and the pleasure swamping her body, and she couldn't get it under control. Jamie was smiling down at her as he fucked her, his hips slamming into hers, never slowing down. But soon his smile turned to a baring of teeth as he shivered, and she stopped giggling. He was shaking all over. "Now!" His voice was a hoarse groan. "Come, baby."

He pressed onto her clit with his fingertips—she didn't even need it. Her body exploded, sensation like a thousand points of light inside her, searing her with pleasure so intense she really was blinded for several long moments—or minutes. She didn't know. It didn't matter. All she knew was their trembling bodies, every hot, silky place where their skin met, where flesh touched flesh. The smell of him all over her. His cries and her own.

Finally the only sound was their panting breath and the low, chirping hum of the cicadas outside. Jamie collapsed on top of her, then rolled onto his side and pulled her into his arms. He held her loosely at first, but when he tightened his arms around her, tears pooled behind her eyes.

Damn it!

She pulled in the humid, come-scented air and blew out a few breaths in a row.

"Hey, baby. What is it?"

"It's . . . nothing. Really. I don't know. Just an emotional night, I guess. I'm good, though. I am."

"You trying to convince me or yourself?"

"Both of us, maybe?"

"Good girl."

"Jamie—"

He lifted his head to look at her, catching her chin with his fingertips. "Hey. I'm not mocking you, sweetheart. I mean it. I like that you can be so honest with me. And it's okay. Anyway, if I called you a bad girl you might kick me, and I've already known the mighty power of your wrath tonight."

One corner of his mouth quirked and she smacked his chest, pausing to appreciate the solid wall of muscle there.

"See?"

"Oh, there's much worse where that came from," she told him, her mood lifting.

"Don't think you're gonna convince me to switch, sugar, 'cause that ain't happening."

"Ha! As if I ever thought it might."

He grabbed her as he rolled onto his back until she was on top of him. "No? You never thought you might try to do me with a strap-on?"

Summer rolled her eyes. "I don't know that I've ever wanted to do anyone with a strap-on, but if I did, it sure as hell would not be you, Jamie Stewart-Greer! I may be a lot of things, but I'm not stupid. Or delusional."

"Then kiss me like you're the Top here."

She giggled. "Well, I *am* on top of you."

"Shut up and kiss me, my good girl."

"Just for that I might have to be bad."

"Oh, really?"

He arched one dark brow before pulling her face down to his by her hair and kissing her so hard she could barely catch her breath.

She began to melt instantly, but when he let her go she couldn't help sassing him. "Being bad is still sounding like an attractive option."

"We'll see about that."

Before she had a chance to think about it he'd flipped her onto her stomach and was straddling her, one arm pinned behind her back. She loved the way he manhandled her—her greedy sex was pulsing with a hot, stinging desire already. Still, she said, "I can be bad from down here, you know."

"Summer Grace?"

"Hmm?"

"I'm getting hard again."

"And?"

"And we're about to find out if you like being at the other end of a strap-on made of flesh."

She blinked twice before she fully understood what that meant. "Ohhh."

He chuckled but kept a firm grip on her arm as he leaned over her, and her head was at the right angle to see what he took from the drawer: a tube of lube, a few condoms, and a pack of baby wipes. Even knowing what he had in mind had her squirming.

"Hold still, my little sugar girl, and I might go easy on you. Nah, who am I kidding?"

"Jamie—"

One sharp smack on her ass and she bit her tongue to keep quiet.

"That's better. Now I need both my hands but you're to keep your arm behind your back. In fact, up on your knees . . . yeah, that's it, but keep your face on the bed. You can use one arm to stabilize yourself—you're gonna need it."

She closed her eyes and waited, trying not to move as he spread the cheeks of her ass and rubbed a good amount of the anal gel lubricant on with his fingers. She hadn't been touched there by a man in far too long. And now it was going to be Jamie. And it felt so damn good.

Oh yes.

He slipped his other hand around her waist and played with her clit while he teased the tight hole of her ass with his lubed fingers. She wanted to push back into him, to impale herself, but she was trying to behave, to comply. And her head was sinking into subspace—something that had always happened to her during anal play, even though she hadn't always known what to call it. There was something very submissive for her about giving up that part of her body to a man. And with Jamie . . . well, anything that had felt even remotely submissive to her before was magnified by a hundred with him. By a thousand.

"Breathe in," he instructed her, and she did, her body instantly going loose as she anticipated what was about to happen.

"Good, yes. Relax, sugar."

He slipped one fingertip inside her. She wanted more—so much more. But she also understood this was how it was done—a little at a time until he knew what she could take. He pressed it in the tiniest bit farther, slid it out, and pleasure was a long, wistful sigh in her body.

"Breathe," he commanded.

She did, and he slid a second finger in with the first. This time she had to really let her muscles go slack to allow the two fingers in past the tight ring of muscle. There was a small burning sensation, but his other hand teasing her clitoris was helping. That and the fact that she loved the sensation of her ass being filled, that she'd been yearning for this kind of play.

He pressed deeper, and she couldn't help it—she surged back.

Immediately his hand left her clit and pressed onto the small of her back. "Easy there. You will get what I give you. Remember? You can answer me."

"Yes. I remember."

"Good girl."

That melting sensation again—with the small part of her mind not otherwise engaged she figured she'd better get used to it.

When he started a slow pumping inside her ass pleasure poured through her system like some slow, warm liquid. She could almost picture it in her head like a length of heavy silken rope, twisting and turning as his fingers did inside her body.

"Mmmm."

"You like that, baby? I can tell you do. And I love that you're into this—into having me violate your sweet ass. Because my cock is going in soon. As soon as I feel you're ready for it. But I have to tell you, sugar, I am so damn ready. So damn hard. I can feel the blood like a pulsebeat in my cock. And I want nothing more than to plow into you. To fuck your beautiful ass. But first let's see how many more of my fingers you can take."

He pulled his fingers out and she felt him add a third at her opening, felt him twine his fingertips together into a point before pushing back into her.

"Ah!"

"Too much, baby? Tell me."

"No. It's good. So good."

"That's what I want to hear."

His fingers pushed in slowly, and she couldn't deny there was as much pain as there was pleasure for the first few moments— or that she loved the pain as much as the pleasure. She breathed into it, converting the pain, breathing it in, breathing out nothing but the lovely sensations of being filled and commanded and *taken* by him. By *him*.

Several minutes passed in which his fingers surged into her ass, then out again, in again, pausing to twist, then turning as he pulled back once more. He was pressing and tapping her hard clit with his other hand, his fingers dipping in and out of her swollen, needy sex. Her mind was a blur of sensation, her body full of desire, overflowing with it.

He pulled out of her and said very quietly, "Have to fuck your pretty little ass now, my sugar girl."

He spread more of the lube on her anus, then parted her cheeks. She inhaled, taking in the scent of the clean, crisp sheets and pulling it deep into her lungs. His sheathed cock rested at the opening, and then he began to push. Ever so slowly—too slowly, yet at the same time it was perfect. The thick head took a few moments to pass the tight ring of muscle, then it slid in and she couldn't help but clench for a moment as if to hold him there.

"Easy," he told her.

She forced her body to relax once more and he pushed deeper, then deeper still, and she felt the weight and girth of his cock inside her body. He was big, but she could take it. She wanted to. Needed to.

He pressed deeper and she felt that point where his cock widened close to his body push into her, his hips tight up against her ass, his strong thighs right behind hers.

"Ah . . ."

He laid his hand at the small of her back once more and exerted some pressure—just enough to make her feel his authority. She fucking loved it. All conscious thought drained from her as sensation took her over completely—as Jamie did. His arm came around her waist and he held her tight, a small gasping pant escaping him as he tilted his hips and pressed into her as deep as he could go.

She was panting then, in short, sharp bursts. So much need, so much pleasure. So much being under Jamie's command. At Jamie's mercy. And she felt it vaguely as something clicked in her mind—or maybe it was in her chest—some new level of emotion and vulnerability. Some new level of trust.

Then he pulled back and began to fuck her. He kept his strokes long and slow, moving in and out of her sinuously while the hand on her back slipped up her spine until it was on the back of her neck and he was pressing her cheek down hard into the mattress.

Yes. His.

"His," she whispered, wanting to feel the word on her lips.

His hips moved a little faster, his thick cock surging into her, pulling out almost to the tip before he buried himself in her once more. Desire jabbed deeper into her system with every slow thrust. She wanted to come—needed to—and almost thought she could just from this. He fucked her harder, his cock plunging deeper, and she was shaking all over with pleasure. With *yielding*.

"Still good, baby? Tell me."

She tried to speak, but she was drowning in sensation—physically, mentally.

He paused. "Summer? You good? Talk to me."

She forced her brain to engage. "I . . . Jamie . . . It's so damn good. God . . . I can't . . . Please don't stop. Don't stop."

But rather than taking away from what she was feeling, saying the words only made it hotter. Her sex and her ass tightened, making Jamie groan.

"Jesus, that's good. Need to come. Fuck, I need to come. Need to fuck you harder. Yeah . . ." His cock jabbed into her, hard and deep, a few savage thrusts that had her gasping. "Ah, baby . . . *my* baby. Fuck, yeah!"

He roared as he came, his hands on her digging into her flesh. And she gave herself over to it—to Jamie and pleasure and pain. She felt so acutely his cock pulsing inside her ass. Felt him trembling. And even before he was done he was rubbing at her clit with the heel of his hand. Almost instantly her body shivered with heat, her climax slamming into her, a wall of sensation, lightning-hot ecstasy. His still-hard cock was buried deep in her ass as she came so hard she saw stars, the room going black. He kept working her clit, his cock moving inside her, milking her climax until she couldn't take any more.

He bent over her, his breath heavy in her hair, the front of his body pressing against her spine so that she could feel every muscled plane of his torso, every contraction of his abs, every delightful shiver that went through him.

"Jesus Christ, sweetheart. I swear you are gonna kill me. But I've never felt anything like I do with you. Never."

She smiled to herself, knowing she felt the same. She didn't need to say it—couldn't say anything right now, with her muscles and her brain turned to goo.

Jamie leaned his weight into her, pressing her body down onto the bed. Then he began to pull out of her very slowly, making her want to come some more. Or maybe just to never let him go.

Never let me go.

She sighed. Sank into the idea of never. Of forever. With Jamie.

She was too far gone for it to even make her blink. No, she'd blink later.

"Okay, pulling out now. Take a breath."

She tried to do as he said, but she was absolutely limp. With coming. Maybe even more with submission itself. She was down deep in subspace. Full of sensation and endorphins and love. Too far gone to even want to really fight it.

Fuck.

But no—it was fine. She had always loved him. Always. Even when he made it hard to.

He pulled out of her, moving slowly, and it only hurt a little. Not enough to matter, except the pain *always* mattered in that it was what she wanted from him.

I am not making sense.

It didn't matter. Nothing did except that they were there together and she was his. *His.*

"Come on, my sugar girl," he said gently, his voice rough. "Let's get us both into a nice, hot shower."

He rolled her onto her back and took her hand, his fingers joining with hers and folding over them. When she simply lay there one corner of his mouth lifted and a dimple flickered in his cheek. "You gonna get up, sweetheart?"

"Mmm. Yes, Jamie."

"Oh, you are totally out in space, aren't you? God, it looks good on you, my sugar girl. To know I took you there. It's a beautiful thing. Mm-mm, if I hadn't just come twice in a row I'd have to fuck you again. But maybe after we've had that shower."

She smiled and he bent down to pull the red blanket from beneath her and covered her with it. "You stay here until I get the water going. I'll be back for you in a sec."

She watched the perfection that was his ass as he walked away from her and disappeared into the bathroom. Idly playing with the soft edge of the blanket, she blinked, watching the reflection of the dark, rainy sky through the open shutter on one of the windows. The streetlamps made tiny prisms of the droplets slipping down the glass, each one a reflection of the amber light splintered into pink and green and blue. It must have been two or three in the morning and somehow light had found a way to make a rainbow, as if just for her.

She let out a small laugh. She really was high as a kite on those wonderful endorphins. And oxytocin and dopamine and whatever else was released in her brain during play and sex and being touched by Jamie.

"Okay, beautiful, up you go."

Jamie lifted her, and her head was light, but she wanted to walk. She looped her arm around his waist and he kept his firmly around hers as they moved into the steamy bathroom, then into the shower stall.

She loved that he'd made it so big and luxurious when he

remodeled the house. The dark-green slate was so *him*, somehow. He'd even built a small bench seat into it. A bamboo rack held shampoo and soap and a few other items. She took the warm air into her lungs, savoring the earthy scent of Jamie's soap.

"Hold still, sugar," he said. "I'm gonna wash you."

Oh, she loved when he took care of her like this, the washcloth gliding over her skin as he carefully lathered every inch of her body. He kept his other hand at her waist or the small of her back, knowing she wasn't entirely steady on her feet. How was it she flew so hard with so little pain play? But it was Jamie, and everything was different with him.

"You need your hair washed, sweetheart? Yes, you do." He leaned in close and spoke softly into her ear, "I think you need to be thoroughly fucked and have your hair washed every day."

She couldn't quite take in what he was telling her, what he might be insinuating—she was too floaty still. All she knew was that she loved him saying these things to her, the husky tone of his voice.

He slipped a hand under her hair and behind her neck to hold her steady, and with the other he used the pressure point in the center of her breastbone to push her back under the water—just enough pain to direct her. She sighed in pure pleasure at the warm water gliding over her skin, at the little bit of pain, his command of her. The way he cared for her.

"No one has ever taken care of me the way you do, Jamie," she said, the words a soft murmur that came out before she could stop them.

"No, that can't be true. Your family at least . . ."

"Sure, when I was a kid. My parents. Brandon. But after he died, everyone who was left just sort of disappeared. We talked about that."

"Yes."

"So . . . since then I've been on my own, for the most part. You know, no one made me breakfast ever again. Not once. No more birthday pancakes with bananas and whipped cream. No Christmas trees or camping or any of the other million little things that made up our life. Our family." She opened her eyes as he finished rinsing her hair and grasped his strong forearm, looking up at him. "I'm not sinking into self-pity, Jamie—really, I'm not. I'm just realizing how much I've missed this sort of thing. It's the kind of stuff I haven't risked looking at all these years."

He stroked her wet hair from her face. His eyes were so green, but dark, like the slate tile in the shower. A little shadowed.

"Of course, sweetheart. How could you look at it, dwell on it, without it tearing you up? A lot of people would have done just that, but you stayed strong."

She nodded. "But can I tell you a secret, Jamie? I've craved it the whole damn time. I had a little of it when I went over to Dennie's house. Her grandmother, Annalee, has been so good to me all these years, but there was always the awareness that I didn't quite belong to her, even though she made every effort to make me feel included. But some part of me always knew in the back of my mind that something was missing, because I used to know what it felt like to really belong."

He searched her face for several long moments, but it didn't make her afraid. She felt wide open to him and it felt good, as if at that moment she could tell him anything. There was no fear for once. She simply waited to see what he would ask her or tell her or do.

"And now, Summer Grace?"

She bit her lip, took what felt like a risk even in her current state of happy serenity. "And now I'm beginning to feel like maybe I belong somewhere again."

He blinked hard but he didn't pull away, didn't let her go. His hand on the back of her neck flexed, then slid around to cup her face while his free hand moved up to hold her other cheek. Some time passed while he stared into her eyes, the warm water falling, soothing her skin while her heart tried to hammer its way out of her chest—his gaze was that intense. Anticipation was that powerful.

"You do, sweetheart," he said. "We can work everything else out, but know that you do. *Know* it. You belong to me."

Her chest went tight, then was flooded with heat. With love. *Love him.*

She could only nod and wait to be kissed.

He watched her face for another moment before he bent his head and pulled her up on her toes and crushed his mouth to hers.

His kiss was hungry, but it wasn't sex. Or, it wasn't all about sex, anyway—there would always be sex between them. The chemistry was far too hot. But there was as much emotion and stark honesty right now. She curled her body into his as she sought his warm, sleek tongue. As his strong arms held her tight. As the warm, lovely water fell in the shower and the rain fell in the New Orleans night outside.

JAMIE SLID ONTO a stool at Flynn McCool's, the local pub he and Mick and all of Mick's brothers had been going to since they'd each hit drinking age. He liked the casual atmosphere of the Irish pub, the long wooden bar, the old wide-plank floors, the vintage beer signs. It was a quiet place, where games of darts and pool took the place of the usual television blaring some sports game or another found in most other bars. They'd been coming for years, hanging out, playing some pool. It was also one of the places they went to confide in each other, male style.

He grinned as he nodded at the bartender, who knew him well enough to pass him a pint of Guinness, then automatically drew another from the tap when Mick came in and sat next to Jamie.

"Hey."

"Hey, Mick."

"Is this an emergency meeting or are we here to shoot the shit?"

Jamie shrugged. "I'm pretty sure you've talked to Allie, who I know damn well has talked to Summer Grace, so you tell me."

Mick tossed a tip on the bar as the bartender slid his pint of ale to him. "I'm not hearing any complaints, and anything else she's keeping to herself. I figure Summer is safe enough with you, you wicked bastard."

"Hey, don't go questioning my heritage," Jamie warned, letting a little of the Scottish come through in his voice.

Mick gulped at his beer. "Your mother could have been seduced by a wayward mailman," he countered. "Wait—do they have mailmen in Scotland?"

"Postmen. Same thing. But Mum would have gone for the milkman first. I hear he was a smart, dapper dude."

"Hearing you say 'dude' with that accent is fucking with my brain."

Jamie slapped him on the back. "Ha! Then my work here is done."

"You're awful damn cheerful."

"And you, as usual, are not."

"Fuck off, Jamie," Mick said cheerfully.

Jamie clutched his chest. "You're breaking my heart."

Mick smacked at Jamie's arm. "Whatever. Tell me what we're doing here, lover boy."

"You're one to talk."

"Damn right I am," Mick muttered into his pint.

Jamie took a long swallow. "All right, all right. So, it's been a little over a week since I dragged Summer Grace out of the cemetery—"

"Caveman style," Mick interrupted.

"Yeah. So?"

Mick raised his glass. "So, nothing. Just marveling at your luck. Not everyone gets a second chance at fucking up so royally."

"Thanks for the reminder."

"I live to serve. How's it been going?"

"Good. Really good."

"Why do I have a feeling that's the understatement of the year?"

Jamie shrugged. "Maybe because it is."

"We're about to get all mushy and shit, aren't we?" Mick huffed.

"'Fraid so, buddy."

"Okay. Let's have it."

Jamie sipped his beer, set his glass down on the old wood bar and stared into the brown liquid. "I don't know, Mick. Things are pretty damn amazing between us. I feel like it shouldn't be this good. This easy. I didn't expect it to be."

"Why not? Because you think you don't deserve it?"

"No, of course not."

"Bullshit."

He shot a look at his friend. "What the fuck does that mean?"

"Forgive me for saying so—or hell, don't forgive me—but in my opinion you don't believe you deserve it. Happiness. Her.

Maybe especially with her. I know some of the demons you've been fighting to even be with her, Jamie. Don't forget how well I know you, or for how long. I was *there*, man. And I know exactly why you've kept your distance from Summer all these years. Frankly, I think it was a mistake. I think you could have been more of a comfort to her."

"Well fuck me, Mick, don't spare my feelings."

"I don't intend to. But did you come here to hear the truth or to have me blow smoke up your ass? Because if it's the latter, you've come to the wrong guy. Which I think you know."

Jamie blew out a breath. "Yeah, I do. I just hate that you're right about this. About me having wasted all these years staying away from her. I feel guilty as hell."

Mick shook his head. "That, my friend, is wasted time, which I know all too well. The thing to do is whatever you can *today*. You have to stop running from the past one of these days, bud. You have to live in the moment."

"Wow."

Mick raised one dark brow from over his pint glass. "What?"

"Words of wisdom from Mick Reid, ladies and gentlemen."

"There has to be a first time for everything."

"Seriously, Mick, you're right. I know you are. And I've been trying. But it seems like the past keeps cropping up for both of us."

"Sure, everyone's got their baggage. But what's happening with you two right now?"

"Things are great. The sex is fucking off the hook—and it feels weird as hell saying that to you about Summer Grace."

"Nah. Don't even sweat it. What else?"

Jamie had to sip his Guinness to cool off. "She's taken to kink like someone who's been thinking about it her whole life— like she was born to it."

"I kinda think she was."

"Yeah. Maybe."

"Maybe hell yes! Allie has said the same about her—that she dove in headfirst and never looked back. That the stuff she asked for in her first scene made Allie nervous. Not that Maîtresse Renee agreed to give her everything in that first session, but apparently the girl has no fear."

"She has her limits, but nothing really scares her."

"Summer's never been afraid of much—that's her nature. It doesn't surprise me that kink doesn't intimidate her. Good thing, too, given how you play."

Jamie was quiet for a minute or two, thinking. It was true that his Summer Grace was brave, in so many ways. And when had he started to think of her as *his*? He wasn't sure when it had happened, but she was his, as he'd told her the other night. And just as true was the fact that not seeing her the last few nights because she'd had to work late stocking the store was driving him crazy. It had only been three nights without her and he felt like his skin was too tight for his body. Like he couldn't hold still. Which was why he'd asked Mick to meet him tonight. He had to see her. And he really wanted to play her at the club.

"Hey, are you and Allie going to The Bastille tomorrow night?"

"Maybe. I haven't talked to her about it yet. There's the usual Friday night demo, isn't there? What is it this week?"

"The schedule said Master Lucan is doing his talk on mentoring newcomers early in the evening, but that's not why I'm asking. Will it be weird to see me play Summer Grace there?"

Mick shrugged. "Allie saw Renee play her. We've both seen you play plenty of other women."

"This will be different."

"I'd assume so. Will it make you uncomfortable to have us there? Because if so, we'll hang out at home. I have a full toy bag and a few heavy-duty eyebolts set into the ceiling—that's never a problem." Mick flashed a wicked grin.

"Yeah, maybe. I might need to work my way up to getting used to you and Allie seeing us together. Hell, we haven't even been out to dinner with anyone else."

"It's only been a few weeks, hasn't it?"

"Yeah. But it's Summer Grace, not some girl I just met. Maybe it's been two weeks that we've been seeing each other, but it's also been most of our lives. I *know* her. We're just learning about each other as adults, but we have so much history. All that stuff you learn when you're first dating a woman—about her family, what she likes to eat, her taste in music—that stuff I already know. We don't have to waste any time on the background details. You know what I mean?"

Mick grinned again. "It was like that with me and Allie. Kinda fast-tracked things because we'd known each other forever."

"Yeah. Sort of. I don't know how fast we're moving."

"Don't kid yourself, buddy."

"What do you mean?"

"If I can see it, dense as I am, then the whole fucking world can see it."

"See what?"

"That you're in love with her."

Jamie bit his lip, took a sip of his ale, then another before setting his glass down very carefully. Keeping his eyes on the drops of moisture clinging to the glass, he said quietly, while his chest sort of exploded with an aching warmth, "Yeah. I guess I am."

Mick let out a snort. "It's more than a guess. And I'm not above shoving your face in it, considering the shit you gave me over Allie. Wake up, Jamie. Do something about it. Don't fuck it up."

"I'm trying really Goddamn hard not to."

Mick slapped him on the back. "Good man. Now how about you let me beat you at pool?"

CHAPTER

Eight

S UMMER'S STOMACH WAS fluttering, tight with nerves. Jamie had been sending her texts all day telling her he had wonderfully wicked plans for their evening at The Bastille and she'd better be prepared, and even though she'd sassed him in response as she often did, most of his messages had carried an undertone— or an overtone in some cases—of real menace. It frightened her a bit, but it also turned her on like crazy. When he'd shown up at her door dressed all in black, from his big black boots to his tight black T-shirt and fitted leather pants that he sported like a rock star, her knees had literally gone weak. When they'd stepped off her front porch she saw he'd driven the Corvette, even though they were going to the club in the warehouse district. And she'd known tonight would be special, different from anything she'd ever experienced with him.

Now they were at the club and Jamie was taking his time

talking to the corseted woman behind the front desk, leaving Summer to stand next to him, fidgeting. Totally unlike her, even in bottom mode, but the way he'd handled things today was certainly doing its job. She was shaken up, off balance. And so turned on already she could barely stand it. Which, she was sure, was exactly what he'd intended. How had he known she'd respond like this to his stern approach when she hadn't known herself?

Finally he was done at the desk as a group came in behind him to check in, and he took her hand and led her onto the main floor without a word. Tonight the lighting was all in shades of purple with the occasional red glow from some of the sconces that decorated the highly lacquered black walls. The music was dark, too, rumbling, rasping hard rock with a heavy bass line that made the floors tremble. She could feel it in the pit of her stomach as they walked across the polished wood floors, passing those who were already playing at the different stations: spanking benches, St. Andrew's crosses, simple chains hung from the ceiling with spreader bars attached to them where male and female bottoms alike were suspended by heavy leather cuffs. At the edge of her vision she caught sight of a beautiful Domme strapping a naked submissive male into an interrogation chair, a trio using one of the padded tables suspended by chains, a tall Dom spanking a petite young woman turned over his knee on one of the plush chairs in a seating area. There were moans and groans of pain and pleasure and the startling snap of a whip from somewhere. And all of it enveloped her, adding to her head-space, making her feel her submission in a way that was energizing. Empowering, somehow, despite the tremors of fear running like a small, live wire just beneath her skin.

Jamie stopped in front of an enormous web made of chain that stood on a giant frame. He placed his bag on the floor to one side of the gleaming web and pulled her closer to him, smiling down at her.

"We'll play here tonight."

. . . said the spider to the fly.

She almost had to grin. But the anticipation was building, making her dizzy. And being at the club with Jamie was overloading her in some way she didn't quite understand. But she loved that aspect of what was happening.

She nodded, waiting for instructions, her head sinking so fast she was having a hard time focusing on anything but Jamie, the beat of the music, the heavy chains she knew he loved and that she was coming to love, too. She could almost feel their cold touch against her skin.

Yes.

Jamie stroked her cheek, his hand trailing over her long hair until he reached the ends, rubbing the strands between his fingers, as he often did. But tonight he seemed more introspective.

"Jamie?"

"What is it?"

"You seem . . . I don't know. A little distant tonight."

"My mind is going. Thinking about the evening ahead. Is it alarming you, sugar?"

"No. Of course not."

He grinned crookedly—a roguish grin. "Maybe it should be."

Oh, she loved that he messed with her head like that, as ridiculous as it sounded to her turning the words over in her mind. But she was going wet already from the mind-fuck, from simply being there with him. From everything she was seeing. From the ambience of wicked sensuality.

She smiled. "Yes, maybe it should. Maybe I'll find out later that I should have been more nervous than I am."

He tilted her chin up with one commanding finger, leaned in as if to kiss her, stopping inches from her lips. He whispered, "Are you nervous at all, Summer Grace? About what I might do to you tonight? About how much you might like it?"

She swallowed, tried to laugh, but it didn't quite come out right. "I am now."

"Excellent." Jamie straightened up, ran a hand down her arm as he spoke, sending delicious little chills through her. "Tonight will be a bit different," he told her. "I'm going to demand a lot of you. I want you to be very conscious of your safewords. Use them if you need to. I don't care how brave you think you should be, or how strong. We both already know how strong you are, sweetheart—you have nothing to prove. But this will be a test of sorts. We're going to try some new toys, see how much you can really take. Because I don't think we've truly tested that yet, do you?"

"No, Jamie," she answered truthfully. "I know I can take much more. And I want to. It's something I've been thinking about. Something I've been craving."

For him.

He yanked her in hard suddenly, his mouth next to her ear. "Get ready for some testing then, sugar. Because I'm going to be hard on you tonight. Oh yes, very damn hard. And I will take the greatest pleasure in your screams."

She shivered, unable to answer as he brushed a kiss across her cheek.

He dragged her over to the chain web so suddenly, so forcefully, she lost her footing in her stiletto heels, but he held her up with one strong arm, keeping her from falling. Keeping her safe. And the contradiction of it was a mind-fuck in itself—sweet, gentle Jamie, who was beautifully rough with her at exactly the right moments. And never more rough with her than he was tonight.

He grabbed her chin and forced her gaze to his. "Where are you, Summer Grace?"

"I'm right here."

He shook his head. "You're not. I'm asking you again, where are you?"

"I don't know . . . In my own head too much, maybe?"

"Better. And I agree. Let's see what we can do to get you more grounded in the moment. Do you remember your safewords? Tell me."

"Green if everything is good. Yellow if we need to pause or change toys, if I need you to ease up. If I need a drink of water. Red to stop the scene completely."

"Perfect. Now take off your clothes while I get set up—all but your shoes."

He released her, turning his back on her to pull different implements from his black toy bag, setting them out on a long table. She swallowed hard when she saw him lay out several long canes in different sizes—both wood and Lucite—but she started to undress, ordering herself to breathe.

She pulled her short black knit dress over her head, then took off her black lace bra. Jamie turned around and put his hand out, nodding his chin. She gave him her clothing, but instead of pulling his hand away he just stood there, watching her with one eyebrow raised.

"All of it."

She knew she should take her thong off, too. She *wanted* to. But she felt momentarily frozen. She didn't know if it was because the way he was treating her was working so well, or if some defense mechanism was kicking in.

Finally he said, "Summer Grace, this is not the time to get bratty with me. And that's the last warning you're going to get."

"I . . . I'm a little disoriented tonight, to be perfectly honest."

"We don't need to have any discussion right now. Simply do as you're told."

His stern tone rocked her. And made her entire body clench with need. Yearning.

So this is what it's like to be a true submissive, and not just a bottom.

She felt a little shocked that she wanted this—the real D/s dynamic and not just sensation and some role-play. A little mad at herself. At Jamie.

"Fine," she said, yanking her lace thong down and handing it to him.

He took it and put her clothes in the toy bag. When he turned back to her, his eyes were green fire. Green ice. Something was going on with him tonight. And she liked it.

He approached her slowly, and she felt the moment as if it were happening in slow motion. He grabbed her, swinging her around and forcing one arm behind her back, gripping her wrist hard enough to hurt. His other arm went around her throat, and God, she loved when he used breath play on her—constricting her air just enough for her to feel his command, for her to give him her trust completely. Her nipples went hard and her pussy clenched again, desire lancing through her. Fear made her shiver. And beneath it all was that little bit of anger still, preventing her from giving in completely.

Jamie leaned in, his tone low. "Stop struggling, Summer Grace. I understand what you're going through—a kind of quiet rebellion. You're not used to this—me refraining from tempering my dominance with gentleness. But you know it's there if you truly need it. Trust in me that I will give you what you need. But tonight is also about what I need. And I need you to serve my desires. Do you understand that I won't harm you, no matter how rough the play gets?"

He loosened his hold on her throat and she pulled in a gasping breath. "Of course, Jamie. I wouldn't be here with you otherwise. And . . ." The words came out in a whisper. "I want to serve your desires. I *want* to. And maybe I even need to."

"Ah, there's my good girl."

Those words, his approval, melted away the last of her anger. Melted her all over. Her mind was emptying out, her head starting to buzz. And he hadn't really done anything yet. She realized in some distant way that *this* was where the power was in the D/s roles. It wasn't in the pain play, although more would manifest once that began. She could hardly wait.

He pressed her back a few steps, then a few more until her back came into contact with the web of chains. They were cool against her bare skin, and she shivered.

"Cold, sweetheart? I'll warm you up, baby."

With a hand on her throat, his fingers pressing, he kissed her hard. His mouth was so lush and sweet—he tasted like mint and pure Jamie. Her Jamie. Like sex and familiarity.

He pulled back. "Warmer?" he asked.

"A little."

He smiled down at her, his dimples flashing, and for one moment he looked like her sweet Jamie again. Then his grip on her throat tightened and he crushed her lips with his, his big body pressing her hard against the chains, until they dug into her flesh a bit. But she was nearly swooning at the feel of him—his tall, muscled frame, the ridge of his arousal against her belly. She moaned into his mouth as his tongue slid into hers, exploring.

Demanding. She could barely breathe—literally, as his big hand tightened on her throat. When she gasped he released her and she sank into him, her legs weak.

"You like it when I choke you."

"Yes."

"So do I."

"God, Jamie—"

"Shh. Quiet now. You'll talk only when I ask you a question, or if you need to safeword. I'm going to cuff you to the chains. Can you stand by yourself?"

"Yes, Jamie."

He made sure she was steady on her feet before stepping back to get the padded leather cuffs. He gave a nod of his chin and she held her wrists out for him. He fastened the cuffs, then clipped them with a pair of carabiners to the big web so that her arms were spread wide. Then he pulled another pair of larger cuffs from his back pocket and knelt to shackle her ankles to the web, as well. She felt exposed, beautifully wanton in her pretty high-heeled shoes and nothing else but her ravenous desire.

He rose to his feet and brushed a quick kiss across her mouth, then nibbled on her lower lip. "Beautiful girl," he said before stepping back, and she watched as he looped the small leather handles of three canes onto a hook on his belt.

She closed her eyes and waited.

Jamie began to stroke her skin—her arms, her sides, then her breasts. She arched into his hands as much as she was able to, but she was bound tightly. Her nipples were so hard they hurt, and when he stroked them with his thumbs she moaned quietly. She was soaked already—her clit, the lips of her sex, tight and swollen with need. He kept stroking the two hard peaks, then pinched them lightly. When he bent to take one nipple into his mouth, sucking hard, she groaned, pulling against her bonds.

"Oh, you like that, baby. But I think you'll like this even better."

He straightened up, looking down at her with a half-smile on his handsome face as he slipped a hand behind her neck and began to tap her thigh with one of the smaller canes. It didn't hurt at first, and she understood he was establishing a rhythm. The tapping became harder, stinging her skin as she sank into the quick cadence of it. It felt good, her body, her brain, converting the small pain into pleasure that shimmered through her system. Then there was one sharp smack and she yelped. He stopped. Looked into her eyes.

"Are we still green?"

"Yes. We're green." She wanted more. Wanted it harder.

He started once more, harder this time, and pleasure swarmed her body in a warm tide. Her head was sinking into the rhythm as much as her body was. Then he hit her with one vicious smack across the front of both thighs and she cried out.

"Oh!"

He smoothed a hand over the hurting places and the pain became pleasure. Desire. The need for more.

More, more, more . . .

"Here we go now, sweetheart," he whispered in warning. It was soothing and threatening at the same time. She loved it.

He hit one thigh with the cane, a sharp snap of the wood, and the pain reverberated through her system, followed by an enormous release of the lovely brain chemicals that helped her to handle it, to float in subspace. He hit her again, a quick volley of smacks over the front and sides of her thighs, and she gasped and groaned, but he didn't stop to let her ride out the pain from each strike. Just when she thought she'd have to call yellow, he pressed a hand between her spread legs and began to massage her, rubbing her hard clit, two fingers thrusting inside her. The caning went on, and at one point she thought he switched to a heavier implement. The pain was more intense, but it only caused more of the lovely endorphins to be released in her brain, until she was nothing more than a being of pure sensation. There was only one thought in her head, over and over.

Love him. Love him. Love him.

JAMIE FELT HER soft, hot inner muscles squeezing his fingers, felt how wet she was, swollen with desire that echoed with each stroke of the Lucite cane. He wasn't even sure she was aware that he was using it on her—this heavy cane with the evil, sharp-edged twists in the Lucite, making it an incredibly high-pain toy. No, she was high as a kite on sensation. He could see it in the way her tightly bound body bowed a little with each hard stroke. In how gorgeously wet she was. In the heavy cadence of her breath. She was moaning, but he recognized it more as low sounds of pleasure than pain.

He kept up the quick cadence while he thrust his fingers inside her. She was welting gorgeously, the red marks rising on her skin. He could smell her desire, the scent of her hair, mixing into some intoxicating perfume. And he was hard as steel, as hard as any of his canes. She was so damn beautiful it was overwhelming, and never more so than at this moment, as her body surrendered what her psyche didn't want to. But even that inner struggle was beautiful to him.

Her hot little pussy tightened and he ordered her, "No, Summer Grace. Do *not* come." He gave her left thigh a hard smack that had her crying out. "That's right. Your climax is your gift to me. It's *mine*. Say it."

She's mine. She belongs to me, damn it.

"Yes, it's yours. I come for you, Jamie."

Her words hit him like a small blow to the chest. It wasn't the first time he'd made her say such a thing to him, but the words carried more power than ever before. He had to pause and take a breath, shaking his head.

Get it under control.

He gave her thigh another sharp crack with the evil cane.

"Ow! God . . ."

He did it again, spreading his fingers inside her, opening her up.

"Jamie . . ."

"Are you safewording?"

"What? No."

He hit her across both thighs.

"Ah, God!"

"Wrong name, sweetheart."

And again.

"Ah! Fuck. Jamie."

She was writhing, and he could see the pain and pleasure warring in her body. And she was soaking wet, flooding his hand with each stroke of the cane, which told him pleasure was winning. He wanted to bring her pleasure. Wanted to bring her pain. For her. For him. He needed to know she trusted him this much. That she wanted this. That she wanted him to be the one who did these things to her. Only him.

Fuck.

He dropped the cane and bent to unhook her ankle cuffs, then her wrists, and she fell into his arms. He kissed her cheeks, her closed eyelids, as he carried her to the leather love seat next to the giant web. He sat with her in his lap, stroking her hair from her flushed cheeks. And cursed himself as tears spilled from beneath her closed eyelids.

"Baby, baby," he murmured.

"Jamie," she gasped, blinking, her arms winding around his neck.

"What is it? Are you okay?"

She buried her face in his neck, and he loved the warmth of her breath there, but he had to have an answer. He took her face in his hand, forcing her gaze to his. Her blue eyes were glazed with tears and need, her lids heavy. And Christ, he'd never seen anyone more beautiful.

"Tell me, Summer Grace."

"It's just . . . You've never played me so hard before."

"Too hard?"

She shook her head, her blonde hair all over the place, like scattered corn silk. "It's like everything I've ever needed. I had no idea—no idea! It's not just the pain. It's the way you command me, Jamie. I didn't know I would love it this much."

"Ah, sugar, those words are like gold to me. You have no idea."

And he couldn't tell her. He couldn't give voice to the fact that she was probably as close to perfect as any woman would ever be for him. That he didn't think he could survive if he lost her now. Because that little fact scared the shit out of him. But she was here. He could be with her. Touch her, hold her, play her. Make her come in a way neither of them would ever forget.

He kissed her cheek, her lips, opened up her eager mouth with his tongue, sucking hers in. Sweet as pie, his girl. And her hot mouth was as hungry as his. She was squirming in his lap as he kissed her, and he'd never been so damn hard in his life. He was going to fucking burst—just come all over her perfect ass in his lap like some kid.

He groaned, pulling his mouth away. She started to pout until he pressed a hand between her thighs once more, forcing them apart. He dove into her hair with his other hand, grasping it tightly at the roots, and pulled, forcing her to lie back against the arm of the love seat while his fingers plunged in and out of her.

"Not yet," he warned, and she groaned in answer, biting her lush lower lip.

She ground down against his erection and he slipped his fingers from her. "Look at me," he ordered.

Her lashes fluttered and she focused her gaze on his, watching him, her pupils widening as he slid his fingers, wet with her juices, into his mouth and sucked.

"You want to come, sugar girl?"

"Yes, please, Jamie. Please . . ."

"Wait for my command."

He lowered his hand and began to squeeze and pinch her clit, then pushed his fingers into her tight pussy once more.

"Ah . . ."

"Hold it back."

He began a slow rhythm, fucking her with two fingers, then three, and her hips were arching, working his fingers. He let her hair go to wrap his other hand around her throat, and her eyes opened wide as he pressed down a bit, carefully listening to her restricted breathing even as he continued to thrust inside her, his thumb on her hard clit.

"Oh yeah, you feel so damn good. So wet for me, sugar. Do you know how hard I'm going to fuck you? Do you know how badly I need to lick you? To eat you up? To taste your come on my lips?"

He moved his hand faster, plunging into her while she panted. Her struggle to hold her orgasm back was a beautiful thing—the exquisite beauty of her face torn in an agony of pleasure. When he told her, "Now!" her face twisted, and she screamed as she came.

Her body shook as he fucked her hard with his hand, faster and faster, deeper and deeper. Her eyes rolled back and he released her throat, sliding his hand to her breast, pinching the luscious pink nipple. And had to order himself not to come with her as he worked her up again. Her body rose, arching into his hand, and her breath was a sharp, panting rasp as her inner walls clenched around his pumping fingers, as she started to come once more. His whole body ached to be inside her, but he kept working her with his hands, watching a dark blush rise on her breasts, her face, as her climax made her shake, her voice a raw cry.

She was still trembling, her muscles spasming, when he lifted her in his arms and stalked across the dungeon floor to the hall that led to the private rooms at the back of the club. He went through the first door he found open—a room with black-painted walls and nothing in it but a high canopy bed draped in black and silver brocade and a side table supplied with condoms, lube and bottled water. But all of that was nothing more than a blur at the edges of his vision. The rest was filled up with Summer Grace—her smooth babyskin, her gorgeous breasts.

He laid her on the bed as gently as he could, which wasn't very gently at that moment. He was too shaken by her, by the overwhelming lust he felt for her. The pure need that went far beyond even the raw physical desire—that went to that place where he needed to be as close to her as possible.

He stripped his clothes off as quickly as he could, the damn leather pants slowing him down, But finally he was naked. He grabbed a condom and climbed on top of her. She was still panting, languid and spent. But he intended to spend her more tonight—and himself.

She watched him through hazy blue eyes as he knelt over her to roll the condom onto his painfully hard cock. As he spread her thighs wide, pushing her knees up to her shoulders and holding them there, he paused to take in the beautiful sight of her pink pussy, the lips and clit swollen and tender-looking, before he plowed into her wet heat.

He threw his head back, pleasure momentarily stunning him, driving deep. His legs, his arms, shook, his cock pulsing. He bit back a groan and slid slowly out, every inch agony, beautiful, orgasm building inside him like a thundercloud ready to burst. He surged back into her, and desire rolled through him—sharp. Dazzling.

She gasped, reaching for him, and he pinned her arms over her head, holding her delicate wrists in one of his hands. Blinking up at him, her lovely lips parted, and his gaze locked on hers.

Jesus.

Simply looking at her was almost too much.

Control.

He sucked in a breath, arched into her once more. And again she gasped.

He pulled back, thrust hard.

"Ah! Jamie . . ."

He bent and kissed her mouth, ran his tongue across her pink lips. But when her tongue darted out he had to raise himself up again, watching her watching him.

Jesus.

Pleasure shivered through him, rattling him to the core. He bit it back.

Control, damn it.

Once more he pressed into her.

"Kiss me," she begged.

He shook his head, knowing it would send him over the edge.

"Kiss me, Jamie," she pleaded again.

Instead he pressed a thumb between her parted lips, and she took it and sucked it into her luscious mouth, swirling her tongue over the tip as if it were his cock. And suddenly sensation wrapped around his cock as if her wet mouth were there. The storm raged through his body, pleasure a roar that rendered him deaf to anything but his own cries. His body shook with the force of his orgasm. Coming was painful, it was so intense. Painful and fucking amazing, and like nothing he'd ever felt before.

"Ah! Ah, Jesus. Jesus, baby . . . So good."

"Jamie."

"Come again for me, my sugar girl."

He ground into her, his cock still hard, still coming a little, maybe. And in moments he felt that hot clench of her sleek little pussy. Pleasure shafted into his belly, into his balls, and as she came, her cries rending the air, it was almost as if he was coming again, too.

Then he did kiss her—he had to. He took her mouth, pushing his tongue inside, meeting her panting breath with his own. He couldn't kiss her hard enough. Couldn't get enough of her mouth. Couldn't get enough of her. It was the most incredible feeling. And even as the last of the storm passed through her, and through him, he knew that this girl could either be his heaven, or his undoing.

Rolling off her, he disposed of the condom, then reached for her, pulling her close while he tried to catch his breath. She snuggled right into that pocket at the juncture of his shoulder and his chest as if she belonged there.

She does belong. She belongs to me.

Wishful thinking, maybe? He didn't want to overload her. He wasn't sure what she was ready for. Hell, he wasn't sure what he was ready for. And then there was the whole death magnet thing hanging over his head, the black cloud he carried with him everywhere he went. It had been with him his entire life. First Ian. Then Brandon. His parents' marriage. Then what had happened with Traci. And the one thing he'd never spoken to another person about. Not Mick. Not Allie. And it sure as hell wasn't something he could tell Summer Grace. Was it?

Don't fucking think about it.

With a practiced mind, he turned away from the shadowed thoughts plaguing him. Pulling Summer Grace closer into his side, he sought comfort in the warmth of her body. She was so trusting, and it was some weird kind of turn-on—or maybe not so weird for a Dominant. Wasn't that part of the package? With great power came great responsibility. It was something he craved. He turned to kiss her forehead and found her long, thick lashes resting on her high, flushed cheekbones. So damn lovely, this woman.

"You sleepy?" he asked her.

"Mmm, yes. Sleepy. Needy. Wanting more. Why can't I ever get enough of you?"

His body immediately responded—so damn sexy. Her husky tone. The words that echoed what he felt whenever he was with her. She squirmed, shifting, and he felt every sinuous curve of her petite, feminine form: soft hips and delicate legs, the flawless curve of her breasts, her hardening nipples pressing against his ribs.

"Jamie? More, please . . . ? I mean, if you're not done with me."

He narrowed his gaze in the dim lighting and focused on the black-painted steel crossbars in the canopy overhead—and remembered that all the canopy beds at The Bastille had a built-in suspension system. His imagination kicked into high gear—into hot, screaming overdrive.

"Oh, sugar, the night is far from over."

"I'm ready. For whatever you want to do to me."

He slipped his hand down her thigh, over her baby-soft skin, his fingertips reading the welts from the caning like Braille—and it all spoke the language of desire. Of pleasure derived from pain. "Can you come again?"

"I can do whatever you want," she purred.

He grinned as he sat up and got on his knees on the firm mattress, pulling her up with him by the leather cuffs still attached to her wrists. He got her on her knees and held her arms over her head by the carabiners still attached to the cuffs, and clipped them to the rings on the overhead bars.

"Jamie . . . what . . . ?"

He put a hand over her mouth, which he knew she loved. "Shh, now. You're going to like this. Or I'm going to like this. Mmm . . . both. All you have to do is get comfortable in the cuffs and straddle my face, pretty girl."

She blinked, smiled, batted her long lashes. "Ohhh."

"Cuffs feel okay?"

She flexed her fingers. Good girl. "Yes."

He smoothed his palms over her thighs as he lay on the bed and slid down, positioning himself until her plump, wet pussy was right over his face. So beautiful. He licked his lips, simply looking at her for several long moments. Then he pulled a pillow under his head so he could reach her. And dove in.

He licked her first, one long, slow slide of his tongue up her slit to the tight nub of her clitoris, then down again. She sighed quietly. He licked again, went a little deeper into her slit this time, the tip of his tongue delving inside her, and she ground her hips against his mouth. He pulled back.

"Ah, ah," he warned. "Bad girl, Summer Grace."

He held on to her hips, his fingers digging into her skin, but she only moaned in pleasure. He knew she was too far gone to really control herself, and decided to do it for her, as much for his sake as for hers. Grasping her hips harder, he moved them back and forth as he lapped at her, pausing to suck on her clit, then back to lapping at her sweet juices. Soon they were working together, her hips following his lead, undulating, a seductive, sinuous motion. She was so wet he couldn't believe it. So wet he had to let her hips go to sink his fingers into her—two, then three. *Had* to. He pumped into her and she groaned, murmuring his name. He pulled back an inch to watch her, eager to see her desire. Her pussy was like a ripe fruit, so pink and swollen, so sensitive. And she was so lost in the moment. Lost in abandon. Wanton. It was an old-fashioned word, but it fit. And she was so thoroughly trusting, which was a turn-on in itself, something he was discovering with her might be a new fetish for him.

He smiled, his fingers sliding in her wetness, slipping back until one fingertip was pressing on that tightest of holes. She gasped, then let out a whispered, "Yes please, Jamie."

He pressed his wet finger against her, then slipped the tiniest bit of the tip into her ass. She pulled in a breath, and as she exhaled, he slid in a little further.

"Oh God, yes.

He took her clit in his mouth again, sucking, flicking the tip with his tongue, letting his finger rest in her beautiful ass, loving how she felt like an impossibly tight velvet glove there. But soon she was grinding onto his finger, and he slid it in and out slowly as he worked her clit with his tongue.

She panted harder, her hips arching into his mouth, then back onto his probing finger. Her panting was loud and hard, and in moments her entire body clenched. She shook all over for several long moments before she really started to come. Then it was a savage clenching of her ass and her pussy, her thighs. And she called his name, then screamed it.

"Jamie . . . Ah . . . Jamie, Jamie!"

He let her ride the waves, his body buzzing with a deep pleasure that had nothing to do with his own spent cock. Or maybe it did—he didn't know. All he knew was a sense of satisfaction he'd never quite felt before. At having brought this woman—*this* woman—so much pleasure.

He couldn't think about what it all meant right now as he sat up and cleaned his hands and face with the wipes in a basket next to the bed, then carefully wiped her clean. Getting up on his knees, he faced her, pressing his bare chest to her breasts, pressed harder until he could feel the plush cushion of them, her hard nipples. She let her head fall back as he kissed her throat, her lovely collarbones, her shoulders. Then finally her mouth. Pressing his lips against hers, he wanted to drink her in all over again. She was nearly limp, but she kissed him back, her mouth soft on his.

When he unclipped her wrist cuffs from the bed frame she sank onto the mattress with him. Shifting her onto her side, he curled behind her, spooning her, his arms around her, listening to her breathe. He refused to let his mind try to dissect what had happened tonight. Between them. In his head. It was getting too complicated and he wanted to enjoy the moment. The hour. The night.

THEY'D SLEPT FOR a while, although Summer wasn't sure how long. Twenty minutes? Three hours? Did it matter?

All that really mattered was that she was there with Jamie, her body sore and worn out from play and sex—and God, the sex! The kink play aside, the sex was spectacular. Was it that she'd finally been able to give herself over to the submissive role with him? A part of her still held back, but she'd never let go before the way she had tonight. Was it the setting—being at The Bastille? Or was it simply the evolution of their connection?

Her body was still buzzing with orgasm . . . seemingly endless orgasms. The blood pumping through her veins seemed to be moving in time with the rhythmic *thump thump* of the music playing in the dungeon, driven by that orgasmic buzz. And if she really listened she could hear Jamie's heartbeat—could almost feel it with his chest still pressed against her back.

Hers suddenly jackhammered for no apparent reason, a tear forming in her eye.

Ridiculous!

She wiped at the tear with her thumb.

"Hey, sugar." His voice was a quiet, rasping murmur. "You're awake."

She bit her lip. "Kind of. Are you?"

"Kind of." He gave her a squeeze and she realized he'd held her in his arms this whole time. "We had a good workout—we earned some rest."

"What time do you think it is?" she asked, more to distract herself than because she really wanted to know. There was too much going on her head. Or in that space in her chest that had remained empty for too long.

Damn it.

"No idea. The Bastille is pretty much a place without time, and I didn't wear my watch tonight."

She loved the watch he usually wore—it had a wide, black

leather band and a large square face edged in brushed steel. Utterly masculine. Utterly Dom-like.

"Why didn't you wear it?" she asked idly, stroking the soft hair at his wrist.

"Mmm . . . too distracted by the idea of bringing you here tonight, I guess. You mess with my focus, woman."

She laughed. "I think that's a good thing."

"You would." He tickled her ribs, and she squealed, kicking. "Hey!"

"Hey, yourself, sassy wench."

"That's right. And don't you forget it."

"Apparently being caned until you scream makes you bratty."

"Nah. I'm always bratty."

He chuckled against her hair. "True." They were both quiet for a bit. Then he said, "Summer Grace—you know what I want to do tomorrow? I want to go to City Park and hang out at the lake and lounge around on those old, bent live oak trees. I want to drink some iced chicory coffee with too much sugar and have those amazing beignets at the coffee stand there like the tourists do."

"They *are* some of the best beignets in the city. Fuck the tourists."

"Oh no, you're saving that for me, sugar."

She was quiet, her heart hammering. "Am I, Jamie?"

"Yeah. You are if you want to, Summer Grace. I can't make that demand of you, you know."

She sat up, her heart tumbling in her chest, her hair tumbling around her shoulders. "Jamie, this has to be more than just the consent of kink. You have to tell me you want this. For us to be exclusive. I mean, I have been, but . . ."

"So have I. But yes, I want that. Damn right I do, sugar girl, who tastes sweeter than chicory coffee in the park." He pulled her down and kissed her hard, then let her go. "You want to skip this place and hit Café Du Monde for some beignets? They're not as good as City Park, but I think they may be the only place open this time of night—whatever the hell time it is."

She laughed. "Now?"

"Yes, now. I'm starving and my girl wants beignets. Come on and let's get you put together."

She looked up at him as he unbuckled one of the cuffs and slid it from her wrist. "Jamie?"

"Hmm?"

She bit her lip, watching him closely. "*Your* girl."

He shifted his focus to her face, let the leather cuff fall to the mattress and twined his fingers with hers, smiling in a way that made her heart melt like a hot pool between her breasts. "Yeah. *All* mine."

CHAPTER
Nine

CAFÉ DU MONDE at four in the morning was like few other places on earth. Even in July, which was usually far too hot and damp for most of the tourists, it was full of the after-bar and after-dinner crowds, as well as the tourists who braved the heat of a Louisiana summer. People wore everything from formal evening wear to shorts and cheesy T-shirts. Jamie quickly spotted a corner table that looked out onto Decatur Street and Jackson Square on the other side of the boulevard, where a few of the horse-drawn carriages were parked, the horses and drivers napping in the pre-dawn heat. The air was damp and smelled like sugary-coffee heaven as he led Summer to the table and helped her into her seat, then sat down next to her, scooting his chair close enough that his long legs tangled with hers.

He leaned in and murmured against her cheek, "I will never

smell beignets and chicory coffee again without it reminding me of you."

She pushed against his shoulder. "Don't be silly, Jamie. You've lived in New Orleans most of your life."

"Yeah. But I'm here with you right now, and that's all that counts."

"You're just high on kink and sex."

He pulled her close and nuzzled her ear. "I'm high on you."

It was everything she'd ever wanted to hear from him. She didn't give a damn how corny it might sound to anyone else. She tried to ignore the tiny voice in her head that told her it was too good to be true.

The waiter interrupted them and Jamie pulled away to order their coffees and enough beignets for a small army while thunder rolled overhead. Rain began to spatter on the sugar-covered sidewalk outside the green and white striped awning that covered most of the café's seating area, adding to the intimate ambience, making the café seem more like a haven. The fact that the place was crowded with wall-to-wall people didn't even matter.

"So what do you say we get to know each other better?" Jamie asked.

Summer laughed. "We've known each other almost forever."

"We have. But it's like when you live someplace and you take certain things for granted, so you never really think about it on a conscious level. How many times have you passed historic homes in the Garden District without giving them a second thought beyond how beautiful the architecture is?"

"Hmm, I guess I see what you mean. Where do you want to start? Like . . . what's your favorite color?"

He grinned, his dimples creasing. He was damn adorable, despite the salacious things they'd done tonight. His dimples were maybe the only thing that could allow her to think of him that way.

"The cornflower blue of your eyes, sweetheart," he said.

She groaned. "Oh God, Jamie—if we were still just friends I might have to gag."

He laughed. "It's kinda true. When I'm not at the club, I wear a lot of blue."

"Yes. And green and brown and still a lot of black."

He raised his eyebrow, the barbell catching the light from the fluorescents overhead. "You've noticed."

"So what if I have?"

"Just another fact to file away."

"In that Domly-Dom mind of yours that must notice every tiny detail to use against me later?"

"As a matter of fact, yes. I'm also marking off that smart-ass remark on my mental ledger of infractions where I keep track of how many spankings I owe you."

She sat back in her chair, crossing her arms over her chest. "That doesn't scare me."

He leaned in and said quietly, "Which only motivates me to find something that will."

And just like that, her body was on fire again. But the waiter came by their table with their coffee in thick white ceramic cups and pastry on white paper plates, the powdered sugar drifting in the air and settling on the green-and-white plastic tablecloth. Jamie picked up a steaming beignet and held it to her mouth.

"You get first bite, despite your errant ways."

She opened for him and he let the edge of the hot little piece of heaven rest on her tongue. She bit in, the sugar melting in her mouth. "Mmm."

He reached out and thumbed some powdered sugar from the corner of her lip, and she picked up a napkin and wiped.

"Okay, so what else do you want to talk about?" she asked.

He shrugged, biting into his pastry. "I don't know. Everything. Like . . . what was your favorite cartoon growing up?"

"Really? That's what you want to know?"

"Why not?"

"*Ninja Turtles.*"

"Ha! That *so* does not surprise me."

"What about you? Do you still watch any cartoons?"

"Only anime porn."

Summer rolled her eyes and took another bite. "Which *so* does not surprise *me*," she said, her voice muffled as she chewed. "Okay, next question. Have you ever wanted a dog?"

"Yeah, actually. Always. But I'm at work too much. It doesn't feel like it'd be fair."

"Couldn't you adopt an older animal and have it at the shop with you? It could be your mascot."

"Huh." He sipped his coffee. "Maybe. That's a pretty good idea."

"What breed would it be?"

"Probably the mangiest mutt available. I always root for the underdog."

"Aw, that's sweet."

He glanced down at his lap, then up again. "Come on, Summer Grace, don't give me a hard time. I'm serious. And I'm not sweet."

"I know you are. Serious and sweet." She took his hand in hers. "I know, Jamie. I know you're a Dominant, and that it's no poser thing—that you're the real deal. But you're also still human. Maybe more than most people I know."

He grinned, picked up her hand and brushed a kiss across

the back of it. "Sugar, you sure know how to flatter a guy," he teased. "But seriously. Thanks. You're the real deal, too, you know. You dove into this kink thing head-first, and that's not something most people can do. But I saw it that first moment in the club—the way you respond, the way your body moves, like you're dancing to the beat. Or to the beating." He grinned. "But it means you're right *in* it. That's not something you can fake. It's a beautiful thing to see. And . . . I'm gonna give the dog some thought. How do you think Madame would react if I brought a dog over to your place?"

"With as much disdain as she responds to everything else."

He grinned once more and nodded, letting go of her hand to eat another beignet. She watched him chew, the motion of his throat as he swallowed, the way his big hands curled around the white coffee mug, everything about him purely sensual. She loved this—sitting in the quiet café while the rain fell on the awning and the street. Watching the sleepy carriage horses, the acrid scent of chicory and the sweet scent of powdered sugar. But mostly she loved talking with him, getting to know each other in a way they'd never really taken the time to do. And the feeling that at last she *belonged*. To Jamie. She sighed and bit into another beignet. Did she even want to think about what the future might hold? Or did she want to simply live in this moment?

She sipped her coffee and her gaze wandered back to Jackson Square across the street. It was dark, other than the flickering candlelight of the fortune-tellers' tables set up all around the perimeter. They were there every night, rain or shine, with their fluttering tablecloths, their animal bones and Tarot cards, their incense and candles.

"Jamie?"

"Hmm?"

"Let's go get our fortunes read."

He laughed. "What?"

She grabbed his hand and tugged. "Come on. Maybe they'll tell you about your dog."

"That's nothing but tourist stuff, sugar. You don't really believe all that, do you?"

"I was raised in New Orleans just like you were. Of course I do."

"I was raised in Scotland until I was seven, which lent me a healthy dose of cynicism."

"Actually, I've heard the Scots are a superstitious people. And some of those stories may have come from you, Mr. Cynicism."

"Superstitious, yes. Gullible, no."

She batted her lashes at him. "Please? It's even stopped raining."

He rolled his eyes. "Okay. But I'm finishing my beignets first."

She leaned over and kissed his cheek, and he turned his head to capture her mouth. He tasted like coffee and chicory and man. She smiled as she sat back in her chair.

"Hurry, Jamie."

He stuffed the last pastry into his mouth, wiped his hands on a napkin and got to his feet. "Lead the way, sweetheart—just remember you won't have the opportunity often. You're lucky I'm feeling generous tonight."

She laughed and winked at him. "I have my ways of getting my way."

He swatted her behind as they stepped onto the sidewalk. "Watch yourself. That's another mark on the spanking ledger."

"Promises, promises."

He yanked her in close and growled in her ear, "You know damn well I'll make good on those promises."

"Mmm, I do. And I can't wait."

"Then let's get this silliness over with and go back to your place."

"Yes, sir."

"That's better," he muttered, but she could see his cheek dimpling as they crossed the street.

They milled around the edges of the square, gated for the night. The feral cats who lived in the park-like square itself hissed in warning when they walked too close to the iron fencing, checking out all the fortune-tellers' tables until they found the one Summer wanted.

"This one," she said, stopping in front of a woman with a small crescent moon tattooed between her eyes. She wore bloodred lipstick and an embroidered shawl, her dark hair hanging in long curls. Her dark eyes were lined in black, and she had a mysterious expression, as though she knew a secret. Summer wasn't certain it was all for show.

"Have your future told?" the woman asked, her voice low and husky.

"How much is it?" Jamie asked.

"For you two? Twenty-five dollars for both. No, twenty. I like you."

Jamie started to reach for his wallet.

"You pay me after," the woman said. "Please. Sit." She gestured to the two folding chairs in front of her table and Jamie took Summer's hand as they seated themselves. "I am Madame Rain. I can read the Tarot cards for you, or your palms. I can also read energy."

Suddenly Summer felt nervous, the tiny hairs at the back of her neck prickling. "Tarot, I think. Jamie? What should we have done?"

"This is your game, sweetheart. It's your choice."

She nodded with more certainty than she felt. "The cards, then."

Madame Rain smiled and picked up a worn deck and began to shuffle. "Did you have a specific question? Or just a general reading?"

Summer glanced at Jamie, but he shrugged. "Just general, I think."

"Ladies first," the woman said, nodding toward Summer. She laid the cards out in a row and studied the beautifully intricate designs for several long moments, her brow furrowing. Then she reached out. "May I look at your palm, miss?"

Summer placed her free hand in Madame Rain's. The fortune-teller moved her fingertips over Summer's upturned palm, hovering there, then lightly touched it in places before looking up. "You've had a great deal of tragedy in your life. You have lost much, but you have also recently gained. You must learn to open yourself, my dear. You must learn to trust—that's an ability you lost far too early in life." She let Summer's hand go and lifted one of the cards. "The Lovers. This card is about choices to be made, but it is also about relationships—friends as well as lovers." She shot a quick glance at Jamie before refocusing on Summer. "You have good friends, very strong ties. But there is a new lover about whom a choice must be made. Perhaps not now, but soon." She turned the card over and over between her fingers, her brows furrowed. "Yes, very soon."

Summer's heart was pounding and she didn't dare to look at Jamie. But Madame Rain was lifting another card. "This card is The World, Key twenty-one of the Major Arcana, the card of attainment." She gestured toward Summer with the card still in her hand. "But that attainment must be earned, and in this case it is dependent upon your choices. Ultimately, we are each responsible for our own destiny. Next we have the Ace of Wands, signifying change and growth. This card tells us that this is a crucial time for you. A wonderful time, but change can be stressful. Your life is moving in a circle, the continuous motion of Ouroboros. Do you know what that is, my dear?"

"It's a symbol, isn't it? A snake swallowing its own tail?"

"Yes. The serpent is a symbol of eternity, of the eternal cycles in life. You find it in nearly every ancient culture. Greece, Egypt, in South America, and the Norse have their own very powerful version. But it always speaks to the same things, always pointing to cycles, to the times when we find ourselves back at the beginning somehow. But it also means we have the gift of starting over. Starting anew."

Summer squeezed Jamie's hand and he squeezed back. This time she did turn to look at him, to smile at him, but his features were closed to her. She had no idea what he was thinking—probably that this Tarot reading was pure crap. But she knew the magic of New Orleans, and she felt the truth of Madame Rain's words.

"I think . . . I think I know what you're talking about," she said.

They spoke for a few more minutes about the details in her reading, then the fortune-teller gathered the cards back into the deck and shuffled again, turning to Jamie. "Now for you, sir."

Jamie shrugged as the woman laid the cards out on the table. The first one she picked up had an image of a knight on a horse, the face in the armor a grinning skull. "This card is Key thirteen of the Major Arcana. Death."

Jamie dropped Summer's hand and got to his feet. "That's enough."

"But, sir, the Death card does not necessarily signify death itself—there's no need for alarm. Please sit down and let me explain."

"I'm done." He pulled some bills out of his wallet and tossed them on the table. "Summer Grace," he said gruffly.

She knew not to argue. She apologized to Madame Rain quietly and stood, letting Jamie take her arm and lead her away. She had some idea of what had triggered him, but the severity of his reaction surprised her. He'd lost his brother, then hers— his best friend. She knew his losses perhaps better than anyone. But he didn't even believe in the cards, did he?

She had to hurry to keep up with his long strides, trying not to think of what had happened in terms of the losses she had suffered—Brandon, then her family in a different but nearly equally tragic way.

No. Can't think about that now.

The rain started again when they were still a good block from his car. He grasped her hand tightly and moved faster as the big drops pelted them. By the time they reached his Corvette the rain was a heavy downpour—it was as if someone were dumping enormous buckets of water down on them. Jamie unlocked the 'Vette and opened her door. She paused.

"Get in, Summer Grace."

"But I'll get your beautiful leather seat wet."

"Just get in," he growled, and she did as he demanded. The smooth leather was cool beneath her damp bottom, which was still sore as hell from the caning, but rather than luxuriating in her bruises as she had earlier, now they only made her all the more aware that something was very wrong with Jamie, and therefore between them.

He swung the driver's side door open and slid in, starting the powerful engine without a glance or a word other than, "Seat belt."

She buckled in and shivered as he raced across town, splashing the water already pooling in the streets up onto the windows. She normally loved the rain, but not like this—not with the atmosphere in the car so tight with tension. Not when it seemed as if it was freezing-cold water trying to drown them rather than the gentle wet of a New Orleans summer.

She glanced at his stony profile and decided this was not the time to talk to him. It wasn't that she didn't dare—that wasn't her, and certainly not when she wasn't deep in subspace, although she still felt the last tendrils of it in her body. But she felt fear like a dark shadow creeping up her spine. He was so completely closed off to her—she'd never seen him like this and she needed some time to figure out how to handle it.

When they arrived at her place he pulled up to the curb and sat there, staring straight ahead through the windshield, not even cutting the motor. She waited. And finally, she exploded.

"So what the fuck, Jamie? You're not even going to say good night?"

He sighed, rolled his shoulders. Said quietly, "Good night, Summer Grace."

Something in her chest—the empty place that had been filling up and warming lately—went ice cold so fast it nearly choked her. *Again.* He was doing this again! It was several long moments before she could say anything.

"Seriously? That's where we're at? You freak out over something and I . . . what? I cease to exist? Just 'see ya later'? Actually, not even that. And after a night of play? And fuck, Jamie . . ." She had to pause, to take in a breath, to swallow the tears forming in her throat. "God*damn* it, Jamie, you played me and fucked me and *talked* to me, and it was one of the best nights of my life and here we are again, with you running off like I was one of your vacuous dungeon groupies! I deserve better than that. I am worth more than that. And if you don't know it . . . Fuck."

She shook her head so hard she felt her neck crack, heard it echo in her hollow ears. Then she fumbled with numb fingers until she'd managed to unbuckle her seat belt, then pulled the door handle. From the corner of her eye she saw Jamie starting to unbuckle his as well, but she wasn't waiting for him. He could fucking talk to her, or he could leave. But she wasn't going to sit in his car, shivering in her drenched clothes, waiting for him to make up his mind.

She grabbed her small purse from the seat and jumped out of the car into the pouring rain. She could barely see as she made her way to the door. Just as she stepped onto the first step leading to her porch she felt a hand on her arm and Jamie whipped her around to face him.

JAMIE FELT HER trembling under his hands and he wanted to kick himself. He'd just felt so stunned. His brain had shut down so damn fast he couldn't have explained to anyone what was going on inside him right then. But now . . . now he could see the tears on her face even through the rain and he felt like absolute shit.

"I'm sorry," he said. "And you are far from being a dungeon groupie, and you deserve everything. *Everything.* I'm being an ass. I'm sorry, Summer Grace."

She folded her arms over her chest. "You damn well should be. You can't keep doing this to me. I won't have it. I mean it, Jamie."

The knot that had tied itself up in the middle of his chest back at Jackson Square gave a sharp twist. "I know you do. Can we get out of this rain so I can apologize to you properly?"

She cracked a smile, even though he could tell she was still hurting. "Which I suppose means with your ever-ready cock?"

He gave her a wry grin. "I'd like that. I really would. But I think this time we really do need to talk. I figure I'd start by clarifying a few things."

She bit her lip, then dropped her arms and turned away from him. "I suppose that's okay. As long as we end up with your cock telling me how sorry you are."

He smiled, but not too broadly as he followed her into the house. He knew her sass was cover-up for real distress. And knew that he'd caused it. He had to man up and try to fix things, to make it right with her.

It was warm inside the house. She dropped her keys in a big green glass bowl on the old sea chest by the front door and went off down the hall.

"I'm getting a towel," she called over her shoulder. "If we get pneumonia, it's your fault."

His stomach tightened. It would be.

Fuck. Stop it.

No one was dying tonight.

She came back and handed him a towel, and he wrapped it around her shoulders and began to dry her hair.

"Jamie, you don't have to do that—I can do it myself."

"I know."

He was glad she didn't argue any further. Despite ending their quick argument on the front steps with teasing, he needed a little time to think. To process. He bunched the ends of her long hair in the towel and pressed, moved the towel and did it again before patting at her damp cheeks. She was watching him, blinking fast, her thick lashes coming down on her pale cheeks.

He cleared his throat. He didn't want to have this discussion with her. With anyone. But he knew he had to do it.

"You're probably wondering what the hell is wrong with me. Well." He rubbed a hand over the stubble of his hair. "Sometimes I wonder, too. But at this point I owe you an explanation."

"Yes, you do," she said calmly, pushing the towel from her. "Dry yourself, Jamie."

He scrubbed the towel over his head, his face, buying a little more time.

"Do you want to sit down?" he asked.

She shrugged. "Is this one of those conversations I need to sit down for?" she asked, and he saw a flash of fear in her eyes.

"Aw, no, sugar. No, not one of those talks. But it's been a long night and I thought you'd want to be comfortable."

Her shoulders dropped. "Good. Let's go sit in the kitchen."

He followed her into the old black and white kitchen with its vintage tile. She'd redone the old wood floors after Katrina and repainted the white cabinets, but she'd kept the original feel to the room. It was a cozy spot for a hard talk. He sat at her small table next to the window, his long legs barely fitting. The rain was really coming down outside, thunder rumbling like a lion in the still-dark sky, the sun beginning to rise behind the heavy storm clouds.

"Do you want me to make some coffee?" she asked.

"You don't need to make coffee. And you don't need to tiptoe around me. Fuck. I'm sorry. I don't mean to be gruff with you—I swear I don't. I'm just all kinds of fucked up tonight. It's no excuse. I know that."

She shrugged and sat across from him. "Just tell me what's going on with you."

Of course, she knew some of it already. Most of it. But he

knew he had some explaining to do. He pulled in a deep breath and ran a hand over his buzz cut, trying to sort it out enough in his head to verbalize some of the fucked-up shit that was making him spin out. "Yeah. Okay." He took another breath, exhaled. "Okay. You know I lost Ian when we were seven."

"Of course."

"And then there was Brandon."

"Yes. And then there was Brandon." She ducked her head for a moment and he could see her forcibly swallowing down her own issues around losing her brother before she looked up at him again. "Jamie, I know the Death card freaked you out, and I get that. But your reaction—."

"Yeah," he interrupted. "Except there's more to it."

"More? I'd think that was plenty to shake you up. It shook me up for a minute but then . . . Okay. I don't mean to invalidate what you're feeling. Go on."

"You'd think that would be enough. For both of us. But there's something I need to tell you now." He rubbed his palms together under the table. "It's something I've never talked to anyone about. Partly because it wasn't really anyone else's business, and partly—mostly, I guess—because I felt kind of . . . I don't know. Superstitious about it."

"You? Superstitious? You agreed to that Tarot reading because *I* wanted to do it. I thought you were the eternal skeptic."

"I am, mostly. But I don't know what else to call it, so yeah. Superstition. It's gelled in my head that way and it's been there for a long time. You remember when I was married to Traci?"

"For about a second, yes. You married her right after Brandon died. But to be honest, I don't remember too much about that time."

He nodded. "We got married about eight months later. It was way too soon, and we were way too young."

She nodded. "It made sense that you guys broke up for her to go away to graduate school."

"It did. But there's another part of the story." He had to stop and take in another deep breath. *Just say it.* "There was a baby, Summer Grace."

"A baby?" She looked stunned. She looked exactly like he'd felt when Traci told him about the pregnancy all those years ago. "You have a child, Jamie? You have a *child* and you never told me?"

"What? No, I don't have a child. The baby . . . Traci had a miscarriage."

Summer Grace laid a hand on his arm. "Fuck. I'm so sorry, Jamie."

Feeling as if he didn't deserve her touch, her comfort, he drew his arm back and gripped the edge of the table with both hands. It was hard to look into her concerned blue eyes as he said the words aloud—words he'd never spoken to anyone but his ex-wife. "You'll probably think this is stupid, but . . . I'm a death magnet. I am. The card tonight confirmed what I already know. Everyone I love—truly love—dies."

"Jamie, that's . . ." She stared at him, wide-eyed. "That's what you've been carrying around all these years? You think you invite death somehow?"

"I know I do. The people I care about are in danger, especially those closest to me. It's one reason why I stayed away from you—not just because it was Brandon asking me to take care of you, to make sure you were all right, but because the best way for you to be all right was for me to keep some distance between us."

"Shit." She pushed her hair from her face, shaking her head, then looked back up at him. "That is some seriously crazy stuff."

"I knew you wouldn't get it." He started to stand up.

"Jesus, Jamie, will you sit down and let me talk?"

He grunted as he leaned back in his chair and crossed his arms over his chest. "So talk."

"I said it was crazy. I didn't say I don't understand how you feel. Because I feel it, too. Not death, maybe, but I feel like trouble just finds me. That bad things happen sometimes because of . . . me."

"That's not true."

"It is. It's as true as you bringing death to the people you love. It *feels* true, which is sometimes the only part that counts. But that doesn't mean it's actually the truth in any way to the rest of the world. It's not like we have some dark super-power. It just means you and I are a little fucked up, as you said. It's one of the deeper things we have in common."

He felt like he'd been punched in the gut. Maybe what she was saying was right. Maybe. He couldn't take it all in. "I don't know, Summer Grace."

She reached for him and pulled at his arms until she could cup his hands in her small ones, surrounding his in her warmth. "Shit happens, Jamie. All the damn time. Life happens, and just as often, death. And in case you've never looked at pregnancy statistics, most end in miscarriage. A lot of them are so early the woman doesn't even know she's pregnant, but it happens all the time. It's not anyone's fault. It's *not*. And certainly not yours. Not that baby or Brandon or Ian. Your brother had an accident. An *accident*. And my brother—that was caused by someone else's stupidity. By the stupidity of the driver who hit him. None of that could possibly be your fault. What did you do, Jamie? Go to a Voodoo priestess and have her make some bad gris-gris? Sit in a corner and *wish* them dead? Come on." She blew out a breath. "And I guess . . . I guess I didn't do any of that to make my family fall apart, either."

"When you say it, it makes sense." But even as he said the words he couldn't quite wrap his head around the idea. "I've been carrying this around for a long damn time, though. It may take a while for me to change my thinking habits."

"It may take us both a while. But you can't let fear rule you, Jamie—if *I* did I would never have let you take me out of that cemetery. And I would have missed out."

She stood and moved closer, until she could run her hand over the stubble on his head. He reached for her hand and brought it to his lips so he could kiss her palm. "You are damn smart sometimes, sugar. I mean that."

She smiled and batted her long lashes. "I always knew I got all the brilliance in the family."

"No doubt." He pulled her down into his lap and buried his face in her damp hair. Christ, she smelled good, which helped him to get his brain in order again, for some reason. "We are so alike, aren't we? I've known you for most of my life, but I'm only just realizing it. We're a matched set."

"Are we?"

"Yeah," he said slowly, working it out even as he spoke. "We both keep the hard stuff inside. You do it by being sassy and stubborn. I do it by being nice—or so Allie tells me—and stubborn, or by being an asshole and stubborn—or so Mick tells me. But in the end it's the same thing."

She was quiet for a moment. "Sometimes I hate that you know me so well." She grabbed his jaw in both of her hands, forcing him to meet her gaze. "And sometimes," she said, her voice going soft, "sometimes I sort of . . . love it."

Her eyes were shining. With emotion. With something else. And he understood how deeply he loved her. How much he had all this time. It still scared the crap out of him. But right now that didn't matter. Not one damn bit.

He stood, setting her on her feet

"Jamie?"

He silenced her with a kiss, pressing his lips hard against hers, needing the contact. Needing her. He stuffed the damn fear down and sank into her lips, her small frame tight in his arms. He sank into the contrast of delicacy and unbelievable strength that was *her*. He couldn't stand for there to be the boundary of their clothes separating them one moment longer. He picked her up and carried her into the bedroom.

SUMMER CLOSED HER eyes as Jamie laid her down on the bed and undressed her. Silently. Gently. There was something commanding even about his tenderness, and when she let her eyes flutter open to look up at him and saw the expression on his face in the quiet light of the rising sun, her heart nearly burst from her chest. Everything they'd talked about—his fears and his doubts and his determination to get over it—seemed to be swamping him with emotion. She wanted to think some of that emotion was for her as well. She knew it was, but she almost didn't dare think it. Because in this moment she loved him more intensely, more thoroughly, than she ever knew she could, and it felt like the biggest risk she'd ever taken in her life.

One by one he pulled off her shoes, then her damp black dress, her bra, pausing with his fingertips under the edge of her panties to look down at her, to lock his gaze with hers. Her heart tumbled in her chest once more, and she had to swallow hard to even breathe as he slipped her black thong down over her thighs. Her body was melting already, but it was some simmering, languid sensation that was completely unfamiliar—something that had to do with the expression in his green eyes as much as it did his touch.

When he had her naked he straightened and undressed himself slowly, still watching her, his eyes heavy-lidded, his mouth loose. She recognized that he'd dropped some of the conscious control, and she had some idea of what it meant for him to get to that vulnerable place with her. With anyone.

His shirt came off, and her body softened all over, and she admired his beautifully pierced nipples, the tattoo, *memento mortalitatem tuam*, running up his ribs—symbols of the raw edge that was such a part of who he was. She understood the meaning so much more now. He licked his lips, the damp point of his tongue moistening his beautiful mouth. She wanted him so badly it hurt, but she couldn't move—all she could do was watch. Wait for him.

Jamie.

He toed his boots off, unbuckled his belt, unbuttoned his jeans and slid them down over his lean hips. He was naked underneath, and his cock was swollen with need—the same need her entire system was suffused with, drowning her in liquid desire. Jamie knelt on the bed, first one knee, then the other, straddling her. He reached down and stroked her cheek, her jaw, lingering at her lower lip, which had begun to tremble for some reason she couldn't understand—not in any language, any words she was familiar with. And desire was some untamed animal that churned and snarled as she waited for him to take her—to take what was his.

"Summer Grace," he whispered. He shook his head, his face momentarily crumbling before he pulled himself back together a bit. She thought she might cry. "Jesus, sweetheart. So much time to make up for."

What was he trying to tell her? She couldn't think straight. "Jamie . . ."

He pressed his fingertips to her lips. "No more talking now. Just kiss me."

He pulled her up into his arms and covered her mouth with his, his lips impossibly soft. He kissed her, pulled back, kissed her again and again until she was dizzy. Her arms went around his neck and he pressed his lips to hers over and over, sweet, almost chaste kisses that touched her on some deep level, making her sigh. She was a confused amalgam of need and fear and love—and sorrow for the time they'd lost, for the time they may never have.

No.

Unacceptable.

She pulled a breath into her lungs, pulled in his unique, familiar scent. The Jamie she'd always known.

Yes.

Finally he laid her back on the bed and slid his body over hers, holding himself up on his elbows, touching her cheeks, her mouth, her hair. His brows were drawn in concentration, and she'd never felt more the center of anyone's attention. It was as if he'd found something important in her face. It was an overwhelming idea, but one she could understand as she looked up at him. She loved this face—*his* face—because it was his. Because it was beautiful to her.

She loved him. With every cell in her being. Exquisitely. Painfully. Undeniably.

"Jamie . . ." she started, but she couldn't say the words out loud.

"Baby," he said, cupping her jaw in both hands, blinking down

at her. "Don't say a word. We don't need to tell each other anything, you and I. Not now. Now I need to be inside your body,
to be a part of you. You need that too, don't you, sweetheart?"

What was he saying? Was he as afraid as she was? Or did he
mean it in the sweet way it sounded if she didn't try to read
between the lines? Because he *was* sweet, her Jamie. And he was
right—she needed him to be a part of her, and she of him.

"Jamie, I need . . . everything."

Need to love you. Love you, love you, Jamie.

Finally he parted her thighs and slipped into her, and desire
was met with desire, emotion with emotion. There was still some
play of power between them, but it was more an exchange than
it had been before, because she truly *gave* herself to Jamie, on
every level. And he gave himself to her, finally, in some way he
never had before.

Pleasure was a trembling sigh as it left her lips, a shiver of need
as he closed his eyes and surged deeper into her body. Every touch
was new: his hands on her breasts, his lips on her neck, kissing,
biting gently. His body felt like a gift, like a new discovery as she
traced the hard planes, the ridges of muscle in his back, the softer
curve of his buttocks as they flexed, arching into her.

Sensation built slowly, as if her body knew they both needed
it to last, not to hurry. She drew in another breath, closing her
eyes as she smelled the rain in his hair—or maybe it was hers. It
didn't matter. Another long, lovely breath as he filled her once
more, and the scent of early morning sunshine coming in through
the windows made her open her eyes to see how it lit his beautiful body. She shuddered at the pleasure swamping her senses,
and as her climax approached, tears filled her eyes, spilling over
onto her cheeks.

"My baby," he murmured, kissing her tears, drinking them in.

Emotion and sensation combined, a gentle explosion that was no less intense for the soft edges that surrounded them, and she had to hold back the words she didn't dare speak as he made love to her for the very first time. Her body shook as she came, crying his name. Then he was coming with her, his hands digging into her hair. And as always, even that felt like a caress.

He was groaning, murmuring her name, his hips jerking, then slowing. He began kissing her again, and it was like some slow motion makeout session that went on forever, until they fell asleep with him still buried inside her. Skin to skin. Flesh to flesh. Beautiful.

CHAPTER

Ten

JAMIE SPEARED A piece of sesame chicken from the cardboard takeout container with his chopsticks and held it in front of Summer Grace's lips, waiting for her to open her mouth. She smiled and obeyed his tacit command, groaning as she chewed.

"That sounds almost like sex, baby," he said, leaning back against the pillows they'd propped up against the headboard of her white iron bed the way he had nearly every night since their scene at the club the previous weekend. He couldn't get enough of her lately. And lucky for him, it was Sunday evening and neither of them had had anything else to do but be together. Other than a few breaks to shower or eat, or to feed the ever-disdainful Madame, they'd been in bed since Summer Grace got off work yesterday afternoon.

"Mmm. It's almost as good as sex," she said, her mouth still half full. She smoothed the hand not holding her own takeout carton over her stomach, and he couldn't help but notice the way the peach satin of her short chemise pulled against her breasts, outlining her nipples. "Okay, so it's nowhere near as good as sex with you, but it tastes like heaven right now. I'm starving."

"You always work up an appetite when I let you be on top," he said, winking at her before taking a bite himself. "You're right—every bit as good as sex."

"Jamie!" She swatted at him with a pale purple throw pillow.

"Hey, now. Don't tempt me to put this food down and take you over my knee when we're both enjoying it so much."

She grinned impishly, and his heart caught in his throat, the way it had been doing all week.

"The food or the spanking?" she asked.

"Food now, spanking later. And earlier. And last night."

"I like that about you an awful lot, Jamie Stewart-Greer."

He popped another piece of chicken into her mouth simply to watch her savor it. "I know you do, sugar."

"So," she said when she'd swallowed, "what do you have going on this week?"

"My cousin Duff is coming in from Scotland tomorrow to get things started with the vintage motorcycle shop next door, remember?"

"Oh! Of course. And I only forgot because you keep plying me with food and sex until my brain is exploding."

"That's your stomach. And maybe something else."

Summer Grace rolled her eyes. "Tell me about him again? Since my 'something else' is exploding and a girl just can't think straight without it."

He chuckled. "Duff is a few years older than me, which I guess would make him thirty-three now. He's from Edinburgh. He's always sort of been the bad seed in the family, but I don't know . . . I don't think it's entirely his fault. He's someone I've always looked up to, in more ways than one."

"What do you mean?"

"Well, to begin with, my cousin is huge, a good six-foot-seven and built like a wall—like Rosie's Dom Finn. He has been since he was maybe fifteen years old. Other guys always take it as some sort of challenge to try to fight someone his size, but his parents blamed him for it every time the school called. Then when he was old enough to get into the pubs, which is sixteen in Scotland, he got into a couple of bad fights, even went to jail twice. But I was there for one of them, and I can tell you he was taunted by those assholes, like he had been his whole life. The drinking just made it hard for him to take it. He won't drink at all now. A sad state for a Scotsman, but it became necessary. But he's a good guy, and he knows Harleys like no one else I've met to this day."

"You know your accent just crept in there a bit while you were talking about him."

"Did it?"

Summer Grace smiled. "It did. And I liked it."

"Well, you'd better get used to it, because once Duff gets here it's likely to pop up more than a bit, especially since he's staying with me until he finds his own place. Which means we'll have to have our liaisons here."

"Liaisons? Is that what we're having?" she asked, batting her lashes.

"Sassy wench. You know that's not it. But I don't need my cousin finding me spanking you in the kitchen, even if he's as kinky as I am."

"Hmm, I might have to start dropping by the shop more often. You know, to hear the Scottish accent."

"Enamored of my big cousin already, are you?"

She set her carton of noodles on the night table and climbed onto his lap, straddling him. "I'm enamored of you, Jamie. Or haven't you guessed that after all these years?"

"The feeling is mutual, sweetheart."

"Is that what we're calling the bulge in your lap? Enamored?"

He grabbed her narrow hips and ground up against her warm mound. "Mmm-hmm. Now put those chopsticks down and prepare yourself to get spanked now and eat later."

"But I'm hungry."

"Uh-oh."

"Uh-oh what?"

"This!"

He lifted her small body and threw her over his shoulder as he stood with her in his arms, flipping the hem of her chemise up, revealing her delectable naked bottom so he could spank her.

She squealed.

"Summer Grace," he said, his tone firm. His cock was even firmer. "Are you going to behave?"

"Yes," she gasped, even as she continued to struggle in his grasp.

He just held her tigther as he walked with her through the old house until he reached the kitchen. Without bothering to turn the lights on—there was enough moonlight coming through the high window over the sink—he started opening drawers.

"Do you have any zip ties?" he asked.

"Shit," she muttered.

"Is that a yes?" he demanded.

"In the junk drawer. Next to the stove."

He yanked the drawer open and saw a bundle of them. "Black. Perfect."

"For what?"

He laid her roughly on the kitchen table, holding her down

with a hand on one shoulder. "Do you really think this is the time to ask me questions?"

She bit her lip. "Um . . . No."

"Good girl."

Even in the pale moonlight, he could see the sheen of subspace gleaming in her blue eyes at the words. He knew they did something to her. Hell, it did something to him to say them. Especially to her. Because she was *his*.

He looked down at her, drinking in her beauty, the struggle still evident in the set of her lovely mouth. He'd rid her of that rebellious streak quick enough.

Taking her delicate wrists in his hands, he drew her arms to either side—then he stopped and grinned at her. "It fucks with your head when you can't see what I'm going to do next, doesn't it, sugar?"

"Yes, Jamie."

"Shall I blindfold you, then?"

"Um . . . is that a trick question?"

He grinned. "Yes."

Flipping her over onto her stomach, he drew one wrist down and slipped the zip tie around it, then around the table leg, locking it tight. Before doing the same to the other wrist, he grabbed the scissors from her knife block and set them close by on the counter in case she panicked and he had to get her out quickly. Once he had her securely bound, he pushed the satin chemise up slowly, allowing himself to enjoy her smooth buttocks, the curve of her tiny waist, the small, rhythmic movements of her body as she pulled in one deep breath after another. When he laid a hand between her shoulder blades, he could feel those heavy breaths, and knew her well enough to understand she was taking herself down further into subspace. But the wicked streak in him didn't want her to center herself. He wanted her off-balance, wanted to fuck with her head a little. Because he needed it. Because she loved it.

He lifted both hands, paused, and slapped them down hard on her buttocks.

"Ow!"

Without warming her up or giving her time to ride out the pain, he did it again, then again and again, until his palms stung, until he felt her skin welting and she was making little mewling sounds between gasping breaths. She was squirming hard on the table, and he paused to massage her wrists, to be sure the zip ties weren't cutting into her flesh, but they seemed fine. He leaned over her until he could feel the heat of her ass cheeks against his belly, loving that they were so hot because of his hands on her flesh—that *he'd* done that to her. That she took it *for him*.

She let out a small sigh—or a small sob, he couldn't tell—as he kissed the back of her neck. He kissed his way down her spine, pausing to move the crumpled chemise out of the way. When he'd worked his way down to her beautiful ass, he bit into the sore flesh.

"Jesus, Jamie!"

In answer he did it again, harder this time, then immediately pinched her in the same spot.

"Ah! Fuck!"

"But you love it," he murmured. "Tell me you love it, Summer Grace."

"I don't. I could kick you, you know," she said stubbornly, making him chuckle.

His laughter died as he slipped his hand between her thighs, found her as wet as he'd known she'd be. He slid two fingers right inside her, his cock jumping when he felt the velvet clench of her pussy.

"Oh, really? You don't love it? Try it again, sweetheart." He smacked her ass hard with his free hand, smiling in the half-dark when he heard her gasp. "Only this time get the answer right."

"I *don't* love it," she said as her body moved, her hips grinding onto his fingers.

He thrust up into her, hard and fast.

"Okay! But Jamie . . . I don't just love it. I need it." She groaned. "God, I need it."

"Good girl."

He picked up a metal spatula he'd placed within reach when he got the scissors out and smacked her ass with it hard enough to leave a visible mark—a rectangle of red on her tender flesh. He ran a hand over the sore spot, leaned down and placed a kiss on the mark. She breathed out a sigh, such a beautiful sound. He wanted to spend the rest of his life making that sound come from her lips, then kissing the pain away.

He straightened up. What the fuck had he just said to himself?

The twisting he'd felt in his chest all week bloomed into a frightening heat he tried to swallow down.

Love this girl.

No.

Just play her. Play her hard. Fuck her hard. It'll be okay.

He focused on her gorgeously welted skin, using it to focus him once more before smacking her with the spatula again on the other cheek, and she cried out. Again he bent to kiss the sore spot—he couldn't help himself—then he ran his tongue over it.

"Mmm."

He pulled back and slapped the metal tool down hard on her damp skin, knowing it stung like mad.

"Oh, God!"

He did it over and over, moving from one lovely cheek to the other as he fought down that twisting sensation, then rained blows over the backs of her thighs, hard enough that he felt the echo of the impact reverberate in his wrist. He still had his other hand inside her sweet pussy, and the more he hurt her, the wetter she got. He stopped to concentrate on pumping his fingers inside her, angling them to hit her G-spot, and her juices pooled on his hand even before she came, screaming his name, her body shuddering.

His cock was so damn hard he could barely stand it.

That's right. Focus on the sex. Just fuck her.

He reached for the scissors and cut the zip ties. Then, tearing off the jeans he'd pulled on long enough to answer the door for the food delivery earlier, he pulled her body down, forcing her legs apart. He took his heavy cock in his hand and plowed into her.

"Oh, yes, Jamie."

With one hand on her hip and the other buried in her hair, pulling her head up until her slender neck was high off the table, beautifully elongated, he rammed into her, burying his cock deep. He did it again, and again, the physical pleasure warring with emotion for dominance. But he was out of control already—he knew it. Finally, he gave himself over, letting her hair go to wrap one arm around her waist and pulling her hips up as he thrust into her. He allowed the warmth to flood his chest as sensation made his cock go unbelievably rigid inside her body.

Her beautiful body that belongs to me, as I belong to her.

His stomach went tight, and he knew he was doing this wrong.

"Fuck, Summer Grace."

"Jamie?"

He pulled out of her long enough to turn her over, to pull her upright, picking her up and pressing her back into the wall as he pushed inside her once more. Her arms went around his neck, her legs wrapping around his waist.

Yes, just right.

He slung his hips, driving deeper as he kissed her throat, his fingers digging into her buttocks. But it wasn't about causing pain this time. It was simply about his *need* for her.

"Baby," he murmured, his breath catching. "Need you, baby."

Her voice was a quiet sob. "I need you, Jamie." Her arms tightened around his neck.

He kissed her hard and kissed the darkness inside her he'd never dared hope might be there. His mind buzzing, he drove into her harder, needing to go deeper. Her pussy was hot and sweet, her mouth hotter, sweeter. She was driving him crazy, his body, his mind, and he found himself unable to process what he was feeling. Exquisite pleasure. Burning emotion. His body poised on that edge as he waited for her to come again. He surged into her in slow, sinuous movements, keeping his pelvis close to hers, and soon he felt her insides squeeze him as she gasped and moaned.

"Ah, Jamie! Yes, yes . . ."

Her pleasure made his spiral, and he fell into that lovely abyss with her. They came into each other, their mouths locked in a kiss full of heat and sweet desire.

Hot and sweet—that was his girl.

They were both panting as he carried her through the house and fell onto the bed with her. They were still twined together. He didn't want to let her go. He didn't know if he ever could.

Panic tried to grip him, but her warm body against his, the soft *thud* of her heart against his chest, chased it away.

Maybe because it's her, it'll be okay.

Or maybe he was completely delusional.

He wasn't going to think of that now. Not with her still warm in his arms. Still his. Until he let her go.

* * *

S<small>UMMER SKIRTED AROUND</small> a crowd of tourists and pushed through the doors of The Grill on Chartres Street in the French Quarter, the same place she and Dennie had been coming to for lunch or breakfast since middle school. The place was an offshoot of the reknowned Camellia Grill out on Carrollton. Both locations had only diner-style counter seating, and the menus were simple Louisiana fare—omelettes and pancakes and some of the best waffles anywhere in the world, not to mention the gumbo. But they came mostly for the staff, who habitually argued with one another, slung food at the diners and generally misbehaved. After all these years the guys who worked there all knew them, and their plates were slid in front of them with a wink and a free cup of coffee.

She slid onto a stool and was looking over the menu when Dennie sat down beside her and gave her a one-armed hug.

"What's up, sweetie?"

"I just got here. Do you want something to drink? A sweet tea? Yes?" Summer turned to the waiter, who had ambled by their spot at the counter while pretending to ignore them. "Andre, two teas for us, please."

"You ladies can have anything you want—you know that," he said, flashing a wide grin at them, his voice running thick with his Cajun accent. "How 'bout a big plate of waffles covered in whipped cream? Some hot chocolate? That's our Tuesday lunch special."

Dennie laughed. "It is not. And we're not thirteen anymore, Andre. And it's hot enough to grill those waffles on the sidewalk."

"Mmm-hmm. You are definitely not thirteen anymore. You want me to kick my wife out so you can be the one to resist my charms every night, Miss Dennie?"

Dennie shook her head. "You should be ashamed of yourself, Andre."

"Oh, I am ashamed of m'self, ladies. But you can still come on over to my place anytime you want." He winked at them and ambled off to get their teas.

Dennie chuckled. "He always has to try."

"At this point I'd kind of be insulted if he didn't. God, I'm starving. I need waffles!"

"You're sassy today, missy."

"Am I?" She looked at Dennie, who just sat there with her brows arched, waiting for Summer to tell her what was up with her. "Okay, I guess I am. And I know I'm beaming like a little girl with a new kitten."

Dennie cleared her throat and muttered, "Your words, not mine."

Summer shook her head. "I know. I know! I'm being ridiculous. You'd think I was sixteen again, only this time Jamie didn't turn me away. I've actually got *butterflies*. Me, of all people."

Dennie's expression softened, and she reached over to cover Summer's hand with hers. "Come on, hon. We've both always known the only man who would cause you butterflies was Jamie Stewart-Greer. And about time, too."

"I'd just about given up on him. Well, I had. God, men are stupid."

"They certainly are. So, how are you feeling about everything? Because I've known you practically our entire lives and I can tell there's something going on behind that blissful smile."

"I was sorta pretending there was nothing but the butterflies," Summer said, her shoulders slouching.

"I'm sorry, Summer. Do you want to just keep pretending? I didn't mean to bring you down."

"No, I guess not." She bit her lip. "No. That's probably why I asked to get together today—not that I didn't want to see you, of course, but I knew you'd call me on my shit, and I need it."

Dennie looped an arm around her shoulder. "You just tell ol' mama Den what's bothering you, honeypie."

Andre dropped off their teas and Summer paused to sip hers before taking a long breath and blowing it out slowly. "This whole thing is just sort of a mind-fuck for me. It's pretty damn scary to have my fondest dreams handed to me on a silver platter."

"What are you afraid of?" Dennie asked gently.

"That it'll end up in some awful mess."

"Because?"

Summer wiped the droplets off her ice tea glass with her thumb, keeping her gaze on the cool amber liquid. "Because that's how things always go. My whole life."

Dennie gave her a small shake. "Summer, my darlin' friend, you listen to me. You do not deserve to lose out on this, you hear me?"

"What makes you think—"

"Because I *know* you, that's why," Dennie interrupted. "I know your fatalistic attitude. I know that's why you've never let yourself connect with any man—that and your feelings for Jamie holding you back. But—and forgive me, but I'm going to be hard-ass honest with you right now—I also think maybe the reason you stopped pursuing Jamie was because you knew on some level that you'd both reached a point in your lives where he'd stop turning you away."

Summer's stomach went tight at her friend's words. "Wow. You really know how to not hold back."

"You know it's because I love you, right? And because I think you have a few demons to face if things are going to work out with Jamie. I don't want to see you keep getting in your own way."

Summer nodded, taking a few moments to absorb it all. "You're right. God, you're right. I think maybe I've been getting in my own way my whole life, and not just with Jamie, or even just with men, but *everything*. Until recently, I never even allowed myself to get too close to any of my friends, other than you. I didn't realize it until I started to really bond with Allie when she got back from Europe, and then with Rosie. It's something I've been thinking about lately. It's hard for me to get close to anyone, but I think I'm learning. I'm trying. And maybe it had to start with my female friends before I could get close to a man. To Jamie. I'm not sure I'm completely ready for that. I don't know . . . I just don't know if I can do it."

"You have trust issues, honey, and I don't blame you. But maybe it's time to try to let that go."

Summer's eyes were pooling with tears. She sniffed, blinking as she squeezed Dennie's hand. "Thanks for not pulling any punches. I needed the hard talk. You're the only one I'd be able to hear it from. You're the only one who would even know."

"Except maybe Jamie," Dennie suggested.

She nodded. "Yeah. Except for Jamie."

Andre stopped in front of their spot at the counter with his notepad. "What are you two beautiful ladies going to have?"

They ordered, and after a bit more flirting Andre turned to get their food on the grill.

"You okay?" Dennie asked.

"Hmm? Yeah. Just thinking about what I need to do. What I need to tell him."

"What haven't you told him, honey?"

She turned to Dennie, her heart beating a thousand miles an hour. "I need to tell him that . . . I need to tell him I'm in love with him."

*   *   *

JAMIE PEERED AT the computer screen on his desk at the shop, poring over figures for the build-out on the space next door where he and his cousin—who was due any minute—would open the motorcycle division of SGR Motors. He was excited about both things—seeing Duff for the first time in a few years and expanding the business. But Summer Grace was on his mind no matter what he tried to distract himself with.

He was out of his mind over this woman. He couldn't get enough of her—her delicate little body, her beautiful blue eyes, the perfection that was her skin. The flawlessness of her submission—and he'd better not even think about that or he'd have yet another raging hard-on at work. But it was more than the sexual part of it—there was the emotional component, which was pretty damn potent.

Back to work.

He squinted at the computer screen, but all he could see was Summer Grace's face. He ran both his hands over his buzz cut, rubbing his scalp.

"Headache, cousin?"

He whipped around to find Duff dwarfing the doorway of his office. He broke into a grin as he got up and grabbed Duff in a hug. His huge cousin pounded him on the back hard enough to make him cough.

Jamie pulled back. "Jesus, what the hell do they feed you in Scotland?"

"Haggis. Maybe you should have had more of it before you left, puny boy."

"I'd hardly call six-foot-two puny, other than in comparison to you, you circus freak."

"Aye, that I am," Duff agreed good-naturedly. "Want to arm wrestle over it?"

"Fuck you. Hardly. How was your flight? And why wouldn't you let me pick you up from the airport?"

"Ah, those airport greetings are far too emotional for me."

Jamie grinned. "Are you telling me you might have cried, cousin?"

"No, but I thought *you* might, and I wasn't prepared to deal with that—haven't carried a hankie since . . . never. So what's all the head rubbing about? Business?"

"What? No, the business stuff is all good. When you've had a chance to rest up I'll show you the figures. Meanwhile, do you want to take a look at the space in person?"

"Fuck, yes." Duff gave him another breath-stilting pounding on the back.

"All right—follow me."

Jamie led the way outside, and used his new key to open the heavy padlock on the rusted metal door of the old building next to his.

"Welcome to SGR Motorcycles, your new baby."

He swung the door up with a flourish and turned to catch Duff's wide grin. The place was a mess of stained and crumbling concrete floors, with piles of junk left behind by the last tenants, but he could see Duff was as excited as he was about the place.

"I can't believe we had to wait so damn long for this spot to be available," Duff said, looking around the space. "Seems we've been talking about it for a good five years or more."

"Well, we wouldn't have had the money to do it right until now, anyway. I thought you could have your office up front, and all the bays over there, with plenty of secure storage in the back."

Duff nodded his big shaved head. Jamie had always thought his cousin looked like a Scottish version of Mr. Clean.

"I'll want to keep a good dozen bikes here at any time," Duff told him.

"That was my thought, too. And maybe as many as twenty if we build in a riser so we have two levels."

"Good idea."

"We have a lot to talk about. The architect will meet with us in ten days."

"Can't wait. Meanwhile, cousin, where can I get a sit-down and a cold drink around here?"

"For me, you mean, since you don't drink?" Jamie grinned at him. "Flynn McCools isn't far—you remember the place? If you don't mind the Irish, that is."

"It'll do since I'm off the booze and on the cola."

"You feel up to walking?"

"I feel up to wrestling a fucking bear."

Jamie laughed as he locked the metal door behind him. "Same old Duff."

"Yeah. I'd say same old Jamie except something's different."

"Jesus. Really? I'm that transparent?"

"Apparently."

They moved down the sidewalk while Jamie turned over in his head how much he wanted to reveal, how much he was even ready to deal with himself.

"I'm in love," he blurted out, then muttered, "Fuck."

Duff let his head fall back as he let out a roar of laughter. "So the bug finally bit you, did it? I'd guess it's that same girl."

"Yeah. It's never been anyone else."

"She sounds like a good one, anyway."

"She is. She's fucking amazing."

"So what's the trouble, then?"

Jamie shrugged. "Same shit as always."

They were both quiet for a bit. The tourists were out in force, and it was only Duff's unusual size that allowed them to pass through easily—people tended to part like the Red Sea for him. A few minutes later they stepped into the half-dark pub and found seats at the old polished wood bar. They ordered Jamie's ale and a Coke for Duff, then sandwiches, and the barkeep set their drinks in front of them.

Duff took a long swallow. "Ah, that hits the spot, doesn't it?"

"Yeah."

Duff turned to look at him. "Happy to see me, are you?"

"Shit. I'm sorry, cousin. My head is all fucked up about Summer Grace."

"Yeah, it is. You should do something about that."

"Like what?"

"Like tell her you love her and want to marry her and bear her children and all that crap."

Jamie laughed. "Get right to the point, why don't you? And no one's bearing children, and if they are, it sure as hell won't be me."

Children? With Summer Grace? He immediately shoved the thought to the back of his mind.

"Well, why not?" Duff asked. "No point in bullshitting you. Is there any point in you bullshitting her?"

"Maybe there is."

"Well, you'd better figure it the fuck out, cousin, because we have business to attend to."

Jamie ran a hand over his head. "Yeah. You're right. Don't worry—I'll keep the business end of things going."

"Damn right. I didn't move halfway across the world to have you slack off."

"You are one hard-ass motherfucker."

Duff grinned. "Yeah, I am." He downed the rest of his Coke and ordered another. "You going to tell me what you plan to do about the girl?" he demanded.

"Maybe after I figure it out myself."

"Take some advice from an old bastard who knows nothing about women—don't wait too long. Women only have so much patience, you know. Don't fuck it up the way I did with Bess."

"You shouldn't be so hard on yourself about that," Jamie started.

Duff arched one dark brow. "Oh no? I can't agree with you, cousin. But let's leave that argument for another day."

He shrugged. "No problem."

He'd leave Duff alone about why his ex-girlfriend had left him just over a year ago, but he couldn't leave himself alone about Summer Grace. He was afraid his cousin was right—that if he didn't figure out what the hell was up with him and what he wanted, the woman of his dreams would decide she'd waited long enough for him. And he was equally afraid—maybe more so—that if he told her how he felt and the relationship went any deeper, he'd end up losing her in some terrible way. There didn't seem to be any happy scenario when he turned it over in his head.

But Goddamn it, he loved her. And Duff was right—he shouldn't wait any longer. As he downed another long gulp of the cool ale he decided: he'd get his cousin settled into his apartment, then he'd go find Summer Grace and tell her.

His gut twisted, but he ordered himself to calm down. Control was everything—always had been—and this was no different. He needed to man up. And apparently he'd needed his giant of a cousin to remind him. He'd go to her tonight.

* * *

JAMIE HAD STOPPED by his place to take a quick shower, then left Duff there to sleep off his jet lag before heading over to Summer Grace's place in the Gentilly district.

He downshifted the Corvette as he turned off the busier street and into her quiet neighborhood. Pulling to the curb in front of her house, he got out, stretching his long legs, his hands shoved in the front pockets of his jeans. He had to pull in a long breath, blinking up at the sky, which had just gone dark. There were some clouds backlit by the moon and the stars, and the air was heavy and sweet with the tang of flowers. A typical New Orleans summer night. Except there was nothing typical about it—not in his lifetime. He was about to tell Summer Grace he loved her.

His stomach started to go tight but he forced himself to calm as he strode up the front steps and knocked on the door.

She opened it a few moments later, and even in her white denim shorts and her simple black cotton halter top she was so damn beautiful it took his breath away.

"Hey, Jamie." She smiled up at him, her long lashes shadowing her high cheekbones.

He took it all in—her corn silk hair bundled up in a messy bun, making him want to pull it all down and fist his hands in it. The soft pink blush of her mouth—a mouth that wanted to be kissed. Begged for it.

"Hey, sugar."

Stepping in, he blinked at her, letting his eyes adjust to the bright light in the entryway before grabbing her face in both hands, cupping her delicate jaw. He spent a few seconds simply breathing her in, his lips inches from hers, then he pulled her closer and heard her quiet gasp. And that just did him in. He went hot all over as he leaned in and kissed her, losing himself in the softness of her lips, the scent of her all around him. Kissing her again, he brought her up on her toes, and her tongue was warm and sweet as it tangled with his. When she moaned, he wrapped her up in his arms and lifted her, kissing her long and hard, until he felt her smiling against his lips.

He set her on her feet without letting her go. "What's that for, sugar?"

"Just happy to see you," she said, her blue eyes shining, brilliant.

"I'm happy to see you too, sugar. Want to walk with me in the garden? I want to be out in the air with you. I want to be under the stars."

She smiled and took his hand, leading him through the small house and out the back door. Madame curled around their legs as they moved onto the garden path. The scent of flowers was even stronger out here, mixed with the herbs Summer Grace grew. The magnolias were blooming and the fragrance of their creamy blossoms was pure heaven. He pulled her against his side, looping an arm around her slender shoulders, and felt her lean into him. She felt so damn good. Being with his girl out here beneath the night sky, the stars glowing in the heavens as if for them alone, felt damn good. Knowing she was his, knowing how he felt about her . . .

"So I got your text about Duff arriving. Did you get him all settled? I didn't think I'd see you tonight."

"He's just fine. I left him sleeping like a baby. But we can talk about him later, okay, sweetheart? Right now I just want to be with you. Let's take a walk around your pretty garden."

He slipped his arm down to take her hand, and she nodded,

a quizzical smile on her lovely face, but then her features relaxed and she leaned into him again as they moved slowly down the brick path. Madame crisscrossed her way back and forth in front of them like some sort of feline wraith in the dark, then finally wandered off to catch mice, or whatever mysterious things cats did in the night.

When they reached the back wall where the pair of magnolias grew, Jamie stopped and pulled Summer Grace into his arms. "Hey. Can you believe we've only been seeing each other for just under a month?"

"You've been counting the days?" she teased.

He turned her body into his, catching her gaze and catching her waist in his hands. "You know, recently I started to. I've started to think about a lot of things lately."

She rested her hands on his chest, which was as high as she could reach, but he didn't mind—he liked it. "Oh? Like what?"

"Like . . . like what would things have been like if we'd got ten together years ago?"

She laughed. "We'd probably have killed each other by now. I know I wasn't mature enough back then to conduct a relationship."

"Yeah, apparently me neither. But think about it. How many nights like this could we have had, you and me and Madame, maybe? How many times could we have hung out with Mick and Allie? You know, gone to dinner or camping."

"We haven't exactly done any of that, Jamie."

"No, because I've wanted you all to myself. And we've needed time to figure this all out before we brought other people into it. But we could. We will, I hope."

Her head tilted to one side as she asked, "Do you?"

"Yeah." Why did he find his voice going rough? "I do want that. Don't you?"

"Yes. But I'm the girl, so you're supposed to say it first."

He smiled down at her. "Then consider it said. There are a lot of things I want to do with you, and not all of them are sexual."

She smacked his chest playfully, laughing. "Now that I find hard to believe."

He caught her hand in his and held on tight. He said quietly, "I'm serious, Summer Grace."

Her face suddenly sobered. "What are you saying, Jamie?"

He wondered if she could hear his heart hammering, his pulse racing in his veins, causing a roar in his ears, inside his head.

"What I'm saying is that I want all kinds of things with you. I want to hang out with Mick and Allie. I want to get in my 'Vette and take a road trip, maybe go down to the Florida Keys and lounge on the beach. I want to go to the zoo with you."

"The zoo? I love the zoo."

He smiled. "I know."

"I'm kinda liking this scenario. What else?"

"I want us to talk to each other like we have a future together, and not just like we're making plans for the next time we'll see each other. I want us not to date or play with anyone else, and not just for health reasons. I want it to be about *us*, because we both want it. I want it to mean something. Because it already does." He grabbed her shoulders and leaned down so he could look into her face—he felt like he *had* to. "I want it all because I love you, Summer Grace."

"Oh, Jamie!" she said, and burst into tears.

"Wh—" His throat went tight with anxiety and he swallowed. "Sweetheart, what is it? Is it too soon to tell you that? Baby, what's wrong? Fuck. Forgive me. Maybe I should have waited. Just . . ." He'd never felt so lost in his life. "Just tell me what the problem is."

"The problem is nothing!" She sniffed, but she let the tears course down her flushed cheeks. "The problem is that I was going to tell you the same thing. Because I've been in love with you forever. And I really never thought I'd hear those words from you."

He kissed her, just pulled her in tight and crushed his mouth to hers. Then he pulled back, peering into her face to make sure this was real. That she was real. But she was—real enough that she grabbed his cheeks and demanded another kiss. When their lips broke apart they stayed there for several long moments, their foreheads pressed together until he realized something.

"Summer Grace. Do you love me?" he asked.

"Of course I love you. Seriously, Jamie?"

"Serious as a hand grenade."

She shook her head. "You are one dangerous man to mention a hand grenade in almost the same breath in which you tell me you love me for the first time."

"Well, to be accurate, it was actually in the same breath in which *you* told *me* you loved me for the first time."

"This is true."

"I do love to be right."

She laughed. "You're the second person who's said that to me this week. Wonder what it means?" Looping her arms around his waist, she buried her cheek against his chest.

He wrapped a hand up in her hair and held her there. "Maybe it means you hang out with unbelievable egomaniacs?"

"Probably," she said, her voice muffled. "Must be the masochist in me."

All he could do was shake his head. Then all he could do was kiss her, there in her little garden, under the dark Louisiana sky, with the stars shining down on them like coins of good fortune.

He felt that good fortune down to his bones. Which also kicked off the old tapes in his head that were trying to tell him the sky was falling. But for now his girl loved him. For now he had Summer Grace—in his arms, in his life. And he planned to spend the foreseeable future drinking that in, maybe even until he was whole again.

CHAPTER

Eleven

It had been seventeen days—not that Summer had been counting or anything—since Jamie told her he loved her, and she was still flying. Things had been more amazing than ever between them. The sex, the kink, and every simple and complicated moment in between. They'd been to the zoo and it had been one of the most romantic days they'd had together. And tonight they were having dinner with Mick, Allie and Duff before everyone headed to The Bastille for a special burlesque performance, followed by a night of play.

Before she'd met Jamie's hulking cousin, she might have thought it would be uncomfortable being at the club with him there, but despite his gruff exterior and his unarguably Dominant ways, she felt incredibly comfortable with Duff. She'd been bringing the guys lunch on her days off, and sometimes dinner at the end of the day while they worked on getting the new half of the shop pulled together, and she and Duff had had the opportunity to get to know each other. It seemed important, and he was coming to feel like a big brother to her.

Jamie was working harder than ever, but they still found ways to make every moment count. He was at her cozy little house almost every night, and she loved waking up in his arms in the morning. It was those quiet moments she loved most—when the sun was rising and the whole world was just coming alive. But tonight was going to be *fun*—their first big social night in a while.

They'd decided to meet at Muriel's, despite the fact that it was just off Jackson Square in the heart of the busy tourist district. But the food was some of the best Creole fare to be found in the city, and Allie and Summer were both in love with the décor: the exposed brick walls, the sheer curtains hanging from the high ceilings that divided the tables, even—or most especially—the Voodoo symbols all over the bathroom stall doors. It had such a New Orleans feel to it, and they'd all decided to brave the tourists packing the sidewalks in favor of a great meal in an environment that held such gritty charm.

The cab pulled up in front of the restaurant and she and Jamie got out. He held her hand as they crossed the narrow cobblestone street.

"You looking forward to this, sweetheart?"

"Yes, to everything—dinner with our friends, the food, then getting to The Bastille later."

"It's been too long," he said, smiling down at her, his green eyes gleaming in the lamplight.

"It has. I'm sure you'll manage to make that my fault."

"Of course I will. All the better to punish you with," he said, leaning in to steal a kiss. She loved the quiet threat in his voice—it always made her shiver.

"Ach, that's enough, you lovebirds," Duff said. He was waiting for them at the door to the restaurant.

"You're just jealous," Jamie said.

"I am at that," his cousin agreed before taking Summer in
one of his usual bear hugs. He let her go and stepped back. "But
maybe tonight my luck will change." He wiggled his dark brows,
making Summer laugh.

"You haven't had time to try your luck," she protested.

"True enough. And about time I took a night off to see if
your dungeon girls are to my liking."

"I'm absolutely certain they will be," Summer told him. "And
Allie and Mick will be able to introduce you around. Oh—and
I'm pretty sure Finn and Rosie will be at the club, too."

"All right, all right, enough cuddling with my girl," Jamie
said in mock irritation, pulling her gently away from Duff.

"What? I don't cuddle," Duff protested.

"Of course you don't, cousin. Come on—let's go see if Mick
and Allie are here yet," Jamie suggested.

They went inside and found their friends at a long table half-
hidden behind one of the sweeping chiffon drapes. It took a minute or two for everyone to say hello—Duff had already met Mick
on a few of his previous trips to New Orleans, and Allie's curiosity had gotten the better of her, so she'd dropped by the shop
the week before. It was a comfortable group, and they lingered
over their meal. As the men's discussion of vintage motorcycles
hit the second hour of the night, it left Allie to nudge Summer
about her relationship with Jamie.

"So, how are things with you two?"

Summer knew she was beaming. "Amazing."

"And?"

"And what?"

"Have you two talked about the future? Moving in together or anything?"

"I don't know. He's with me almost every night anyway. And he and Duff have the new business to think about. Anyway, we've only been seeing each other for a month and a half."

"You've known each other forever. That has to count for something, doesn't it?"

"Well, yeah. But the dating part, the being a couple part, is still relatively new."

Allie lowered her voice. "But there's a commitment, right? Since I've been traveling with Mick off and on the last few weeks we haven't really had a chance to talk, and I *have* to know." She grinned. "I'm sorry, hon, but Rosie and I have been *dying*. You've been so busy with him we haven't heard anything, and of course Mick isn't saying a damn thing, if he even knows. That 'bromance' pact of silence."

Summer couldn't help but smile. "Yes, there's commitment. We don't see anyone else, even play with anyone else, while we figure this thing out."

"It seems to me there isn't much to figure out. And I'm rarely wrong about these things."

"Jesus. What is it with everyone being right lately?"

Allie shrugged and tucked a small piece of bread in her mouth, chewing thoughtfully. "It is what it is, hon. And in this city, you'd do best not to ignore the signs."

Summer bit her lip. "Maybe. It can be a little scary if I think about it too much, though. Like I'll . . . jinx it or something."

Allie rubbed her hand over Summer's back. "Aw, I'm sorry, honey. I'll shut up now. Let's just enjoy our night out. I'm looking forward to the burlesque troupe they're having at the club tonight."

"Me, too," she agreed.

But her own words were sticking in her mind, making her roll and unroll the napkin in her hands beneath the table. She'd been ignoring the small fear in the back of her mind that she really could jinx the wonderful thing happening between her and Jamie. It was stupid, she knew, but she couldn't quite shake the thought. And the closer they got, the more there was to lose. Anytime she wasn't with him or staying too busy to think, the fear came creeping over her. Her only comfort in those times was going out to her garden and digging in the earth—and oddly, the aloof Madame had recently taken to curling up next to her on the sofa or the bed and letting Summer pet her. Stroking the old cat's fur was soothing, whether she was stressing or not. Not that she really needed to be soothed. Did she?

She gave herself a mental shake as she reached for Jamie's hand. He paused in his conversation to glance at her, to bring her hand to his lips and brush a kiss across her fingers.

Tonight was not the time to worry over silliness. Allie was right. They had a wonderful evening ahead, and she planned to enjoy every moment of it.

Just in case . . .

THE BASTILLE WAS busy when they arrived—everyone had come out for the burlesque show that was about to begin. Summer stood between Jamie and Duff, which always felt as if she had a pair of bodyguards with her. She had to admit she sort of loved it.

The lighting in the dungeon tonight was more red than amber, with a spotlight on the stage at the back of the main room. The music started, and from offstage came a saucy, rich alto voice singing "You Can Leave Your Hat On." The headliner strutted out in her gorgeous finery, followed by eight backup girls, and the performance began. There were cheers and whistles from the crowd, and Summer lost herself in the show as they sang and danced and peeled their way through four more sultry songs. When it was over Jamie grabbed her hand and their group found an empty social area with three couches. A few moments later they were joined by Finn—a towering blond Aussie who was as tall as Duff and even more packed with muscle—and Summer and Allie's friend Rosie, a dark-haired, heavily tattooed beauty. The guys set down their play bags—all of them black duffels— and she, Rosie and Allie sat down, followed by the men. She was discussing the burlesque performer's gorgeous costumes with the other girls when Duff let out a low whistle.

"That stunning bit is exactly my type," he said, nodding his chin.

They all followed the direction of his gaze to a lovely woman whose smooth caramel shoulders were bared above the black satin corset and tight black pencil skirt that showed off her curves. Her dark, curling hair was piled high on her head, and with her back to them, Summer could see the vertical line of heavy Tibetan script tattooed down the back of her neck and disappearing beneath the edge of her corset.

"I don't think so, cousin," Jamie said.

"What do you mean? Why not?"

"No way, Duff. That's Layla," Rosie said. "She's a Domme."

"So she thinks," he said.

"You'd be in trouble with her," Finn told him cheerfully. "Pure Top, and a wicked sadist, too. Never seen her bottom."

"There's a first time for everything," Duff responded, narrowing his gaze in Layla's direction.

Summer watched as Layla turned around and her gaze met Duff's. She stopped what she was doing and stood there for several moments, blinking. Then her features went hard as she crossed her arms over her chest defiantly, her green eyes blazing from across the room, and Duff grinned.

"Challenge accepted," he murmured.

Mick shook his head. "That won't be a challenge—it'll be a fucking battle."

"What is she, some raving bitch? I don't see that in her at all. Oh, she's hard enough on the outside, and I like it. But bitch? No."

"She's a sweetheart," Allie put in. "But being a female Dominant, some of the male Doms give her a pretty hard time. She's got her defenses up. Anyway, more than one good Dom has tried to get her to bottom for them, and it hasn't happened yet."

Summer nodded her agreement. "I like Layla—I've talked to her in the women's changing room a few times, but as sweet as she can be she has plenty of salt, too. I don't think I'd try it if I were you, Duff."

His grin spread, and from the corner of her eye Summer swore she saw Layla flinch. "Luckily you're not me, sweet Summer Grace. And lucky for Layla, too."

Jamie groaned. "Okay. But it's your funeral, cousin. Just don't come crying to me when she hands you your toys and tells you to go home."

"Ha! Not likely."

Mick shook his head once more. "All right, kids, I've had enough of your charming company. Now I need to take my girl and test out my new jute rope on her." He slipped an arm around Allie's waist and they got up.

Allie bent to give Rosie and Summer a quick hug, a happy smile on her lips. "I'll see you two later?"

"Of course," Rosie said. "Anyway, you have a tattoo appointment with me at Midnight Ink on Sunday."

Allie beamed. "I wouldn't forget—I'm so excited!"

"Tattoos later—right now my rope is calling," Mick said, and Allie took his offered hand.

"We're out, too," Finn said, pulling the tiny Rosie to her feet then throwing her over his shoulder. Rosie yelped and pounded on his back.

"Like a flea, my beautiful girl," Finn said, smacking her ass. "Apparently my girl here needs a little lesson in humility. 'Night, all."

As he carried her off Summer could hear her muttering, "Goddamn it, Finn. You and your fucking caveman act."

"Which you love," he said, smacking her ass again.

Rosie giggled as he carried her away.

"You'll be fine on your own?" Jamie asked his cousin.

"Sure I will be," Duff answered, his eye still on the beautiful Creole woman across the room, who was ignoring his glances, bent over her own toy bag.

"I'll order the coffin, just to make sure I'm prepared," Jamie said.

Duff chuckled. "You do that, cousin."

Jamie offered his hand to Summer, helping her to her feet, and immediately her stomach fluttered with anticipation.

They hadn't gone far when he yanked her into his side and whispered in her ear, "Time to see how much heat you can take, sweetheart."

"Wh . . . what?" she stammered.

"Hot wax, sugar. And it will be *very* hot. Extra hot for my extra-hot girl."

He kept his arm around her and his hand gripped her waist, his fingers digging in, making her feel owned. Making her head sink into subspace even as they maneuvered their way through the crowded club. And as her mind sank, her limbs going warm and loose, the people faded away and the world narrowed into a pinpoint bubble where only she and Jamie existed—them and the throbbing beat of the music, which was some dark, edgy metal with a hard drum line that reverberated in her belly, in the blood pounding through her veins. It was perfect for the mood Jamie had already set with those few frightening words—frightening in the best way possible.

He guided her into one of the hallways off the main play space, where she knew some of the club's theme rooms were. He paused in front of the open doorway to the medical room, and Summer shuddered as she looked in on the old dentist's chair, the padded table with the shining chrome stirrups, the white walls that seemed more intimidating than the sleek black and red walls found elsewhere at The Bastille.

"Hmm, fascinating, isn't it?" Jamie murmured. When she instinctively started to pull out of his grasp, to back away, he only held on tighter. Leaning in, he whispered, "Scary as hell, this room, huh, sweetheart?"

She swallowed. "Yes."

"You have nothing to worry about. I'm not taking you in there. But . . . never mind that first part—you still have *plenty* to worry about."

"Fuck, Jamie."

He only chuckled in answer as he led her past the dreaded medical room to the one next door, and they stepped inside. The walls were painted a deep red, which seemed oddly comforting and threatening all at the same time. There was a long table padded in red vinyl in the center of the room, and a heavily carved wooden table—probably an old Spanish piece—against one wall. A few red leather chairs and a double-wide lounge chair piled with pillows filled the space, and dim lamps glowed with a golden light from sconces on the walls.

Jamie left her in the middle of the room to set his toy bag on the wooden table. When he came back to her, he took her face in his hands and looked into her eyes, stroking her cheeks with his thumbs. As he'd had her do before, she focused on aligning her breath with his and he smiled in approval. And as that sense of utter connection kicked in, he moved in closer, until his forehead met hers. She breathed him in, exhaled, and felt her limbs go even weaker with exhilaration, anticipation. Love.

"Hey, baby," he said quietly, "you ready?"

"Yes. I'm ready."

"You love me?"

She smiled. "Oh, yes."

"Love you, too, my sugar girl."

When he kissed her, she sighed against his mouth as he opened hers with his soft, sleek tongue. He tasted of man and desire, and her body melted into his. He held her face more firmly, controlling the direction of the kiss, his fingers squeezing just hard enough to hurt. She loved it—every tiny signal of his authority over her. She loved that he could make her concerns and all the minutiae of the day disappear. And she loved the sensation of his lips on hers—so soft and sweet yet utterly commanding at the same time. How did he even manage that? But it had been that way with him from the very start.

Jamie.

Love you so much.

He let her go and stepped back. "Perfect that you're wearing what I told you to. Such a pretty dress. But let's not ruin it. Strip."

"Oh. I . . ."

He took one step toward her and pressed his fingers into the tender space below her collarbone, into the pressure point there. "Do it now, love," he said quietly.

She nodded, swallowed, realizing in some distant way that being a little afraid of him was a huge turn-on. Not knowing exactly what to expect, how much the hot wax would hurt, was a huge turn-on. The fact that all of this was happening with the man she loved was maybe the biggest turn on of all.

Oh, yes . . .

Pulling the straps of her little black lace dress down, she shimmied her way out of it. Jamie gave a nod of his chin and she handed the dress to him before slipping out of her lacy bra, then undoing the garters on her black garter belt and sliding the sheer black seamed stockings down her legs. She had to step out of her high black stilettos to get the stockings off. Picking up the shoes, she silently handed them along with her bra and stockings to Jamie, who watched her with a sharp gleam in his green eyes. The barbell piercing his eyebrow glittered wickedly in the low lighting. Why did his piercings, his tattoos, make him seem all the more devilishly sexy when these things never had the same effect on her with any other man? But his demeanor and knowing what was coming were making her wet.

She was brought back into the moment by Jamie reaching out and pinching her nipple, hard.

"Oh!"

"Where were you, baby?"

"Right here, Jamie. I promise."

"See that you are," he warned.

She nodded, then got out of her garter belt and black lace thong. It felt so good to be naked—the vulnerability of it always took her down to another level of subspace when they were in-scene.

"Don't move, my girl," he said before turning to carefully

fold each article of her scant clothing and setting the small pile on the long wooden table, leaving her to shiver as an exquisite anticipation spiraled in her.

With his back still to her, he began to pull chains from his bag, and the primal clink of metal on metal made her nipples go hard, made her skin itch to feel them on her body. He worked slowly, making it pure torture to watch him. To wait. She took a deep breath and tried to calm her racing pulse as she reminded herself that everything he did was part of the beautiful mind-fuck they both loved.

Finally he turned back to her and moved in closer. He smoothed his palm over the small of her back, and even that simple touch made her tremble with need.

"This is how it's going to come down, sugar. I'm going to lay you out on this vinyl table and cuff your wrists and ankles to the chains, which will be attached to the table by the steel bars on the sides. They're incredibly strong, so no matter how you squirm you can't get away. No matter how bad the pain gets, the only thing that gets you out is using one of your safewords. Tell me you understand."

"I understand, Jamie."

"Tell me your safewords. I want them foremost in your mind before we get started."

Oh God. How bad was this going to hurt? But she *wanted* it to. Wanted to do this for *him*. Wanted the pain, to test her limits. Her mind was buzzing.

"Yellow if I need to pause or to change toys, which I have a feeling is not an option tonight—"

"It's not."

She nodded. "Red if I need to stop the scene completely."

"Good girl. Hands clasped behind your back."

Good girl.

Her legs went weak as she did as he asked.

Jamie kissed her cheek, her temple, his hands going to her shoulders, sliding down to cup her breasts, then gripping until she groaned. He moved his hands lower, over her buttocks, squeezing and kneading, harder and harder, finding the pressure points. When she came up on her toes to get away from the pain, he smiled.

"Your skin is so hot under my hands," he said. "This is going to be so good. Come here."

Lifting her, he set her on the edge of the vinyl table. She had one moment to realize how cool the red vinyl was against her naked thighs, her burning naked sex, then he kicked her legs apart, stepped between them and thrust his fingers inside her.

"Ah!"

She reached for his broad shoulders to steady herself.

"That's it, sugar. You love it when I fuck you, whether it's with my cock or my hand, don't you?" His voice was rough with desire. "You are so damn wet. Fucking beautiful. Makes me so hard." He pumped his fingers into her, deeper, faster.

"Ah, God . . ."

"Yeah, that's it, baby."

He thrust hard into her pussy, over and over. She grew wetter and wetter as pleasure poured into her system, until she was soaking his hand and the table beneath her. Until she was moaning and panting, ready to come.

"Ah-ah. Not yet." He pulled his fingers from her swollen and needy sex and pressed her down onto the table on her back.

She started to fold her thighs together, unable to help herself, but he forced her legs apart with strong hands. Leaning over her he ordered, "Eyes on me, Summer Grace."

As she looked up at him, the only thoughts in her head were how beautiful he was and how badly she needed to come. How much more she needed to please him. *Needed* to.

"You know I see your desire, that everything I do is to make it good for you. And I think this is going to be so good for you. The wax is going to be hot. It's going to feel like it's burning your skin, but I will not let you walk away with blisters. The point is always to hurt, but not harm. You know I believe in that. Do you trust me?"

The answer came easily. "Of course I do. I trust you."

He kept his gaze on hers, his eyes brilliant, letting her know how deeply immersed he was in Topspace. He bent and brushed a kiss across her lips, then over her cheek, whispering, "Love you, my sugar girl. You are infinitely precious to me. I would never harm you. Never. But I'm going to hurt you now because we both love it so much. Because it'll make you fly so high. It'll make me fly, in my own way. The pain always brings us closer, and I can't seem to get close enough to you." He paused, stroking her hair. "Stay here now, love. Stay still and wait."

She smiled as he straightened up and reached behind him, coming back with a length of chain with one of the leather cuffs already clipped to one end. He attached the chain to the table, then he took one of her ankles in his hands and buckled the cuff around it.

"Comfortable?"

"Yes, Jamie."

"Not cutting off your circulation?"

"No, Jamie."

He did the same to the other ankle, leaving her legs spread wide. She loved how it made her feel. Wanton. *His.*

Standing at the foot of the table, he watched her. "You'll find that I've left a little slack in the chains. I love the sound they make when you pull against them." He paused, his gaze roving over her face, her body. "So, so pretty. All of you. And your pussy is beautiful right now, so pink and wet I can't stand it."

To her surprise he bent over her and placed a kiss there, right on her aching clit, making heat pound like a hammer of pure desire, bringing her pleasure even as it tortured her. He stood up and licked his lips.

"Like honey. Like sugar, my sweet girl."

Tracing the lines of her body with his fingertips, keeping contact as he moved around the table attaching the chains, he placed her wrists in the cuffs and secured them, then checked in with her again.

"Still good? Circulation okay?"

"Yes. Still good."

He stepped back to survey his handiwork, and as she watched him through the glaze of subspace, he unbuttoned his dark shirt and took it off. A frisson of heat trembled through her system, between her thighs, at his stark male beauty. She pulled a little against her bonds, writhing on the table, hearing the metallic clink of the chains. And she loved the sound, maybe because he did.

Need him to touch me.

But he turned away from her to pull a few items from his bag—two tall pillar candles in glass containers, a long fireplace lighter, his first-aid kit, the big hunting knife he'd carried since he was a teenager. He laid it all out on the table, lit the candles, and she breathed in the scent of warming wax, the earthy scent of the burning wick. She felt her muscles tensing a little—there was no denying she was nervous. She knew some people used less potent candles in sensual play and massage, but this was Jamie, and although he was always sensual, he was also always a sadist.

He played with the candles for several minutes, letting the wax melt and pool. When he turned back to her with one of the candles in his hand, she had some idea of what was coming. Her pulse tripped, revved up a few notches.

He laid the palm of one hand flat on her stomach. "Hold very still," he warned her before he poured.

The wax landed on one thigh, and at first the shock of the heat made her yelp. Then for a second or two she thought it wasn't as hot as she expected. But when he poured again in the same spot, the second pour sealing in the heat of the first, the pain was like a simmering buildup that took a few seconds to hit her brain.

"Ah, fucking Christ!"

"Breathe," he commanded, and she pulled in a gasping breath.

He gave her a minute, then he poured again, this time on the other thigh. The wax had obviously had time to build in temperature, because the burn came right away, and she cried out.

"God, Jamie!" The chains clinked and crashed as she yanked on them, her body convulsing in pain.

He stroked a hand over her skin, his touch soothing, helping her to convert the pain to pleasure. "Shh, you'll be okay. You can take it, Summer Grace."

She bit her lip, then made herself pull in and blow out a few breaths.

"Okay?"

"Yes. Okay. I want to take it. For you, Jamie."

"Good girl."

This time he moved his hand between her breasts and poured onto her stomach and she yelled again.

"Fuck!"

"Breathe," he told her, his hand smoothing over her breasts, caressing them, pausing to feather his fingertips over her nipples, bringing some pleasure to help her ride out the pain. She sighed.

"Summer Grace."

Blinking, she looked up at him, and he held her gaze while he played with her nipple, teasing it into a hard point. Still holding her gaze, he drew his hand back to pour the melted wax over her breasts.

"Ah! Jamie . . . Goddamn it, that hurts!"

With a small smile he bent to kiss her lips. "Yes it does, sweetheart."

It did—it hurt like hell. But at the same time her body was being flooded with endorphins and dopamine—the lovely brain chemicals that made her fly. That and the fact that he called her those sweet pet names while he hurt her really did something to her head.

He did it again and again and she lost track of time, of their surroundings. All that she was had to do with Jamie's touch, the burning pain, the sound of her own cries in her ears. And all of it while he stayed close enough that she could smell his skin, his desire. All of it while her body burned with a need so intense she thought she might come as he poured the wax onto her skin.

Impossible.

But nothing was impossible with Jamie.

She flew, safe in his command, under his hands, in his love. And it was *everything*.

JAMIE PRESSED DOWN on Summer Grace's skin, the heat beneath his palm melting into his skin. For some reason he couldn't quite understand, he welcomed the pain. Welcomed that moment of connecting with what *she* was feeling.

He glanced up at her face, so lovely and soft. So lost in subspace. So entirely *his*.

She was squirming on the table, pulling a little on the chains as her body undulated He was certain she had no idea what she was doing. No idea how unbelievably beautiful she was. How hot it was for him to watch her moan and squirm, to hear the metallic clink of the heavy chains, to see her bound in them.

He licked his lips as he slipped a hand between her spread thighs. She was soaked, swollen. When he stroked her hard clit, she gasped. His cock twitched. He pushed his fingers inside her, and she was so hot and wet it nearly sent him over the edge. He stripped his jeans off, kicked his way out of them and his boots, grabbing a condom from the table before climbing onto the table on top of her.

She looked up at him with that sensual, gleaming blue gaze as he knelt up between her spread legs to slide the condom over his hard cock.

"Have to be inside you, baby," he murmured, hearing the desperation in his own voice.

"Yes. Please, Jamie. Yes."

As he slid his hands under her buttocks, lifting her, opening her up, she bit her lip, her fingers wrapping around the chains that still held her to the table. He shifted, pulled her hips a little higher, and surged slowly into her.

"Ah, Jesus."

She was so wet and tight and clenching his cock already. Pleasure went through him in a rush that made him dizzy. Keeping one hand under her, he stroked her body with the other, finding her skin in between the patches of wax hardening on her stomach and ribs. He began to move inside her, and raised his hand to her face, which was torn with pleasure. Touching her lips he ordered, "Suck," and slipped two fingers into her mouth.

Wrapping her lips around his fingers, her tongue slid over the lips, in between them. She worked them as she would his cock, and he had to force himself to calm, to not explode inside her. He began to fuck her in rhythm with her warm, sucking mouth, losing himself in the cadence, in her body, in her utter submission to him.

Summer Grace.

"You are mine, my sugar girl. My girl. My heart," he muttered, gasping in between the words that didn't do enough to convey what he felt.

She moaned around his fingers to tell him, "I'm going to come. Please, Jamie. I need to . . . Please."

"Yes. Come for me. I'm gonna come, too. Now . . . Right now. Ah!"

He fell on top of her as his climax came down on him like a wave of heat and need that drowned him in sensation. He grasped the chains above her head, felt her fingers searching for his and twined their hands together as she shuddered, as she came with him.

"Baby, baby, baby . . ."

"Jamie. Love you, Jamie."

He drew in a long breath, breathing it all in—the scents of desire and candle wax, their intermingled sweat and come. The scent of her hair and what was left of her sugary lip gloss. And he *had* to kiss her, to drink her in. To drink in this moment. He pressed his lips to hers, heard her small sigh, felt her body give in to his once more. And it was perfect. *They* were perfect.

CHAPTER

Twelve

SUMMER TURNED ONTO the main boulevard and headed toward home. The city was quiet on a Sunday night, and she considered stopping for groceries but decided she could do her shopping tomorrow night after work. She wanted to stay in her head, exactly in this lovely space where Jamie had put her. Her cell phone lit up, but she saw it was her mother's number, and let the call go to voice mail. She wasn't ready to tell her about Jamie, about their budding relationship. And she didn't want anything to intrude on her mood.

Their weekend together had been incredible. Being with all their friends made her feel more like a couple somehow. And then their night at The Bastille . . . She was still flying from the wax play, and even more from the amazing connection she'd felt that night, and still felt. The weekend had stripped away the nagging voice full of doubts that always seemed to be lurking in the back of her mind, waiting to come out and take over. But Jamie's love, his tenderness after they played and even during the play, wiped out everything else. If only they could be together all the time those voices might not ever come back.

A small shadow of self-doubt flitted through her mind, but she fought it down.

"No," she murmured to herself. "Everything is fine. We're together. He's not going anywhere."

She made another turn into her neighborhood and the lights and buzz of the city gave way to the quiet Gentilly district. She passed the rows of old homes, some of them still closed up or showing signs of damage from Katrina, many more restored to their former glory. She was glad to see her neighborhood coming back to life, blossoming in the wake of the terrible storm. She felt somewhat the same inside.

Jamie was making her blossom in a way she'd never been sure was possible. The idea made her smile to herself as she pulled into her narrow driveway. Getting out of the car, she grabbed her purse and her overnight bag. She went up the stairs and unlocked the front door, eager to get inside, to get things ready for work in the morning so she could climb into bed, close her eyes and remember every detail from the weekend.

She shut the door behind her, pulled her cell phone from her purse and, dropping her bags on the floor, she texted Jamie.

I'm home safe and sound!

Good girl. Glad you made it home. Get some good rest, baby. Love you so much. Call me if you need me.

Love you, Jamie.

Her body warmed all over. Even in text she could *feel* him. With a smile on her face she walked through the house, turning on lights as she went, heading to the kitchen to make some tea. She flipped on the lights—and stopped.

No!

Madame lay on the kitchen floor, her fluffy white side sunken in, her legs stiff, her blue eyes wide.

She felt as if she couldn't breathe as she sank to the floor. Reaching out, she touched the cat, knowing she wouldn't feel anything but death. When she finally managed to catch her breath, she smelled it in the room.

"No!" she wailed, her fingers clenching and unclenching in the still-soft fur. "No, Madame. Please don't . . ."

She stumbled to her feet, ran into the living room and came back with a throw blanket, laid it carefully over the cat's body as tears poured down her cheeks. Her mind was going blank. She couldn't think of anything but the tearing ache of loss in her chest.

Closing her eyes, she held on to the counter for support, whispering, "Please no. No more death. No more, no more."

Unwanted visions of Brandon flashed through her mind. She remembered her last day with him. The fight they'd had that she'd never told anyone about, not even Dennie. She'd tried to sneak into the house after a night out partying with her friends and found Brandon waiting for her at the kitchen table, looking tired and annoyed.

"Summer Grace, what do you think you're doing creeping into the house at six o'clock in the morning?"

"You're not my father, Brandon."

"No, but I am your brother, and this is not okay. You're not even seventeen years old yet! You can't have everything your way, Summer Grace, just because that's how you want it. What the hell were you doing all night?"

"*Nothing that's any of your Goddamn business!*"

"*Keep your voice down. Do you want to wake up Mom and Dad?*"

"*What's wrong, Brandon? You don't want the scolding father role taken away from you? Well, I'm not your kid. I'm not your responsibility. So get over yourself.*"

She'd marched upstairs, leaving a fuming Brandon behind, knowing she'd disappointed him. Knowing he cared as much as their parents did, maybe more. Tears had stung her eyes—tears of guilt and wounded pride. What a fool she'd been. And so careless of her brother's feelings. So careless . . .

Fuck.

Her eyes flew open. Had she forgotten to leave food for Madame? She ran to the back door, but there was plenty of food and water in the cat's dishes. She turned to glance over at the blanket-covered body on her kitchen floor, but had to look away.

Pressing her fists against her eyes, she begged, "Please, Madame. Please, please don't be dead."

Hadn't she said the very same words when Brandon died? Hadn't she begged him to come back to her? For months. But he never had. Her parents hadn't, either. Even Jamie had abandoned her. They all had. They'd left her alone and she hadn't known how to handle the world—the entire big, fucking scary world at sixteen years old! She'd felt . . . orphaned. Lost. And she damn well wasn't going through this again. First it was Brandon, now it was Madame, then it could be . . . What?

She couldn't stand to think of it. Couldn't stand to look at Madame's body on the floor. She was dead and there was nothing she could do about it. Death was so damn final. But it was just as final when someone chose to turn away from you and broke your heart.

Brandon.

Her parents.

Jamie.

Madame.

Jamie!

"Oh no," she moaned.

She was so, so cold. She wrapped her arms around her chilled body, but she couldn't seem to get warm. And the tears were coming faster than she could wipe them away.

This was the universe warning her. She was not going to be allowed to keep anything. Anyone.

Jamie.

"You can't have everything your way, Summer Grace . . . "

Brandon.

Somehow she managed to find her way to the front hall, to dig her phone out of her purse, to dial.

"Den? Something's happened." She had to stop as another sob caught in her throat, choking her. "I need you. Please come."

"Oh, honey, what is it? No, never mind—I'll be right there. You just hang on, you hear me? I'll be right there."

It wasn't until she hung up that she realized she was on the floor, but there was nothing she could do about it. She was drowning in helplessness. Powerlessness. All she could do was wait in this house filled with death. God, it was all too familiar, the quiet of it.

The house was so quiet after the funeral, even though her mother and father and her grandparents were there. No one was saying anything. No one asked her if she was okay, if she needed anything. No one offered to read her to sleep, or to make her hot chocolate, and she knew at that moment that part of her life was gone forever, and she was on her own. On her own except for Dennie, and thank God for her.

"She's coming. She's coming," she whispered to herself, wiping uselessly at her wet cheeks. She pulled her knees to her chest, wrapping her arms around her legs and bowing her head as if she could hide from the world. "Please hurry . . . please."

MONDAY MORNING JAMIE was just opening up the shop when his phone rang. He juggled his coffee in one hand, tossed his leather jacket over the back of the office chair with the other before pulling his cell from the pocket of his jeans.

"Hello?"

"Jamie?"

"Dennie? What's up?" His stomach dropped. Why did he know already something terrible had happened?

Death magnet.

Fuck!

"Is it . . . is it Summer Grace? Is she okay? What's wrong? Tell me."

"She's okay. I mean, she's not okay or I wouldn't be calling. She hasn't been in an accident or anything. She's not sick. But listen, Jamie, she's not in great shape, my poor girl, and she asked me not to call you, but I thought . . . I thought I should. I thought you should know."

"Know what? What's going on?"

He heard Dennie blow out a breath on the other end. "She found Madame dead last night—her cat. And she just . . ." She paused, lowered her voice. ". . . she freaked out. I mean total meltdown. She's been at my house since last night crying like the world has ended, and I can't get her to stop. She hasn't slept. Well, neither have I. I won't leave her like this. My grandmother has been helping me sit with her, but we don't know what else to do."

Jamie ran a hand over his hair. "Wait. Her *cat* died? Is that what you're telling me?"

"I know it doesn't make much sense on the surface . . ."

"I don't know. It does and it doesn't. What is she doing now?"

"Still crying. I really think you should come."

"I do, too. I'll be right there. Let me call Duff and see how soon he can get here to cover me."

"Thanks, Jamie."

Ten excruciating minutes later he was in the truck on his way to Dennie's house out in Lakeview. He cursed at the morning commute traffic, his fingers tight on the wheel. On the inside he felt like he could easily burst open—like some torrent of anger and grief would come pouring out. He swallowed it down like bile.

Finally he pulled up in front of Dennie and Annalee's house. He cut the engine and jumped out, stalked up to the door, knocked and waited. Shifting from one foot to the other, he tried not to let this feel like the end of something.

Dennie came and opened the door, and he pulled the screen door wide and stepped into the dim hallway.

"She's in the back bedroom," Dennie said, keeping her voice down. "Come on."

He followed her through the quiet house and through a doorway at the end of the hall. It was dark in the room, with just a small glow of sunshine coming through the drawn curtains, but he could vaguely make out a shape under the pile of quilts in the old high bed.

"Summer Grace?"

"No. No, no, no." Her voice was rusty, as if it hadn't been used in a long while. Or as if she'd been crying all night.

His chest went tight.

He moved closer, sat on the edge of the bed and laid a hand on her shoulder. "Hey," he said gently. "You okay, baby?"

There were several long, quiet moments, then a hard, wrenching sob.

"Ah, it'll be okay," he soothed. "Whatever it is, it'll be okay."

Suddenly she sat up, her hair disheveled, and even in the faint light he could see how red and swollen her eyes were. "No, it will not be okay. It has never been okay. Not *ever*! I've been stuffing it down for too damn long, but that's the reality of it. And God, Den, I told you not to call him. How could you?"

The last came out on a small sob, and his heart broke a little to see her like this. To have some idea of what she was feeling. And to know that some of it, at least, was his fault.

He reached out to stroke her wild hair from her cheek, but she waved his hand away. "Don't. I can't stand it—the sympathy. Don't you think I know how fucked up this is? How fucked up *I* am?" She sniffed, wiped her nose on her sleeve. Muttered, "I didn't even like that cat very much."

"Come on, sweetheart. No one liked that cat much. And we both know this is about more than just the cat."

"Of course it fucking is!" Her eyes were blazing. "It always has been. I thought I'd learned the lesson well: everyone leaves, one way or another. *Everyone*. Even you."

"Summer Grace, I'm right here."

She closed her eyes, bit her lip. "For now. But I've just had another lesson in impermanence. I don't think I can stand one more. And fuck it all, I don't want you to see me like this. Please go."

"I can't leave you like this."

Her eyes flew open. "Just go!" she yelled, then collapsed into tears.

Dennie rushed to her and wrapped her in her arms. Looking up at Jamie, Dennie whispered. "Go, Jamie."

He got up, feeling shell-shocked. He took a step back, watching Summer Grace, *his* Summer Grace, sob while Dennie held her. And felt as if the world had been pulled out from under his feet.

He turned and left the room, left the house, got into his truck and drove off.

HE'D BEEN BACK at the shop for most of the day. Duff had looked at him questioningly when he arrived, but instead of asking questions his cousin had just given him a fond slap on the back and gone next door to keep an eye on the crew doing the build-out.

Since then Jamie had spent a lot of time staring at the computer screen, fielded a few phone calls, but none of it had stuck in his brain. It felt as if his brain *were* stuck, worrying, wondering if Summer Grace was okay. If there was something more he could do. If he could only get her to *talk* to him.

He knew that Madame's sudden death was bringing her old loss issues up and shoving them right in her face—that much was obvious. But why was it taking such a toll on her? Had she never really dealt with losing her brother? She'd seemed okay all these years. Stronger than most. But maybe she'd simply held it all inside, covering it up with the tough-girl act.

That had to be it. Which meant that, given time, she'd get through this. But did he give her the space she'd asked for, or did he step in and *make* her let him help?

He got to his feet, muttered, "God fucking damn it, I've never backed down from a challenge before."

"What's that, cousin?" Duff asked, coming through the office door.

"Duff, there are times in life when you just have to go after what you want."

"Agreed. That's why I'm here. I was about to go over the architectural plans for the two big truck bays, but I see you have other things on your mind. I'll mull it over myself. You need to go to your girl, I imagine?"

Jamie nodded.

"I'll hold down the fort. Shop closes at seven anyway."

"Good. Thanks."

Duff shrugged. No problem." He moved past Jamie and sat in his chair, stared at the computer and pulled up the web browser. "Can I get porn on this thing, cousin?"

Jamie shook his head, almost cracking a smile. "Get whatever you want, cousin. That's . . . I think that's the point today, maybe."

Duff turned with a raised brow but didn't say anything as Jamie grabbed his keys and left.

It seemed to take forever to get back over to Dennie and Annalee's house, but soon he parked in front of their pretty white and yellow clapboard. He jumped out and tried to steady his pulse as he moved up the front steps. Before he even reached the door Dennie's grandmother Annalee opened it. The woman was tiny, with snowy white hair and piercing turquoise eyes. It had been years since he last saw her, but even though there were a few more lines on her face, she still exuded that classic Southern woman thing—grace and charm yet tough as nails. Warm but formidable. He'd always liked her.

"My apologies, Mrs. Harper, but I'm here to see Summer Grace. Whether she wants to see me or not."

Annalee opened the screen door and gestured for him to come in. As he stepped into the house, she stopped him with a surprisingly strong grip on his arm.

"You talk to our girl, y'hear me, Jamie Stewart-Greer? You make her see that death is just the way of the world and something we all have to cope with. Because the shape she's in now is the only other option, and that's not a life. You make her *want* a life, y'hear me, son?"

He swallowed past the lump in his throat. "I am sure gonna try, Ms. Annalee."

Annalee patted his arm. "That's a good boy." He didn't even flinch at the title. "Now you get me my red hat out of the hall closet so I can get to my dinner meet-up. I'll be in my car. You tell my granddaughter to come with me."

He nodded, opening the closet and reaching in to retrieve the requested red hat. He would have been grinning like mad if this had been any other day, if he were there with any other purpose. Annalee Harper was one sassy lady.

"Here you go, ma'am."

She smiled and gave him one last pat on the arm before she took the offered hat and walked out the door.

He stood for several moments, trying to get his thoughts in order. He'd come racing over here on a mission, but Annalee's words stuck in his head, making him realize how important this was. He shook his hands out before walking down to the end of the hall.

The room was still dark. Dennie was sitting in a kitchen chair pulled close to the bed, trying to get Summer Grace to drink some tea.

"Come on, honey. You haven't had anything but a little water since you got here."

Summer Grace rolled over in the bed and turned her back to her friend. Jamie took a step into the room, and Dennie looked up when one of the old floorboards squeaked under his booted foot.

"Oh. You're here."

"Your grandmother asked me to tell you you're going to her dinner meeting with her."

"Her Red Hat Society? Right—it's Monday."

"Sounds like she meant it, Dennie."

Dennie stood, pushing the cup of tea into his hands. "Okay, then. Guess I'm going. I guess . . ."

She gave him a sharp scowl before moving past him to leave.

"You Harper women are no joke."

"No, we sure aren't," Dennie called over her shoulder as she retreated down the hall. "See you don't forget that, Jamie."

He nodded, understanding the unspoken warning to take care of Summer Grace—not that he intended to do anything else.

He stepped farther into the room. "Sweetheart, I know you're awake and know I'm here. Turn over and talk to me."

"Don't you dare try to pull your Dom stuff on me right now, Jamie," she muttered from under the heavy patchwork quilt that covered her from head to toe.

He moved closer and set the tea mug down on the small night table. "Damn it, Summer Grace." He paused, making an effort to keep his voice low. "This has nothing to do with kink. There are no roles right now. This is just you and me, and I love you. Let me help."

She rolled over and pulled the quilt off her face to glare at him, but in moments her face crumbled and, his heart twisting, he rushed to take her in his arms, a little surprised when she let him. She was crying, long, wrenching sobs, and he held her tighter—held her as tight as he could. It was a long while before she pushed away.

"Okay. I need to stop." She hiccupped, wiped at her face with her sleeves, then with her hands. "I can't do this, Jamie."

"Can't do what?"

She waved her hands. "This! All of this. Me falling apart and you coming to my rescue like I'm some broken doll. I *hate* this. I hate that you're seeing this. I hate that you're here now because it drives home even more that you won't always be."

"What? What do you mean?"

She pushed her tangled hair from her face and looked at him directly for the first time that day. Her voice was harder than he'd ever heard it. "Jamie. You left me, too, you know. Left me all alone when I lost Brandon, and then my family fell apart. You were gone. *Gone.* I chose to overlook that somehow, because I was too used to being enamored of you. But I see it now. I remember. So much for you being obsessed with carrying out Brandon's dying wish."

He felt like he'd been slammed in the chest with a sledgehammer. "Fuck, Summer Grace," he said quietly. "Really? That was years ago. I was a sad, fucked-up kid myself. And now . . . now you're going to hold that against me? To let it make up how you see me? I thought things were so amazing between us lately." Anger was welling up in his chest, making his pulse throb hot in his veins, making his head ache. "You said you trusted me— how many times did you tell me that? But how much trust do you really have in me?"

"As much as I'm capable of, given that I lose everyone. Everything."

He shook his head, his fists clenching at his sides. But when the tears slid down her cheeks unchecked, the anger drained away. This was the woman he loved. The woman whose entire history he knew—a history he shared. His shoulders fell as he swept her into his embrace. She fought him, squirming and pounding on his shoulders, his back, but he let it happen. He held her safe until she calmed down. There was more crying, but he knew she needed it. Finally he pulled back and helped her wipe her face with the soggy edge of the sheet.

"Baby. You've held so much in all this time. I know it's because you've had to," he told her. "And I know I could have been there for you, that I could have helped you get through it all. I thought I was the broken one—so damn broken I wasn't good enough for you. And ultimately I held back with you because of that stupid crap in my head about being a death magnet—"

"Maybe I'm the death magnet, Jamie. First Brandon. Now Madame."

"She was a *cat*. And she was old. And two losses in a lifetime don't make you a death magnet."

Summer Grace shook her head. "And three make you one? But Brandon . . . Jamie, I have to tell you . . ." She stopped, visibly swallowed a sob, but it was still in her voice when she continued. "We had a fight that morning. I was so selfish. So immature. I was totally in the wrong, and I was such a bitch to him when he was only looking out for me. That was the last conversation we had. And maybe if he wasn't so pissed at me, so annoyed with me, or fuck, *hurt* by me, he would have seen that car coming." She shook her head again, her gaze on her hands twisting the edge of the quilt. "It really wasn't you who had some fault in Brandon dying. It was me."

His heart broke a little at her words. At her self-condemnation. He knew that feeling too well.

"No, sweetheart. No, it wasn't either of us. Just hearing you say that out loud makes me see it wasn't me or you or *anything else*, and how mistaken I've been all this time in thinking it could have been my fault—Brandon or Ian or Traci losing the baby. It's just the way the fucked-up world happens sometimes. But, Summer Grace . . ." He reached out and stroked her cheek and she looked up at him. He saw the remnants of tears glistening on the tips of her long lashes. "Sweetheart. I am so damn sorry. I should never have left you alone to deal with the whole mess. Maybe if I'd been there for you, if I hadn't been so damn . . . afraid of myself, and what I thought I was, I would have been able to protect you from some of it—the pain and the loneliness and that sense of being lost. From all the times your life broke, then broke again. And I am more sorry than I can say that some of the times things broke it was because of *me*. But I let you down because I was too wrapped up in my own shit. And that wasn't just when we were younger. It was right up until I saw you at The Bastille the first time. Not because you were there, or playing with someone else. But because it made me see myself through your eyes, and I wasn't too happy with what I saw. I was the guy who disappointed you, who let you down. But when I saw you that night, I was also the guy who was done doing that."

She was blinking fast, but not so fast that he didn't see another tear escaping from her eye.

He wiped it with his thumb. "Don't cry anymore. Come on, sweetheart. I'm trying to apologize."

"I know you are. Just give me a minute to pull myself together and absorb everything."

"Jesus on a cracker, you two." Dennie stepped into the room.

"I thought you went with Annalee to her dinner," Jamie said.

"Oh, we've been hanging out until we were sure Summer was okay. And I see she is. So now we're really leaving—and leaving you two to work it out. But first I want to say this: I have never seen two people more in love. I'd kill to have what you have. Don't fuck it up, okay?"

"I love you, Den," Summer Grace said.

"I know you do, honeypie." She turned and left the room, and they both held their breath until they heard the front door slam shut and the distant rumble of Annalee's Cadillac.

Jamie stroked her hair, her cheek. He wanted to kiss her so badly, but he sensed they had more talking to do. That *she* had more to say. "Okay. Talk to me, baby. What do you need to tell me about what's happened?"

She shrugged, but he could see she was turning ideas over in her mind. She bit her lip, opened her mouth to speak, then paused for several moments. Finally she started.

"When Brandon died it was . . . like the end of the world to me. He was my big brother. I worshipped him. My entire world revolved around him, maybe even my crush on you in the beginning."

"What did Brandon have to do with a teenage girl's crush on me?"

"You were the sun Brandon revolved around, Jamie, just like I revolved around him."

He shook his head, ran a hand over his stubbled scalp. "No. There's never been anything remotely sunshiny about me. Brandon was the one with the sunshine. Our whole group revolved around him. That's why it hit everyone so hard when we lost him."

She reached out and took his hand. "But not like it hit us—you and me. They were all hurt by it. We were both . . . destroyed by it."

"You know," he started, his tone low and soft, "I never knew how affected you were by Brandon dying. I thought maybe you were too young to really get it, but now I know better. You hid it so well."

"I had to. My parents were so messed up. I felt everything falling apart. I needed to be the one who held it together." Tears welled, and she let them pool in her eyes. "But I couldn't do it, Jamie. I feel like . . . I failed. My family broke apart. Shattered into a million pieces, like some puzzle I couldn't put back together. And I broke. I broke and you were too broken by it for me to lean on you."

"But fuck, Summer Grace—that was my job. You should have told me how bad things were."

"There were times I wanted to, but you weren't really around after a while. You got married and I couldn't talk to you then. Impossible. Because I loved you even back then, when I was sixteen years old. People say a teenager knows nothing about love, but I did. I knew." She looked up, caught his gaze with hers. "I *knew*, Jamie. I still know."

His throat was so tight with emotion he could barely get the words out. "Summer Grace. Goddamn it, I love you so much."

He moved in to kiss her and she turned away with a sharp laugh. "I love you, too, but Jesus, Jamie—you can't kiss me when I look like this."

He grabbed her face in his hands, forcing her to look at him. "I can and I will. I want to. I want to kiss you all the time. I don't fucking care if you've been sobbing for twenty-four hours straight, except that I never want that to happen again."

He looked into her swollen eyes—they were the same corn-flower blue. His girl's eyes. He smiled at her for a moment before he moved in and kissed her. There was a small hiccup from her, then she gave in, her mouth going loose under his. Her arms twined around his neck and he pulled her closer, held her tight until he could really feel her, heartbeat to heartbeat.

He pulled back to ask, "Okay. What else are you mad at me about? Let's get it all out of the way right now—get it over with."

"I don't think I'm mad anymore. At myself, maybe, but that's just going to take some time. I should have faced this stuff years ago—or at least once I became an adult. I feel like I don't really have an excuse. Except that it was all simply too big for me to deal with. I think . . . I think I've been afraid that if I let myself feel it, I'd end up like . . . well, like *this*."

"But you survived it."

"Only because of you and Annalee and Dennie."

"Hell, I'm half the reason you ended up here. But in the end you survived it because of how strong you are."

She tucked her hair behind one ear. "I don't know about that. I think a lot of the strength I let people see is me covering up the part that's too raw to show anyone."

"You're showing it to me now. You've shown some of it to me every time we've played together. The people who think there's some intrinsic weakness in being submissive have no concept of the strength it takes. And you have it, Summer Grace—you do. You've always had it. You had the strength to hide your pain. It doesn't matter that eventually it kind of exploded. You were strong enough to keep a lid on it all that time."

She cracked a smile. "How do you manage to make me sound so grand when I'm sitting here in tear-soaked pajamas that don't even belong to me because a bad-tempered old cat died?"

He smiled at her, smiled at the light reappearing in her blue eyes. "I wouldn't have you any other way."

"Well I've got news for you, Jamie Stewart-Greer—there's not going to be any 'having' me until I've had a good long shower and maybe some food."

"Deal. But brace yourself, because I'm about to kiss the pants off you, sugar."

He threw back the covers and pulled her into his lap, his arms tight around her slender body, his mouth coming down hard on hers.

Her lips were so damn soft. She opened to him right away, the resistance gone out of her. Her hands went to his shoulders, then his cheeks, behind his neck. She held on to him so tight—tight enough that he knew she was going to be all right—that they would be all right. And all was right with his world.

CHAPTER

Thirteen

S UMMER TENSED AS they walked into her house, but Jamie
had asked Duff to take Madame to a local veterinary office
to have them dispose of her body, and to air out the house. She
inhaled carefully, but she smelled nothing but the sultry New
Orleans air and maybe some of the rosemary and hibiscus growing in her garden.

As Jamie closed the front door, she turned to him. "Jamie?
Is it bad that I didn't say good-bye to Madame? I didn't want
to come home to that—I couldn't—but I feel bad."

"You're more into this spiritual stuff than I am, but don't
you think she knows you loved her? And isn't that the only
important thing—the love?"

"You're right." She smiled up at him as she snuggled into his
arms. "I love you, Jamie."

"I love you, baby. Love you, love you, love you," he whispered into her hair. "And I'll love you forever. I will. Don't you dare doubt it."

Her smile spread until she felt her cheek crease against his muscled chest. "Yes, sir."

"Sassy girl."

"But you wouldn't have me any other way."

"It's true. I only want *you*, Summer Grace, exactly as you are."

"Jamie?"

"Hmm?"

"Can it be time for that 'having' me you were talking about earlier?"

"I think it was you who was talking about it, my insatiable girl," he said, but he was sliding his hand into her hair and up the back of her scalp, pulling tightly.

She sighed. "Mmm, when you pull my hair like that, I am."

He picked her up and she laced her legs around his waist, and he kissed her as he carried her into the bedroom. Setting her down on the bed, he knelt to pull off her sandals, then her yoga pants.

"As much as I love the pretty lingerie you get from work, I think I prefer it when you go without."

"It's only because I didn't have any clean stuff with me at Dennie's."

"Either way, it's working for me." He took her hand and pressed it against his erection under the denim of his jeans.

"Oh, so it is," she agreed, her body melting.

Cupping his hard length in her palm, she remembered what it felt like to have him inside her. Her sex squeezed, ached for him.

He moaned softly, covered her hand with his and pressed down *hard*.

"Sugar, if you keep this up—not that I'm complaining—this is gonna be over before it starts."

She bit her lip. "What if I want to put it in my mouth?"

He groaned. "Christ, you kill me."

She looked up at him. "I haven't even tried yet," she said.

"Oh, you are a sassy girl. Come here and let me teach you a lesson."

He grabbed her, and before she knew what was happening, he had her over his knee, her bare bottom in the air. He gave her a good smack, making her yelp.

"Oh, come on, sugar—that was nothing."

"I'm a delicate flower tonight, Jamie."

"Ah, baby." He turned her over and lifted her into his lap. "I'm sorry, sweetheart."

"Jamie, it's okay. I was joking." She reached up and stroked his strong cheek, let her fingertips trace the metal bar through his eyebrow. "Thank you for being so sweet to me. And I love you. And I'm also needing you. Please?"

She boldly took his hand and placed it between her thighs, holding it there until he began to explore, his fingers slipping into her wet heat.

"Nice." He smiled, kissed her lips, pulled back to whisper, "Very nice," as he rubbed her juices over her clitoris, then began to slide his fingers back and forth over the sensitive nub. "Come on, my sugar girl. Tonight I'm going to be a service Top. I'm gonna make you come, over and over. That's what I want more than anything—to make you feel good."

"Jamie . . ."

"Shh. This is what will please me most. This is what I *need*. Say yes."

What else could she do? "Yes," she answered, a small smile on her face, her cheeks going warm. Her body going warm.

He pulled her tank top over her head and she was glad she'd

tucked her bra into her purse rather than putting it on after her shower. It felt so good to be naked with him, with the man she loved, in the soft, sultry New Orleans air. He laid her back on the bed, then undressed slowly, his gaze on her face as he undid his belt, then his jeans, opening the fly just enough that she got a hint of his beautiful skin, his beautiful cock, underneath. He kicked off his big black boots, then pulled his T-shirt over his head. And in some way it was if she'd never seen his bare torso before—he was so perfectly made she gasped, her sex clenching as she looked from his gorgeously pierced nipples to the tattooed script running up his right side. She wanted to run her tongue over the tattoo, to find the small areas where the skin was still raised with ink. She wanted to take his nipple rings into her mouth, to work them until his nipples were as hard as his cock. She wanted to trace every sleek rise and angle of his tight abs with her tongue. But for now she would focus on what he wanted to do to her. Gladly. Deliriously.

He slid the jeans down over his leanly-muscled thighs, exposing all of his golden skin, and she had to grab handfuls of the bedding beneath her to keep from reaching out to touch him. She'd never seen a more beautiful example of the male form in her life—he was pure art. Pure sex. Pure love.

Hers.

"Jamie?"

"What is it, love?" he asked as he knelt at the foot of the bed.

"I'm yours."

"Oh, yes, you are. All mine."

"And you are mine."

He smoothed his hands over her calves. "Sweetheart, I am as much yours as you are mine. I have been from the start. You have my heart, which means you have all of me." He bent and laid a sweet kiss on her ankle. "Don't you know that, Summer Grace?"

"Yes. Just checking. No, not checking. I just wanted to hear you say it."

"In that case you can ask anytime."

"You're pretty wonderful, you know that?"

His features sobered. "I didn't, until you."

Her smile faded for a moment. "Neither did I."

"We need each other."

"Yeah. We do."

Her smile came back as he lowered his head, stretching up to kiss her lips before sliding down and down, until his lovely, sweet mouth was between her thighs. He kissed her there, too, then started in with his tongue, hitting all the right spots, taking her higher and higher. When her body tensed with her oncoming climax she expected him to halt her, to make her wait. But he only dove deeper, his fingers thrusting inside her, his hot, wet mouth sucking her flesh until she came, crying his name. But he didn't stop, and soon pleasure crested again, and she was coming and coming. She had no idea whether it was a new climax or more of the first—there hadn't been any time for her to separate them. Didn't matter. It was *her* Jamie, bringing her pleasure, making her fly. Flying for the first time with nothing but pleasure and love, no pain. She didn't need it right now. All she needed was *him*.

He took one moment to glance up at her, a sensual smile on his damp lips, then he was on her again, making her squirm. And this time it did hurt a little, she was so sensitive. But in moments she was coming again, and this time she screamed his name, her throat raw.

When she was certain she couldn't take any more, he rose above her, guiding her to wrap her legs around him. Poised at the entrance to her body, he gazed down at her.

"Do you know what it does to me to bring you pleasure?

How it fills me up? And fuck, Summer Grace . . ." He swallowed, and the expression on his face made her heart swell. "I want to do everything for you. And to you. And for us. I want to be inside you so badly it hurts. But I had to tell you how much I love you. How much I love your beautiful body. Your strength. Even the parts of you that are almost as fucked up as I am. Seriously. Maybe we're broken together, but we can also heal together. I think this is the only way I can."

She reached up and touched his cheek, letting her palm linger there. "I think this is the only way I can, too. You are the only man I have ever truly loved, Jamie, the only man I ever could love."

"It's you and me, sugar. This is what was meant to be."

"You and me," she agreed as he slid into her.

What she felt was more than desire, more than sensation, more than pleasure. It was all of those fused with love. Powerful. Intoxicating. And something she welcomed being lost in, drowning in—because it meant drowning in *him*.

"Love you, Jamie."

"Love you, Summer Grace. My beautiful girl. My only girl."

Soon she felt him pulse deep inside her, and her body answered. Together they fell over that keen edge, tangled, entwined, where flesh met flesh and heart met heart. And it was exactly right, exactly as it was meant to be. And she knew their whispered words to each other were true. Together they would heal.

IT WAS THE Saturday night after Labor Day and the weather was warm, the air heavy with the damp of the end of the summer season as Jamie drove through the city in the vintage T-bird he'd just bought. With the top down the air blew through Summer's hair, but she didn't care if it was a tangled mess. She laid her head against the headrest, looking up at the stars whooshing by above, her hand wrapped in Jamie's. There was everything in the world to be happy about, it seemed.

"Jamie?"

"What is it, sugar?"

"I'm kind of surprised you managed to get away, with the motorcycle branch of SGR Motors opening Monday. You and Duff have been working so hard, I've barely had a chance to see you. Not that I'm complaining. I'm so proud of you guys."

"There's always time for a midnight picnic. Anyway, it's a way to celebrate, just the two of us."

"Where are you taking me?"

"You'll see," he said, letting go of her hand to downshift, then turning onto Iberville Street.

"This is the way to the St. Louis Cemetery."

"Can you think of a more appropriate place for us to have a picnic at midnight?"

She laughed, leaning her head back once more, closing her eyes and letting the breeze wash over her. She was dizzy with the night and the wind and love for this man beside her.

She opened her eyes when she heard the engine slow to a purr, and Jamie was parking. He shut the engine off and came around to help her out of the car, then reached behind the seat for a small picnic basket.

"Are you hungry?" he asked.

"Not really."

"Good. Because there's not much aside from champagne in here."

She shook her head, laughing. "You're in a mood tonight."

He leaned down for a quick kiss before they crossed the dark street. "I'm in a *great* mood."

When they reached the back wall of the old cemetery, he gave her a boost up. She straddled the wall while he handed her the picnic basket, then held on to it while he climbed up and over. He took the basket first, then helped her down. They walked hand in hand down the rows, moving slowly, not talking, simply being together in the lovely old place that felt sacred to them both for so many reasons.

The moon was nearly full, shining like a metallic disc in the sky overhead, casting silvery light into the shadows of the aboveground tombs.

"Someone's been here," Summer said. "There are fresh flowers on every tomb. Weird." She stopped in front of one of her favorites, an enormous marble mausoleum with a flat sheet of white marble to one side. Someone had already laid a blanket atop it, along with a bottle of champagne in a bucket, two crystal glasses sparkling in the moonlight, and flowers were scattered over the blanket.

She turned to Jamie. "You did all this? When did you have time?"

Jamie set the basket on the ground and pulled her into his arms. "Where there's a will, there's a way."

"Jamie." She smiled up at him, then looked around her again, taking it in. "These are peonies and white roses—my favorite flowers. I can't believe you went to so much trouble."

"I'd do anything for you, sweetheart. Don't you know that by now?"

"I do. I mean, I guess I do. But this . . ."

He stroked her hair, tucking it behind her ear. His face was soft, sober suddenly. "I mean it. I'd do anything for you. *Anything.* I want you to give me that chance."

"What do you mean, Jamie? I'm not going anywhere."

"Neither am I. And to show you I mean it . . ."

When he dropped to one knee, her breath stuttered.

"Ohhh."

He held her hand, looking up at her, his eyes shining with the light of the moon and the stars. "I love you. I love you in a way I never knew I could. You are and always have been the only one for me, and I want to spend the rest of my life making you believe that, over and over, every single day."

"Jamie." She could barely breathe, emotion welling in her chest.

"Summer Grace. My sweetheart, my one and only girl. I want to fall asleep every night of my life seeing your lovely face before I close my eyes. And I want to wake up with you every morning. I want to be with the one woman who truly understands me. Who knows how broken I've been, and who's the only one I can mend my broken self with. I want my future to be with you, no matter what else it brings. I know we can get through it together.

"Summer Grace Rae, will you do me the very great honor of becoming my wife? Will you wear my ring, and wear my collar? Will you be mine in every way possible? And will you take me as yours? Will you marry me?"

Tears filled her eyes, fell onto her cheeks. "Oh, Jamie!"

One corner of his mouth quirked. "Baby, don't start crying before you give me your answer."

She brought his hand to her lips, opened it and kissed his palm. "Yes, Jamie. Yes, of course. Always and forever. I'll never belong to anyone but you."

He pulled a ring from his pocket, a gleaming princess-cut diamond in a vintage setting that felt enormous on her small hand as he slipped it onto her finger.

"Oh my God. It's so beautiful."

He stood and she went into his arms. He kissed her hair, her cheeks, her temples, and finally, her mouth. He tasted like Jamie, her Jamie. Her love. *Hers*. Forever. When they pulled apart, she was half laughing, half crying.

"Time to get down on your knees, my beautiful girl."

"Oh."

It was all she could say as the awe of the moment suffused her body, filled her, dizzied her as she sank to the ground. Jamie reached into the picnic basket and came back with a collar in his hand, and goosebumps rose all over her skin when she saw it. It was shining silver chrome, studded with pink crystals—perfect for her.

He stroked a few fingers under her chin, forcing her gaze to his.

"You understand how this is different from the ring, sweetheart? How much deeper this goes?"

"Of course. I wouldn't be on my knees if I didn't know, Jamie."

"And do you understand how important it is to me that I do both these things—ask for your hand and deepen that commitment—here in this place where we celebrate your brother's life every year? How it feels like I'm doing this in front of him here?"

"I thought about that, too. It feels like . . . like Brandon is here, giving us his blessing."

"Yes. Exactly."

He looked down at her, studying her face, and she felt such love for him and from him. Her heart was bursting. Full and fulfilled.

"Summer Grace Rae, my beautiful girl," he said slowly. "My only love, will you be with me, belong to me, as *mine*? Will you take me as yours?"

"Yes, Jamie. You are everything to me. *Everything*. I want to be yours. Completely."

He smiled, ran his hand over her cheek, and she turned to kiss his fingertips before turning back to face him. He bent and she lifted her hair as he fastened the collar around her neck. Happy tears ran down her cheeks, but only a few—she was far too happy, too full of bliss, to cry for long. And when he took her in his arms, pulling her to her feet and kissing her long and hard, all she knew was the bliss.

"Love you, Jamie. And Jamie . . . I know I have a ways to go still, but thank you. Thank you for helping me to heal. For being willing to go the rest of the way with me."

"I should be the one to thank you. And I will spend the rest of my life doing exactly that, and thanking the universe every single day for putting you in my life. I love you." He kissed her, then kissed her again. "I love you. I can't tell you enough how much I love you. And that's the *thing*, you know what I mean, sugar? Love is the thing."

She stood on her toes to press her lips to his, aware of the heavy band of leather and chrome around her neck, the heavier diamond on her finger. And as wonderful as these things were, Jamie was right. The thing—the only thing—was love. No matter how broken either of them might be, it was love that would put them back together again, hold them together, to each other. And it was love that made her feel healed already.

Love was the thing.